Trial by Tribulation

Trial by Tribulation

Arthur Woodrow Hanson

VANTAGE PRESS
New York

FIRST EDITION

Published by Vantage Press, Inc.
516 West 34th Street, New York, New York 10001

Manufactured in the United States of America
ISBN: 0-533-12430-1

Library of Congress Catalog Card No.: 97-90580

0 9 8 7 6 5 4 3 2 1

Trial by Tribulation

CHAPTER ONE

Burly Ed Lerner, sheriff of Mallon County, Oklahoma, the county known throughout such oil domains as Oklahoma, Texas, and Louisiana as the "Pipeline of the Southwest," climbed wearily into his service vehicle, feeling the aches and pains of his thirty years on the force. His heavy revolver jabbed him uncomfortably as he attempted to slide his sturdy legs under the steering wheel. Time was when he had a driver to cart him around the county, but with recent cutbacks due to reduced tax revenues combined with increased crime activity, he had to give that up, along with some office conveniences.

The sheriff had been anticipating this day with considerable distaste for what he had to do. Tucked away in an inside pocket of his jacket was an unusually significant document: a warrant for the arrest of Daniel Wayland, the young son of one of Mallon County's most distinguished citizens, Angus Wayland, a powerful man, known thereabouts as the oil baron.

Sheriff Lerner was and always had been a devoted public servant, ready to do his sworn duty despite his own personal feelings; so on this momentous occasion he put his regrets aside as he began the five-mile trip to the renowned Wayland mansion.

Along the way Lerner drove with his car window open to enjoy the cool morning air before the heat of this summer day set in. He lazily cast his gaze over the rolling hills of the land in which he was born and raised. The Oklahoma countryside was devoted mostly to small or medium-sized farms, and was dotted here and there with small groves of low-growing deciduous trees, with their full complement of summer foliage. Prominent along the way were the familiar tall derricks of the fabulous southwest oil wells, such as had meant handsome incomes for many Mallon citizens, and incredible wealth for some. Most of the wells were on pumps, with their huge horse-like heads slowly and rhythmically rising up, then bending down to suck the precious fluid from the earth. As had many Mallon citizens who lacked the good fortune to own oil-rich property, Lerner often dreamed of what might have been--a life free from financial troubles and the stresses of full-time employment--but not at this crucial time, as he approached

1

the Wayland estate and readied himself for the uninviting task ahead.

Angus Wayland's mansion, built during the heyday of the twenties, was situated on a massive estate, somewhat remote from main traffic arteries. The large two-story structure, unlike most other mansions in the deep South and Southwest, was modified Victorian in style, reflecting a growing trend of the era away from Victorian "gingerbread." Prominent in the front was a large portico, facing a broad circular drive that exited from, and led back to, the paved road that took one a good two hundred yards to the main gate. The gate itself was an ornate steel structure that was usually manned but could be electronically controlled from the main house. Attached to the gate post was an intercom telephone connected to the master's study. Behind the house were two outbuildings for the storage of maintenance materials and equipment, and a structure that once provided living quarters for a sizeable staff, before Angus Wayland began contracting for most services on the estate and discharged all of his staff except gate tenders, a house man, and a maid.

The estate, situated amidst a forest of deciduous trees, was completely surrounded by a high masonry wall, topped by two strands of barbed wire, electrified to sound an alarm in the main house if cut. There were no oil wells on the estate, because Angus and his father before him steadfastly refused to permit drilling on the property.

Wayland, a dour man of fifty with thick hair that was starting to grey at the temples, was busy in his study when his main gate telephone rang. Since his house man was off for the day, he answered it himself. It was the sheriff.

"What is your business?" Wayland wanted to know.

Sheriff Lerner, who had known Wayland quite well for a long time, replied, "Let me in, Angus. I have to talk to you."

"What about?"

"Come on, Angus, let me in. I can't talk to you out here in the sticks!"

After a brief hesitation Wayland issued instructions to the gate tender to open the gate. He went personally to the front entrance to meet the sheriff.

Sheriff Lerner looked grim as he dismounted slowly and

walked toward the entrance. "Howdy, Angus," he said, his voice sounding strained.

"Howdy, Ed, what's this all about?"

"Is Daniel home?" Daniel, Angus Wayland's only son, now in his early twenties, was unemployed and still living at home.

"What do you want with Daniel? Has he been in some kind of trouble?" Wayland's voice was now conveying a hint of belligerence.

"I'm sorry, Angus. I've got to arrest Daniel."

"Arrest him? On what charge? What has he done?" Then, "Have you got a warrant that gives you the right to barge in here like this?" The questions sounded much like vociferous challenges.

Sheriff Lerner lowered his gaze and shifted uncomfortably, but then reached into his inner jacket pocket and pulled out the warrant, showing it to Wayland. He explained, "The charge is murder--first degree murder."

Wayland snatched the warrant, reading it hastily. Satisfied that the document was legitimate, he handed it back to the sheriff. As he did so he exploded with anger. "First degree murder--what the hell are you talking about?" he roared.

"Look, can we go inside?" Lerner asked. "I know I owe you an explanation, and I think we can talk better inside. Maybe the missus ought to be in on this too."

"You damn right you owe me an explanation!" Wayland's face was cherry red, and he seemed ready to burst. "All right! Come on in! I hope for your sake you've got a damn good reason for coming here with that crap!" Sheriff Lerner followed the irate Wayland into the study.

At that moment Cheryl Wayland, wife of Angus, having heard the loud talking at the front entrance, appeared, her face showing concern. Cheryl, a handsome woman, slender, looked younger than her forty-four years. She was casually but tastefully dressed in a flared green print skirt and beige blouse. Her lovely brown hair, expertly groomed, fell nearly to her shoulders. In a pleasing, well-modulated voice she asked if there was some trouble.

Wayland roared, "Ed here says he has to arrest Daniel for murder! What do you think of that?"

"I don't understand!" Mrs. Wayland exclaimed, her face suddenly drained of color.

Sheriff Lerner looked as if he was facing the devil himself, but he was determined to do his duty. "Folks, if you'll just have a chair I'll try to tell you what's happened. Please! Please sit down!"

Stirred by the urgency in the sheriff's voice, Mr. and Mrs. Wayland seated themselves on a large leather settee. The sheriff took a chair facing them. Working himself up to what he had to do, Lerner began, "You know about those murders hereabouts lately, where young women were raped and then strangled. The papers called the murderer the 'midnight strangler'."

"We heard about it," growled Wayland. "So what? Are you saying Daniel had something to do with that?"

Lerner ignored the challenge and went on with his prepared speech. "We've been working on that for a long time, along with the FBI. At first we weren't getting anywhere, but we finally got a break, and found the evidence we needed to identify the murderer. There was no doubt about it--it was your Daniel."

Cheryl Wayland's face registered profound disbelief and shock. Her husband's face showed a similar reaction, plus rage, arising from a conviction that a monstrous deception was being perpetrated upon him and his family.

The sheriff was prepared for the Waylands' shock reaction. Hoping to ease the situation, he commented, "Now, I know this comes as a big surprise to you folks. I'm sure you didn't know this was going on behind your backs. Well, it was a big surprise to me, too. I've known Daniel ever since he was a little kid, and he ain't never been a bad kid. He sticks by hisself a lot, never had much to do with the other kids, but he never got in any trouble."

"Dammit," Wayland exploded, "I still don't believe it! Somebody is trying to put something over on us! Who put you up to this?"

"Nobody put me or anybody else up to it!" Lerner expostulated. "The evidence is clear!"

"Just what the hell is this *evidence?*" Wayland demanded to know, spitting out the word "evidence" as he might spit

4

out a bite of rotten tomato.

"My God, man, there's a file on this as thick as a pine log! I can't talk to you about it! The DA wouldn't let me even if I could! Anyway, I'm not saying that Daniel is guilty. That's for a jury to decide. All I'm saying is that there's evidence enough to bring him in, and that's what I have to do!"

Wayland jumped to his feet. "I'm not sure I'm going to let you take Daniel in!"

The sheriff stood as well. "Now Angus, I don't blame you for taking that attitude, but it has to be. I can take him now, or I can come back with an army or whatever else is needed, and I don't think that would help anybody. Now why don't you just back off and let me have the boy."

Wayland seemed ready to fight, but his wife jumped up and physically restrained him, saying forcefully, "Angus! Don't! Let the sheriff take him. We can work this out later, through the law!"

Turning to the sheriff, Mrs. Wayland spoke her piece. "Daniel is in the back. I'll call him. We'll talk to you later!"

Stepping into the adjoining room, Mrs. Wayland shouted toward the back of the house, "Daniel! Come on out here! The sheriff wants to talk to you!"

Very shortly Daniel appeared. He was a rather handsome young man, about six feet tall, blond, good features and good build. He was casually dressed in a plaid sport shirt and blue jeans. He said to his mother, "What's this about?"

Mrs.Wayland looked at Lerner and said, "All right, Sheriff, you tell him!"

"Daniel," Sheriff Lerner began, "I'm sorry, but I've got to take you in. I have a warrant for your arrest for the crime of murder."

"Murder? I don't understand!" Daniel looked genuinely puzzled.

"Come on, you'll hear all about it later. My job is to take you in."

Daniel looked inquiringly toward his mother, who gestured toward the door and said, "Go on, Daniel. We'll get to the bottom of this. We'll be in to see you later. Don't worry!"

Mrs. Wayland seemed almost at the point of breaking into tears. As Lerner prepared to handcuff Daniel she burst out, "Is that necessary?"

"I'm afraid it is, Ma'am. It's the law."

The sheriff applied the cuffs, then took Daniel's arm and escorted him to the car. In a brief moment he was headed out, as the Waylands stood watching, still unbelieving that events of the last several minutes had not been simply a frightful nightmare.

As soon as the sheriff was well on his way Wayland sprang into action. He raced to the phone and quickly dialed a familiar New York number. When he received a reply, apparently from a secretary or stenographer, he shouted, "This is Angus Wayland. Put Henry on the phone! Now!"

"I'm sorry, sir," replied the now frightened voice on the other end, "but Mr. Jacobs is not in at the moment!"

"Look," Wayland exploded, "I've got a crisis here, and I want to talk to him. Wherever he is, get hold of him and have him call me back. Go on! Get going!" He slammed the receiver down.

* * * * *

The sign on the door read, HENRY JACOBS, ATTORNEY AT LAW, and supplied the New York address. Inside, prim Miss Kerri Wilson, loyal secretary to Mr. Jacobs, had just received a frantic, angry telephone call from Angus Wayland. She was a bit frightened, and a bit angry herself; but she was stirred into instant action, more from fear of her own employer's wrath than of what Angus Wayland might do. She wasn't quite sure where her boss was at this moment, but she had two places to try: the Country Club (today was an off-and-on golf day for Mr. Jacobs), or his favorite restaurant, Maison de Marie. He was not at either place. She had one more possible place to try, the courthouse. Just as she was about to place that call, Mr. Jacobs came through the door.

Henry Jacobs was an anomaly. At age sixty-five he was still a powerful man in legal circles, with a nationwide reputation for accepting, and winning, tough cases. Among his celebrated court triumphs had been the political boss, Nathan Wilder, who was charged with gross malfeasance following an illegal break-in to obtain classified records; the Mafia chief who

6

was arrested after a mid-town shootout with Federal officers; the multi-millionaire stock broker charged with insider trading; and several other cases involving persons of equal prominence, all acquitted or their sentences reduced to a mere slap on the wrist. Jacobs was a large man, six-foor-four and nearly two hundred and eighty pounds. With his great size and his extraordinarily loud voice he was an impressive courtroom figure, often intimidating witnesses by sheer force of personality. Then with his exceptionally keen mind (I.Q. about 170), he was indeed a force to be reckoned with. And as might be expected, he was anything but cheap.

As Jacobs entered the office Miss Wilson told him excitedly about the call from Angus Wayland. He remarked, "That reprobate--I wonder what he's up to now. Get him on the phone."

Miss Wilson responded at once, and within three minutes notified her waiting boss, "Mr. Wayland is on the line, sir."

"Hello, Angus--" (He usually exercised his booming voice even on the telephone) "What's up?"

"What's up?" sputtered Wayland. "They've arrested my son, that's what. I want you to get down here right away! We may be in real trouble!"

"Hold on! Arrested for what?"

"For murder! You know those 'midnight strangler' murders? They say Daniel did it!"

Surprised, Jacobs asked, "Did you know anything about this before?"

"Hell, no! I didn't know anything about it until the sheriff barged in here today with a warrant to arrest Dan! How soon can you get down here and look into this? I'd just as soon this thing never got to court. Even if Dan is guilty, like they say, the publicity could ruin me! Anyway, I don't think he is guilty, and I think you're the man to clear this up. I'll pay you double your usual fee if you can get him off!"

"Hold on, Angus--you're talking a quarter of a million dollars here!"

"I don't care what it costs! Get on down here!"

Jacobs consulted his schedule, then responded, "You've caught me at a good time. I've got a couple of things scheduled, but I can cancel them without any trouble. I'll fly down tomorrow." With that he hung up.

Jacobs gave instructions to Miss Wilson to make arrangements for the trip and to make an appointment to see the Mallon County sheriff the next afternoon, and to cancel all other appointments for the next several days. He then retired to his law library and closed the door. It was well past dinner time when he finally left his office.

* * * * *

District Attorney Michael Loudon, age forty-five, was born in Norman, Oklahoma, to parents of English extraction. His father, James Loudon, an oil field worker, was a high school graduate. His mother, Beth, worked some as a practical nurse before the demands of wife- and motherhood necessitated her remaining at home.

Daughter of a Cockney schoolmarm, Beth longed to go to college and pursue a career in teaching, but was denied that opportunity by financial reverses in her family and her own later life, complicated by the early death of both parents in an auto accident. Nevertheless, she was determined that at least Michael, who showed excellent scholastic ability, should have the chance to attend college. Since Norman was a college town, Michael could live at home. The state would pay tuition, and Michael could take odd jobs to help pay expenses. In time, Beth reasoned, perhaps circumstances would permit Michael's achieving what he most wanted: an advanced degree in law.

With Michael's full cooperation, and her husband's willing concurrence, Beth's dream was realized. Michael achieved his BA degree in minimum time, and went on to a degree in law. Because of his excellent scholastic record he was immediately recruited by a prestigious law firm in Oklahoma City, where he acquired valuable experience before deciding to strike out on his own. A few years later he pursued an opportunity to establish a lucrative practice in a fast-growing area of nearby Mallon County.

Here Michael met and married Althea, a beautiful and charming local girl who was active in community affairs. Rejoicing in his good fortune, Michael saw a rosy future for himself, his wife, and his family to be, especially after Althea

8

happily informed him that she was pregnant. Althea carried the child to near full term with joyful anticipation. But then tragedy struck. Due to severe complications, Althea lost the child and her own life.

Michael never remarried, partly through grief and loyalty to the only woman he had ever truly loved, and partly through the pressure of becoming established in his profession. Not long after his tragic loss he was persuaded by loyal supporters to run for district attorney of Mallon County, an enterprise in which he was eminently successful.

In appearance Michael was not outstanding in any respect. Average was the word: average height (about five foot ten) and physique, average weight, and an average face. He was not particularly handsome, but neither was he unhandsome. His dark brown hair, showing only faint signs of balding, was neatly barbered, as befitted one much in the public eye. His now light grey two-piece suit showed signs of wear, but was well-fitting and quite serviceable. Perhaps this unpretentious appearance was an asset in the courtroom, as it would not arouse envy in opposing litigants; and Loudon had many successes to his credit during his seven-year tenure as Mallon's district attorney.

In another respect, however, Michael Loudon possibly was outstanding. Besides being extremely honest and conscientious, and thoroughly dedicated to the ethics of his profession, he was eminently fair, as anyone engaged with him in legal action would have to admit. Yet Michael could be as firm as anyone in prosecuting those to whom the evidence pointed as being enemies of society.

Michael was painfully aware of deficiences in the legal system, but he saw the system not as an entity in itself, but as an integral part of the whole society, and saw the system's flaws as stemming from flaws in the social structure. It was part of his job, as he saw it, to keep the system's flaws from obstructing justice, and to that end he was willing to bend and compromise where such seemed to be prudent.

Alone in his office after the staff had all gone, District Attorney Michael Loudon leaned back in his chair, quietly contemplating a voluminous file on his desk labeled DANIEL WAYLAND.

9

Michael mentally reviewed the sobering history of the vicious crime spree that had alarmed the entire community, involving the rape and murder of almost twenty young women, mostly either prostitutes or runaways. Dubbed the "midnight strangler" case by the press, the crime spree was the occasion for one of the most extensive manhunts on record, to which had been devoted hundreds of hours of detective work and the use of the most sophisticated crime-solving techniques available, many of which had been "borrowed" from New York, Philadelphia, and Washington D.C. The case had attracted national attention, being given media coverage on network television and the leading news magazines.

Although the experts differed on some aspects of the case, they all agreed that one person had committed all of the crimes, largely because of a distinctive modus operandi. It had been determined that all of the crimes occurred within a half hour, either way, of the hour of midnight. All of the victims, it appeared, had been rendered unconscious by one means or another, then taken to a remote wooded area, raped, and strangled by hand pressure. And in every case one item of the victim's clothing had been removed and never found at the scene, indicating what the sheriff referred to as souvenir collecting by the rapist.

The officials had been completely baffled in the case until they got a break totally by accident. A twelve-year-old boy, wandering in the wooded area where most of the crime victims had been discovered, found a woman's garment lying almost completely buried. Normally a person would have ignored such an item, not uncommon even in a remote wooded area; but the child, for reasons that he could not explain, became curious and picked up the garment, in this case merely a woman's sleeveless blouse. As he pulled the garment from its buried position, another garment was uncovered, then another, and still another, until a sizeable stash was revealed. This unusual circumstance so intrigued the child that he ran home and told his parents. Remembering the published stories of the rapist taking items of clothing from the murder victims, the parents notified the sheriff, who dropped everything and rushed to inspect the find.

From that point on there occurred one of the most inter-

10

esting and ingenious developments in detective history. Through prodigious effort a team of officials was able to salvage from the clothing bits of hair, microscopic pieces of skin, and other bits of debris that did not correspond with any of the murder victims, and even a smudged fingerprint. That prompted a trail of investigation that, partly through luck and partly through the genius of a laboratory chemist, to Daniel Wayland. Further investigation, details of which were meticulously kept under wraps, confirmed that Daniel Wayland was indeed the "midnight strangler."

Michael thought pensively of his own involvement in the case, checking with the sheriff and other principles on procedures as required by law, assessing legality of some contemplated movements, making suggestions as to possible avenues of approach, and finally, complying with the sheriff's request for a warrant to arrest Dan Wayland.

Loudon leaned forward, opened the Wayland file, and began to study it with care. After an hour of reading, during which he remained as thoroughly engrossed as a child watching a horror movie, he commented to himself that the job that was done in gathering evidence was brilliant and extremely thorough. There was no doubt about it: according to the evidence, Wayland was the culprit.

Loudon was not acquainted with the Wayland family, least of all with Daniel. He did know that Angus had fathered three children, two girls and Daniel, and that Daniel was the youngest. The two daughters apparently had never married, and had continued living at home, as had Daniel. There had been rumors of conflict within the family, but there had been no trouble that would warrant the attention of the DA's office. So how could this young man, who apparently had everything a young man could want, commit such horrible crimes?

Loudon walked over to the county jail to see if the sheriff was still around. Sheriff Lerner was preparing to leave, but paused to chat with the DA. After an exchange of pleasantries, Loudon brought up the subject of the Wayland lad. "I understand that you got the young man in, all right. Did you have any trouble?"

"Not really," the sheriff replied. "The father made like he wanted to give us some trouble, but the missus stepped in

11

and kept things under control. The boy didn't give me any trouble."

"Have you interrogated him since you brought him in?"

"No," the sheriff replied. "Knowing the old man, I didn't want to get into that until we heard from his lawyer. I haven't heard from him yet."

"A good idea. What is your impression of young Wayland?"

"Well, Mike, it's hard to believe. The fellow is real good looking, and it's easy to see how he could entice young girls into compromising situations. He's also well-mannered, courteous, and not at all hostile or belligerent. In fact he seemed rather puzzled as to why he was arrested."

"Has he tried to talk to you about it?"

"He started to, but I read him his rights and refused to listen to anything he had to say except routine stuff."

"Has he had any visitors?"

"Yeah, his father and mother were in this afternoon late, but I don't have any idea what they talked about."

"Ed, I want to say again that I was really impressed with the job the investigating team did in getting this case together. That file is a masterpiece. I know you had a lot to do with that, and I really appreciate it. Thanks a lot."

"Thank you, Mike. I appreciate your mentioning it."

"Okay, Ed, you're welcome. Talk to you later."

Back in his office Loudon got on the telephone and dialed the number of his favorite companion of recent months, Janice Farley. He proposed a date for the evening, but accepted a counter invitation to have dinner at her apartment.

As Loudon left his office and stepped out into the early evening air he felt a slight chill, and pulled his jacket more snugly about him. Walking briskly along toward his rendez-vous with Janice he noted a gathering of dark clouds on the horizon, portending a coming storm, a fact to which at the moment he gave no further heed.

* * * * *

Janice Farley had been an only child. Her father, Harold Farley, son of Graham Farley, U.S. senator, was a col-

12

lege professor in English. Her mother, Alicia, also an only child in a prominent Maine family, was an interior designer. As a child Janice was extraordinarily precocious, having completed the eighth grade by age eleven, and high school before age fourteen. She was enrolled in college by age fifteen, and had obtained her bachelor's degree in psychology in less than three years. Although she had shown great promise for a future in psychology, she decided to wait a while before selecting an avenue to pursue. For a year or so she cast about, taking courses in philosophy, social welfare, sociology, and even anthropology, before finally deciding to settle down and obtain her master's and PhD in psychology.

Janice had always been a sensitive person, concerned about the welfare and problems of others. Those who knew her well believed that she felt more deeply about others' misfortunes than she did about her own. Paramount in her make-up was a powerful urge to understand, and as a child she at times drove her parents and others frantic with questions about almost everything under the sun.

After obtaining her PhD Janice began looking for a teaching job. Very soon she was offered a position by the college in Mallon City, and because she liked what she had heard and read about the area and its climate, she readily accepted the offer.

Janice had been married, to a commander in the Coast Guard. She lost her husband to pneumonia three years ago. They had no children. After her bereavement Janice lived a solitary life, lost in her teaching and research, until she met Michael Loudon about a year ago, at a fund-raising function. Since that time she and Michael had been intimate friends, although neither had considered a serious romance. Their relationship was solidified by compatibility in philosophy of life and intellectual acuity and principles.

Now, at age forty-two, Janice was still an attractive woman, slender, well-groomed, with a complexion of which any movie actress could be proud. Her naturally-curly, reddish brown hair framed her heart-shaped face in a way that gracefully accented her delicate features. Her hazel eyes had that unexplainable look that revealed intelligence combined with sensitivity.

13

Janice busied herself preparing dinner for herself and Michael. At the moment she was dressed in a flared skirt with a pattern of large checks and a play of reddish-brown colors that almost matched the color of her hair, topped by a long-sleeved, white blouse graced by a flounce down the front. To protect her ensemble from kitchen splashes she wore a small apron. She hummed to herself as she finished setting the table, complete with candles and long-stemmed wine glasses, and checked to see how her dinner was coming.

There was a knock on the door, and doffing her apron, Janice went to admit her guest.

Janice and Michael greeted each other as especially good friends do. The dinner was not quite ready, so Janice had time to join her guest in a martini. They chatted lightly about this and that, nothing in particular.

The cocktails finished, Janice excused herself and went to the kitchen. Within minutes dinner was served, a simple but tasteful blend of cordon bleu, green beans cooked with mushrooms in a light cream sauce, broccoli al dente, and tossed spinach salad. Michael played host with a bottle of lightly chilled blush wine.

After dinner, the table cleared and the dishes washed with Michael's help, the couple settled into easy chairs to relax and sip their coffee. As is often the case with very good and close friends, Janice sensed that Michael had experienced something unusual that day. To make it easy for him to talk, she asked, in her best conversation-opener manner, "How was your day?"

Now that the investigative phase of the "midnight strangler" case was consummated with the arrest of Daniel Wayland, Loudon felt free to talk about it. "I haven't talked much about the case up to now," he explained, "because nothing was settled; but Daniel Wayland was arrested this morning, with all the evidence pointing his way, so it looks like it will be going to trial. This is the most fantastic case I was ever involved in. Did you know the Wayland family?"

"I didn't know the family that well," Janice replied, "although I've heard a lot about them, especially the father. I never heard that Daniel had been in any kind of trouble."

"He never was, at least so far as we know," Michael

14

confirmed. "Furthermore, he has been described as a nice-looking young man, a little shy, with a good attitude. It's hard to believe; but the file shows conclusively that he is guilty. It was a fabulous bit of police work, involving not only the county officials but also the FBI."

"What a surprise!" Janice commented thoughtfully. "From what I've heard about Angus Wayland, I'll bet he was really put out by this."

"He probably was, but I haven't talked to him. I'm sure that he lost no time hiring an expensive New York lawyer. So I don't know what his strategy is going to be. As strong as the case against Daniel appears to be, I don't see how they can expect to wangle an acquittal out of it. And I would never consider plea bargaining in a case like this."

"Do you think Wayland might try getting his attorney to offer you a bribe?" Janice asked.

"Hardly. If he was going to try that he'd use local talent. And the best lawyers don't get that way by using cheap, sleazy tactics like bribery. My best guess is that they'll try to prove that the lad was insane at the time he committed the crimes, and thus incapable of knowing right from wrong."

Janice looked steadily at Michael for a moment, then asked in serious tone, "How do you feel about that?"

After a brief hesitation Michael replied forthrightly, "I don't like it. If a man is capable of doing what Daniel apparently did, I think he should be permanently removed from society. If he was declared insane, he would be put into a mental institution as a sick person. True, they say he would remain there for many years, but under those circumstances there is always the chance that the doctors would declare him cured and release him. I've seen that happen before, and as often as not the 'cured' patient commits further crimes, often violent ones. Take this case a few years ago in San Antonio when a man who had been released from a mental hospital as 'cured' took a rifle up into a tower in the middle of the city and started shooting people at random. He killed eight and wounded eight more before they managed to stop him, this time by killing him. Also, even if they don't release a killer, there's always the chance that he may escape."

Noting the intensity of Michael's dissertation, Janice

wisely steered the conversation into less serious avenues. After about an hour of casual chitchat, Michael said good night and departed, with a promise to be in touch as soon as anything developed.

When Loudon approached his office the next morning he found a cluster of reporters waiting at the entrance to his office building. They had already been to see the sheriff, who dodged their questions and told them to go see the DA. As Loudon arrived the newspeople gathered around him and began shouting their questions about the arrest of Daniel Wayland. "What's the case against Daniel Wayland?" "How come we haven't heard about this arrest?" "What does Angus Wayland say about this?" "What is Wayland going to be charged with?" And so on. Loudon wondered how the press already knew about the arrest, but decided that somebody on the inside had leaked the news.

Loudon admonished the reporters, "Calm down--calm down! I'll give you a statement! As you probably know, the investigation of the 'midnight strangler' murders has been going on for a long time. The results have been kept secret so as not to give aid and comfort to the perpetrator or perpetrators. As you know we were stalled on this for quite a while, but we finally got the breakthrough that we needed. The investigation led directly to Daniel Wayland as the prime suspect. He was arrested without advance notice so as to avoid possible flight."

"Is Wayland guilty?" one reporter demanded to know.

"That is not for me to decide," Loudon replied. "All I can say at this point is that he will be charged, and the case will probably go to court."

"What effect is this going to have on the oil market?" another reporter asked.

"I don't know," Loudon answered dryly. "I'll leave that up to the economics experts."

The reporters pressed closer and continued shouting their questions, but Loudon refused to say anything further and escaped within the confines of his office building.

Later that afternoon the newspapers hit the streets with screaming headlines, SON OF OIL MAGNATE ARRESTED FOR MIDNIGHT MURDERS, WAYLAND SON TO BE CHARGED WITH MURDER AND RAPE, and so on, includ-

16

ing OIL EMPIRE THREATENED BY ARREST OF WAYLAND SON FOR MURDER. News of the Wayland arrest was immediately picked up by national and international news media, and according to some reports, created a shock wave that was felt through every reach of the nation and indeed the western hemisphere and parts of the oil-rich eastern hemisphere.

CHAPTER TWO

It was almost noon when Henry Jacobs' private jet landed at the Mallon City airport and taxied to a stop near the main gate. After exiting the plane, Jacobs entered a waiting limousine, arranged for in advance by Miss Wilson, that was to serve him throughout his stay in Mallon City. His first stop was Chez Alphonse, Mallon City's finest restaurant, for a hearty lunch.

Shortly before two o'clock Jacobs proceeded to the DA's office to inspect the documents essential to his client's arrest. Loudon was not in, but his secretary obliged by producing what could legally be provided to counsel at this time. Jacobs studied the documents carefully to assure himself that they complied with the law. Satisfied, he then proceeded to the sheriff's office, where he was greeted noncommittally by Sheriff Lerner. Jacobs introduced himself as attorney for Daniel Wayland, and told Lerner he wanted to see his client. He asked Lerner, "Has my client been told in detail just why he was arrested?"

Lerner replied, "No. He wanted to talk about it, but I wouldn't let him. He had the Miranda."

"Can you tell me what provided the breakthrough in your investigation?"

"No, sir. You'll have to talk to the DA about that."

Jacobs studied Lerner's expression for a moment to get a sense of the latter's determination not to tell him anything. Finally he asked to see his client.

The sheriff obliged by leading the way to the jail's interviewing room. He instructed a deputy to bring in Daniel Wayland. Having secured the interview room, Lerner departed, leaving the accused and his counsel alone, except for a deputy standing guard at a discreet distance outside the door.

Jacobs shook hands with young Wayland and introduced himself as his attorney. Although he had done business with Angus Wayland for years, he had never met the son. He half expected to see a surly, defiant young man. On the contrary, he was struck by Daniel's friendly, cooperative demeanor, as well as the young man's wholesome good looks. This distinctly un-criminal appearance led Jacobs to consider that despite early indications of a strong case against Daniel, there might be a chance to get him an acquittal.

Jacobs invited Daniel to have a seat, then asked, "You are Daniel Wayland?"

"Yes, sir."

"Do you know why you have been arrested?"

"I'm not sure, sir. They said I committed a bunch of murders."

"Did they say what murders?"

"Yeah, I know it was what they called the 'midnight strangler' murders that we've been reading about in the papers for a long time. I heard there was nineteen or twenty murders committed."

"Did you commit these murders?"

"No, sir, I don't believe I did."

"But they say the sheriff has uncovered a pile of evidence that says you did."

Jacobs was not challenging the young man, but instead was trying to encourage him to tell what he could, or what he was willing to, about the alleged crimes.

"I know," Daniel replied, "but I don't remember doing anything like they say."

Jacobs stared at the young suspect for a moment, trying to get a clue as to what was happening here. He saw nothing. He pressed just a little, pointing out to the suspect that he might be better off to tell the truth--but to no avail.

Through his years of dealing with clients seeking to make the best deal for themselves, Jacobs had become highly skilled at judging when a client was being truthful, and when not; and in this interaction with Daniel Wayland he was convinced that the lad was indeed telling the truth: he actually did not remember committing the alleged crimes!

Jacobs then went on, "Well, where were you on those particular nights when these murders occurred?"

"I don't know, sir. I don't know what nights they were committed. Anyway, I guess I was home in bed." In response to further questioning, Daniel asserted that he always had pre-ferred to stay by himself, and wasn't much for going out at night, going to bars, partying, and that sort of thing.

Sensing that he had gotten all that he was going to get,

19

Jacobs signalled the guard that the interview was over.

After thanking the sheriff for his cooperation, Jacobs walked the short distance to the DA's office, hoping that the DA was back. He was. Jacobs introduced himself as Henry Jacobs, Daniel Wayland's attorney, and Loudon responded with the query, "What can I do for you?"

"You seem to be satisfied that the Wayland case is closed, as far as the investigation is concerned," Jacobs said. "In that case, will you consent to let me see the file now, so that we don't have to go through discovery? It would save a lot of time and expense."

Loudon replied, "Well, I don't see why not. You're right, our investigation is completed, and we're not holding anything back. It's all there." Loudon turned the complete file over to Jacobs, to study at his leisure in the nearby library, knowing that there was a complete copy in the safe in case of loss or alteration. He requested that Jacobs return the file to the sheriff's office if the DA's office was closed.

Loudon explained that the arraignment was scheduled for tomorrow morning, at which time the defendant would be formally charged and a trial date set. He added that the county would recommend denial of bail.

Jacobs reserved comment at this time, and retired to the reading room that had been provided for him. He spent the rest of the day and much of the evening going over the file with great intensity, postponing dinner until he was finished.

Jacobs was deeply impressed with the thoroughness of the official investigation and preparation of the file. His keen legal mind was unable to find even the slightest flaw on which defense could build a case. All details had been fully investigated and reported. Often investigators will get careless and leave some important coverage incomplete, thus allowing defense to build a case on "technicality;" but not here. It was evident that the investigators had been especially anxious to nail this case down. Leaning back in his chair with a heavy sigh, Jacobs had to admit that according to solid evidence Daniel Wayland was guilty, and the chances of an acquittal were virtually non-existent.

After returning the Wayland file to the sheriff's office, Jacobs dined at Chez Alphonse, then returned to his hotel

20

and went to bed.

The next morning Jacobs and Loudon appeared at the arraignment of Daniel Wayland. Others gathered to witness the hearing included Angus Wayland, several reporters, a few curiosity seekers, and next-of-kin (as noted in the following passage). Loudon lost no time in formally charging the defendant with six counts of murder and as many counts of rape. Victims identified in the charges were six young girls varying in age from sixteen to twenty-two (not mentioned in the charges, but noted in the investigation file, was the information that four of the young victims named in the charges had been local prostitutes, and two were runaways from nearby states. It was further noted in the record that next-of-kin for these victims had been located and notified, and the same for the other victims, except for two who had been identitied but for whom no next-of-kin could be located. It was also a matter of record that parents of several of the victims had traveled to Mallon City to claim the bodies of their daughters. Families of two of the victims named in the indictment had recently returned and were present at the arraignment.)

Defense entered a plea of not guilty, although it was understood that the plea would probably be changed at a later date. Defense asked that bail be granted, pointing out that the defendant was a member of a well-established family of good repute in the community, did not have a criminal record, and thus was not apt to evade his responsibility to appear in court. Prosecution argued that due to the seriousness of the crimes bail should be denied, not only to thwart any escape attempt, but also to protect the community. Bail was denied, and the defendant ordered to remain in custody. Due to a fortunate cancellation of a scheduled trial, and the court's estimation that the Wayland trial would be of short duration, a lengthy wait for a trial date could probably be avoided. After checking with the clerk, the judge tentatively set the trial date three weeks hence. Several reporters at the scene rushed to telephone their respective publications and record the events of the morning.

Shortly after the hearing Jacobs contacted Angus Wayland and suggested they get together without delay and talk about strategy. Wayland, angry because bail was denied, jumped into his car and told Jacobs to come on out to the

21

house, then departed in haste. Before summoning his limousine, Jacobs pulled a notebook from his briefcase and jotted down several notations relating to the DA's file, and planned his strategy before heading out to meet Wayland. He knew that Wayland was counting on him to pull a rabbit out of the hat and come up with a scheme for getting Daniel acquitted, but that obviously was out of the question unless all the key officials dropped dead and the DA's file got lost or burned. Even then, he reasoned, they probably had a duplicate file, probably on microfilm, locked away in the county's safe, and with that file even an imbecile could present a solid case for conviction.

Upon arriving at the Wayland mansion, Jacobs found the huge front gate open, obviously because he was expected. At the front entrance he dismounted and banged the ornate knocker on the heavy entrance door. Wayland responded in person almost immediately, as if he had been watching for Jacobs' arrival. After shaking hands, Wayland led the way into the study and closed and locked the door behind them.

After they were comfortably seated Wayland lost no time in broaching the subject. "Well, have you had a chance to look into Dan's case?" he wanted to know.

"Yes, I have," Jacobs replied. "Everybody was very cooperative, and I had plenty of time to study the file."

"Well, how does it look?" Wayland asked impatiently. "Any chance to get him off?"

Jacobs decided that the best way to handle this was the direct approach, no hemming and hawing or beating around the bush. Accordingly he looked his client squarely in the eye and said, "Angus, there's no doubt about it, they've got the goods on Daniel. I've talked to Daniel, and apparently he really has no knowledge of committing the crimes. I don't know how that can be, but it is. I wasn't sure how he could have done all that without being seen, but now I've seen your place here I can see how it could be done. He could easily slip out of the house at night, and could conceal himself in these woods around here. The apparent scene of the crimes isn't too far from here. How he met his victims is a mystery--"

During this monologue Angus Wayland's face was beginning to turn red, and his lips were becoming tightly compressed. "Stop it!" he interrupted with a roar. "I don't want to

22

hear all this! If you can't get him off, what the hell can you do!?"

"Now calm down, Angus. We've got to talk about these things, because it's all going to come out in court if we try to make a case for acquittal."

"What do you mean, *if*?" Wayland demanded to know.

"Well, if you try to fight this thing, with the strong case they've got, it's going to be a long, bitter trial, with lots of publicity; and considering who you are, the whole damned world might want to hear about it. It could even get dirty, in which case your name or your family's name could get smeared."

Wayland's face was getting red again. It was obvious that he did not relish the idea of unfavorable publicity. By this time it was becoming obvious to Jacobs that Wayland cared more about his good name than he did about his son; but Jacobs decided to keep that to himself.

"What about plea bargaining?" Wayland asked.

"Not a chance. With the case they've got they'd be crazy to go for any reduction. No, I think what we should do is go for diminished capacity, that is, plead not guilty by reason of insanity. Since Dan doesn't remember doing the crimes, we stand a good chance of making the insanity plea stick. If we could do it that way it would be a lot easier on your reputation-- father of a sick person, rather than father of a vicious criminal. Get the picture?"

Angus thought a long moment, then with a heavy sigh acknowledged that the insanity plea was the best way to go. "But I don't like it," he growled. "I don't like any of this. But I guess that's going to be my cross to bear. Dammit anyway! Ok, go ahead, do what you have to do."

"All right, I know a psychiatrist in New York who can do this for us. He's done it before, and he's good at it. Let me use your phone and I'll give him a call."

"Yeah, right over there."

Jacobs dialed information. "Give me the number of Doctor Sidney Goldman," he requested, giving the doctor's office address. Upon being given the number he dialed direct. The receptionist answered, "Dr. Goldman's office. May I help you?"

"Hello, this is Henry Jacobs, calling from Mallon City.

23

Let me talk to Dr. Goldman."

"I'm sorry, Sir, the doctor is busy with a patient and cannot be disturbed. May I take a message?"

"I want to talk to him. How long before he's through?"

"He should be through in about ten minutes."

"Well, have him call me. This is important!" Jacobs supplied Wayland's area code and number. Then he settled down to wait.

To make conversation Jacobs commented to Wayland, "This is an interesting house. How old? Twenties? Thirties?"

Wayland wasn't much in the mood for conversation, but he responded briefly, "My father built it about 1925. He was in the oil business too. He liked this country around here, and decided to spend the rest of his life here. That's a portrait of him there on the wall." Wayland pointed to a large painting of a grim-looking, bearded gentleman on the far wall.

There followed a period of awkward silence, that fortunately was interrupted by the ringing of the telephone. Wayland answered.

"Hello, this is Doctor Goldman. I was told I could reach Henry Jacobs at this number."

"One moment. Henry, it's for you. Doctor Goldman."

"Hello, Sidney," Jacobs began. "Look, I know you're busy, but we have a crackerjack of a murder case here, and I think we have grounds for a sanity plea. Are you going to be available to spend some time here for the trial?" Jacobs supplied the approximate trial date.

"Yes, I think so. I'll have to be there a day or so ahead of time to study the case. I'll let you know if there's any problem."

"Good. I'll call you in a day or so to discuss procedure. Thanks."

Jacobs hung up the telephone. Turning to Wayland he commented, "We've got our man. Now all we can do is wait and see what develops. I'll keep you posted, and you let me know if you hear anything."

Henry Jacobs then left the house, climbed into his limousine, and departed.

That afternoon Jacobs arranged to meet with Loudon to discuss the case. Jacobs was not aggressive in these official interviews. Quite the contrary, he was usually cooperative and made no effort to intimidate officials. He believed that the courtroom was the place to do battle, not people's offices. His intent was to learn all he could about each case, and found that with a proper attitude he could learn much more than he would if he got people on the defensive.

Loudon was not acquainted with Jacobs beyond their brief meeting of the previous day, although he had heard of him in the past, and was aware of his reputation for success in difficult cases. In this case he felt that Jacobs would have his hands full if he tried for acquittal. He felt no antagonism toward Jacobs, even though he was sure that in the courtroom Jacobs, if given half a chance, would try everything in his repertoire of attack techniques to intimidate him, discredit him, and of course defeat him. Loudon had been through this many times and had been attacked by the best, so he was not concerned about that. He merely wondered what the man's strategy would be. Briefly he considered the irony of Jacobs probably getting maybe half a million dollars for this case, when he, mere attorney for the people, would get no more than his usual salary, which was in no way impressive. But he was realistic about this, and was aware that he had choices--he was not nailed to this job--and did not choose to live the kind of life that Jacobs was accustomed to. One always paid a stiff price for becoming and being wealthy, he felt, and while many were willing to pay that price, he personally was not. In fact, he saw no advantage to being wealthy, no matter what the price.

"Just thought I'd fill you in on what has happened so far," Jacobs said. "After studying the file I have to agree that you have a strong case, so I talked it over with Angus Wayland and together we decided that it would be in the best interests of Daniel and the family to enter a plea of not guilty by reason of insanity. We have plenty of reason to believe that Daniel actually did not know what he was doing when he committed those crimes, or even that he did commit them. So we believe we have a strong case in that direction. So I have asked a good friend of mine from New York, Doctor Sidney Goldman, to come down here and be a witness for the defense. Will you go along with us on that?" Jacobs' manner at that point was one of confidence that there would be a "gentlemen's agreement" here and now, that Loudon would see the logic of defense's position

25

and readily agree to go along, and they would shake hands on the deal and together prepare a suitable release for the press.

But it was not to be. Loudon leaned back in his chair and heaved a long sigh, then replied, "I appreciate your interest in helping the family, but I happen to believe that Daniel is a very dangerous person and must be removed from society. I know that according to law if he is found to be insane he must be incarcerated in a mental institution, but there's too much evidence that such a plan cannot meet the public's need for security. No, I will not support your plan."

Jacobs' demeanor changed dramatically, from smiling to a look almost of hostility. "I don't understand you," he sputtered. "Why do you have to make a federal case out of this? What harm is there in putting the boy in a mental institution instead of prison?"

"As I've already said, I don't think it is safe. There are several ways an inmate can get out of those institutions. And they do get out. I believe the public has a right to be certain that this man will not have a chance to commit further crimes. The risk is particularly great considering that the man appears to have the capability of blocking out any awareness of what he is doing while committing a crime, thus bypassing whatever normal restraints he might have against engaging in such behavior."

"But don't you believe that with treatment there's a chance he could be cured?" Jacobs asked impatiently.

"A chance? Maybe. But I've heard of several 'cured' persons who committed further serious crimes after release. I don't believe that the psychiatrists have demonstrated a great deal of credibility in that direction. Maybe they'll get better at it, but for now, I'm not convinced. With lesser crimes, maybe it is worth taking a chance; but with the seriousness of this crime spree--close to twenty young women raped and murdered over an extended period of time--I think the risk is too great."

Jacobs jumped to his feet. "We're going to fight you on this," he promised. "Believe me, you are going to hear noises that you don't want to hear, unless you change your stand!"

"What do you mean by that?"

"Just rest assured that you're not going to find it easy to pursue your strategy! This is a lot bigger that you realize, and you're getting in way over your head!"

Jacobs strode from the office, closing the door firmly behind him, leaving Loudon to ponder the ominous threat he had just heard.

Just before closing, Loudon's deputies and his capable secretary, an aging spinster named Madge Thomas, gathered in Loudon's office and asked him what he was going to do. Somehow they had gotten the word that the defense was planning to plead not guilty by reason of insanity, that the defense attorney was a powerful New York lawyer, and that Loudon had said he was going to oppose the insanity plea. One deputy asked, "If they bring in some high-powered psychiatrists who will get on the stand and swear that Daniel Wayland was insane at the time he committed the murders, what can we do about it? Wouldn't the jury be obliged to accept such expert opinion?"

"No," Loudon replied, "the jury would not be obliged to accept the findings of the psychiatrists. There's been a lot of precedent for that. But unless the psychiatrists' findings are countered in some way, the jury would probably go along with them."

"Do you have any idea how they'll go about this?" one deputy asked.

"I'm not sure," said Loudon. "Jacobs, their defense attorney, says they can make a case on the fact that Wayland does not remember committing the crimes. What little I know about it, they'll probably try to make a case of dual personality, or something like that. I won't know for sure until the trial just what they'll try to do."

"How would we fight something like that?" another deputy asked, seemingly speaking for the entire staff.

"I don't know," Loudon replied. "I guess I'm going to have to do a lot of research, since I've never handled anything just like this before. I'll have to hit the books, folks!"

"Is there anything we can do?" a deputy asked.

"In the direct sense, no," Loudon replied. "I'll have to field this one alone. However, this is going to take pretty near all of my time for the next couple or three weeks, so I'll have to depend on all of you to handle the regular work. You can check with me as you need to, but for the most part you'll be on your own."

"We'll do our best," one deputy promised, supported by firm nods of agreement by the rest of the group. The staff then departed, as their chief began to reflect on his next step in what, by any stretch of the imagination, was going to be a difficult undertaking.

* * * * *

In preparation for the upcoming trial, Henry Jacobs was on the phone with Doctor Sidney Goldman, describing Daniel Wayland's "symptoms," and receiving assurance that a plea of not guilty by reason of insanity was probably defensible. Dr. Goldman promised to get a team down there right away to study the case and make a full report of their findings. Jacobs said he would hold off on a change of plea until then.

Michael Loudon busied himself getting the paper work in order. He gave much thought to the proposed plea by defense that Wayland was not guilty by reason of insanity, and to the earlier threat that there would be serious trouble if he refused to go along with that plan; and he was not sure how he would go about countering expert defense testimony in that regard. Loudon believed that to have any chance of defeating the insanity plea he would have to challenge the concept of insanity itself as it related to criminal proceedings, that is, to satisfy the court and the jury that insanity, unless in the unlikely event that it could be demonstrated in court, is not provable and thus not a defense. That would mean, he thought, that true insanity is just as obvious to the average citizen as it is to "experts." That would mean also, Loudon realized with some chagrin, that he, the prosecution, would probably have to "explain" how an accused could commit crimes without knowing it and/or being totally unable to remember doing so. He realized that he did not have the tools to do that, and was unsure as to what expert testimony he would need to bring in for that purpose.

What to do? Loudon thought--give it up, or go ahead and fight the uphill battle against impressive odds? The more he thought about it, the more forbidding his plan seemed to be. At the same time, there was no lessening of his conviction that there was indeed something wrong with the insanity defense, or

28

of his intense desire to make sure that Wayland would have no further opportunity to commit serious crimes. Discussing the matter with fellow attorneys would surely lead to total rejection of his plan, and to possible speculations about his own sanity. In pursuing his plan he would be going against the grain of the entire social structure, including law, government, and education, all of which were thoroughly steeped in the belief that insanity, demonstrable or not, is a reality. And win or lose, what would happen to him? He would be stepping on some very large toes, not to mention vested interests to the tune of billions of dollars. There would be much publicity, most of it probably negative; and one thing was dead certain: the Wayland case would be heard around the world.

The next question was, how strongly would Angus and his powerful friends want Daniel to be insane as opposed to being a convicted felon, labeled a vicious criminal? What difference would that make in Wayland's status as a powerful influence in the world's oil economy? Loudon had not talked with Wayland himself, but he had been assured by Henry Jacobs that Wayland very much wanted Daniel to be found not guilty by reason of insanity. One might assume that "very much" to a man of Wayland's stature was a force to be reckoned with. That would mean that when Wayland learned of a serious plan to oppose his wishes, he would make a point of approaching the district attorney himself, or he would send people of great influence, to "discuss" the matter--with promises of severe consequences for failure to comply.

Obviously the easiest course would be to give in, accept and not oppose the insanity plea: leave it up to the jury, and let them take the heat if they opposed defense's plan. Perhaps he, Michael Loudon, might decide to run for senator, and you don't succeed in such a pursuit by stepping on powerful toes. Quite the contrary, you play ball with powerful people, and get them behind you.

Never before had Michael come so close to the moment of truth, where one comes face to face with his own conscience and must decide which way to go. He liked to think of himself as a highly ethical person with deeply engrained principles, a believer in the worth and dignity of every person, and in everyone's right to individual freedom and pursuit of happiness. He

29

also believed that he would stand by those beliefs and principles in the face of strong counter forces. But now, all that he had worked for, status, a good reputation, acceptance in the community, a good paying job, was possibly on the line, depending on what he did in this momentous case.

Was he being hasty in concluding that a successful stand against the insanity plea would result in such dire consequences? He dismissed the thought immediately. He was no fool, and was not given to wallowing in illusions. Then, how serious? No illusions there either. The consequences would be very serious. The worst might not come at once--it might take two or three years, even longer, to feel the impact of the destructive forces against him. Loudon knew that powerful people work behind the scenes, over lunch, in clubs and functions, to wreak their havoc--rarely out in the open, where they might be openly challenged. Normally the true perpetrators of a personal disaster might never be identified. And such persons are not inclined to give up, or to show mercy.

This was too much for Michael Loudon to handle all at once. He had to sleep on it, think about, feel it out, search his soul. He had the advantage of knowing what he was up against, as opposed to many hapless individuals who bucked power and discovered too late the consequences. He had to decide what he would do if he lost everything--everything, he reminded himself, except his personal integrity, self-esteem, and clear conscience, which no power on earth could take from him.

That night Michael Loudon had a dream. He saw himself attempting to ascend a steep hillside upon which were perched numerous houses, situated closely together in helter-skelter fashion. There were no paths or steps to make the course easier. It was dark, with no light from houses or street lights to illuminate his passage. Because the footing was quite loose in places, he would slip and slide occasionally. He was now quite high up. The earlier part of the climb had not been so bad--it was only in the last hundred feet or so that the going had gotten to be so difficult; and it was becoming more difficult by the minute. As he neared the top he felt a touch of elation as he thought he had about reached his goal; but suddenly he found himself facing a completely perpendicular wall of smooth rock, ten feet or more in height. There was no means of gaining a foothold to ascend the wall. To each side the terrain dropped off precipitously, leaving only the narrow ledge on which he was standing. As he contemplated descending, he could see that the slightest misstep could result in a fall that might terminate only at the very bottom of the steep hillside. A wave of panic swept over him as he realized his dilemma. Suddenly he awoke, much relieved to find himself lying comfortably and safely in bed, although he was sweating and still shaken by the all-too-realistic perception of near disaster.

*   *   *   *   *

Loudon did not know who was feeding information to the press about the Wayland case, but it was obvious that secrecy was out of the question. Reporters were frequently in contact with Loudon, informing him that they knew of defense's plan to plead not guilty by reason of insanity, and wanting to know what he planned to do about it. Loudon held his ground, stating that it was too soon to outline strategy. The defense had entered a plea of not guilty, and any plan to change the plea was thus far mere speculation. Loudon did, however, indicate that he would be opposed to a plea of not guilty by reason of insanity in any case of this kind, on the grounds that the mental hospital is not sufficiently secure to guarantee the public's safety.

"Could the suspect be cured if he was hospitalized?" one reporter asked.

"The suspect cannot be hospitalized for that purpose, but I suppose some effort might be made in that regard by the hospital staff. However, the records available to me show no instance where the 'patient' who had committed this type of crime was ever 'cured.' There have been cases where an inmate was pronounced cured, released, and later committed serious crimes. That is always a possibility in a case of this kind, and I don't believe that we can afford to take that chance."

"What about the public sentiment against punishing the insane?" another reporter inquired.

"I'm not sure that the entire public feels that way about it. In my opinion most people are more interested in security than

31

in sympathy where multiple murders have been committed."

"What about the death penalty if the defendant is found to be sane?"

"I will not demand the death penalty," Loudon declared. "I am not dead set against the death penalty--I think there are cases where it can be justified--but I'm not strongly for it either. You all know my position on this. We've been over this ground before."

The afternoon and evening newspapers all ran front page headlines announcing the district attorney's statement that he would oppose a plea of not guilty by reason of insanity in the Wayland case.

Shortly before office closing time the following day Loudon received a call from Angus Wayland. "What the hell do you think you're up to?" Wayland shouted into the telephone. "I want that insanity plea to stick!"

"It isn't up to me," Loudon countered. "I just state my view on the matter, and the jury makes the decision."

"But if you just stated your position, but didn't try to fight it, the jury would find for the defense, wouldn't they?" Wayland asked gruffly.

"I don't know that for sure. There have been lots of cases where the jury went against what appeared to be a stacked court, where the prosecution and defense appeared to be in harmony."

"Well, be that as it may, I don't want to take that chance. I want you to back off, go along with the insanity plea."

"And if I don't?" Loudon asked calmly.

"If you don't," Wayland declared ominously, "you are for sure going to wish you had!" Wayland slammed the receiver down.

So there it was. Loudon knew that Wayland was not bluffing, and he knew that the man could probably buy all the clout he needed to get his way. Loudon had wondered how he would feel when he finally came face to face with the full potential of the power that could be brought to bear against him. Now he sat back and probed his inner feelings to determine just how he did feel. He wasn't beyond kidding himself, he knew that, so he tried to look past that possibility to get at the true feelings. To assist in that effort he tried to imagine himself being stripped of his job and subjected to public disfavor, accused of serious crimes that he didn't commit, and so on. Oddly enough, at this moment he felt quite calm and unconcerned about what might happen to him. As before, however, he reminded himself that time would tell, particularly since he had not yet faced the sting of reality.

A harbinger of future events was not long in coming. The next morning Loudon had a visit from a stranger, a stern-looking man in his mid thirties, dressed in a well-pressed, single breasted, three-piece suit, wearing horn-rimmed glasses and carrying a briefcase. The stranger introduced himself as Franklin Dupree, Assistant to the Secretary, Department of Vital Resources, Federal Government.

"What can I do for you?" Loudon asked. The Federal man did not offer to shake hands, so Loudon did not offer a hand either. He did, however, invite the man to have a chair.

As he seated himself Dupree began, speaking in a well-modulated, confident voice. "Sir, we have evidence that you plan to oppose the insanity plea in the Wayland case. Is that correct?"

Loudon stared at Dupree, then asked, "How did you find out about that so soon?"

"We have our sources," Dupree replied stiffly.

"Yeah, I think I know who. Yes, I had planned to oppose the plea."

"The Government would prefer that you not do that."

Loudon remained perfectly still for a long moment, staring at Dupree, then said softly, "And just why is that? We're dealing with a very dangerous man here."

"All I am permitted to tell you is that certain key persons in the far east oil cartel, MAPS (Mediterranean Association of Petroleum Shippers), an organization that does a lot of business for us through the Wayland empire, are very sensitive about doing business with criminals. In their view, if there is one criminal in a family, the entire family is criminal. In order to secure our petroleum supplies, we must protect the Wayland family from the scandal of a criminal conviction. Otherwise there is danger that MAPS will shut us off, as the Arab nations did several years ago. I am sure you understand how important it is for us to avoid that risk."

"If the situation is that sensitive," Loudon asked, "Why hasn't the Federal Government taken steps before this to work out a more secure system? That kind of dependence on one family, one empire, one cartel seems pretty shaky to me. How did we get into that kind of bind?"

"I am not prepared to answer that," Dupree replied disdainfully.

Loudon reflected for a moment, then stated firmly, "I'm sorry, I can't believe that such dependence really exists. This whole thing sounds like a scam to me, and I'm having nothing to do with it. I believe that Daniel Wayland is a very dangerous man, and it is my duty to see that the public is protected against such a severe threat. Finding him insane and sending him off to a mental hospital does not, in my view, guarantee that kind of protection." Loudon did not say so, but he was convinced that sending this federal representative here was nothing but a power play, generated by some high federal official, in reponse to pressure applied by Angus Wayland, who probably had something on the official. No, he definitely was not going to be intimidated into changing his plan, and said so.

Upon hearing Loudon's refusal, Dupree looked as though he had been struck. Apparently, Loudon thought, the man had been sent here under threat to get results, or else.

"You don't know what you're doing," Dupree sputtered. "If you don't grant what the government wants, you can be in serious trouble."

"Well, that's my problem," Loudon declared. As the two men stood up he continued, "You go back and tell your boss that he can do what he wants, I have a job to do here and I intend to do it. Case closed!"

Dupree grabbed his briefcase and strode angrily toward the door, slamming the door behind him as he departed.

Loudon struggled with feelings of resentment at this obvious effort to intimidate him. If he had any doubts about what he was going to do at the trial they were now gone--he was going to do everything possible to defeat the insanity plea. The only question was, how to do it? To that end he decided to consult with Janice Farley, and called to make a date.

* * * * *

34

Early in her college work Janice Farley decided that nature is the ultimate truth in everything. Man may create ideas and conceive of things that are not found in nature, but to achieve validity such conceptions must be rooted in nature. This view, she was frank to admit, caused some problems in her striving for her advanced degree, because it seemed even the brightest of her professors often entertained myths and misconceptions that could not possibly be rooted in nature. She learned to endure such deviations, deciding that she could not change the world. After all, she reasoned, our current society is only a few generations removed from a host of ancient beliefs in gods, goddesses, nymphs, fates, and what have you, and little more than a few decades away from probably as many myths about how the human body works. She had been fascinated by a 1902 major retail catalog in which she found numerous ads for potions and electric belts that were said to cure everything from chilblains to sexual problems and even mental problems, and surely, she reasoned, despite the rapid pace of learning and discoveries in modern medicine, one could still expect to find residues of myths from the past, particularly in areas not readily subject to scientific study, development, and control, such as the mind.

As she now waited to greet her good friend, Michael Loudon, little did Janice realize that she would soon become intricately involved in one effort to change deeply-entrenched mythology in an area of immense significance for almost everyone.

It was a pleasant evening, warm, with a hint of breeze bringing scents of lilac and jasmine from the nearby city gardens, so Michael and Janice decided to take a walk in the park. There was a broad, paved path that stretched completely around a central pond, a distance of almost three miles. The surface of the pond was unruffled except for the gentle wakes of swimming birds, and reflected its wooded environment with surprising clarity. A stroller by the pond could gaze upon a host of lily pads with an abundance of pink and white flowers. A single white swan sailed smoothly past in the near distance, barely disturbing the tranquility of the scene.

In this soothing atmosphere Michael felt somewhat removed from the stresses of the last couple of days, and much closer to the calm security of nature. Janice noticed, however, that he seemed somewhat preoccupied. "You didn't bring me out here just to look at the scenery, did you?" she asked teasingly.

"No," Michael grinned. "I have a little problem I'd like to talk to you about, if you don't mind."

"Of course not. Go ahead!"

"I've definitely made up my mind to oppose the insanity plea in the Wayland case," Michael began. "But I'm not sure how to go about it. I thought maybe you could help me work out an approach."

"I'll be glad to do what I can," Janice replied. "Where would you like to begin?"

"What would you suggest?"

Janice paused for a thoughtful moment, then suggested, "Why don't we start from the beginning: with the concept of mental illness. The concept itself is a myth."

"Why do you say that?" asked Michael, puzzled.

"Well," Janice replied, "the concept is based on an ancient belief, which by the way still exists, that the mind produces behavior, that is, people do certain things simply because they put their mind to it. Many great thinkers, fascinated with the workings of the mind, have even gone so far as to assume that the mind and body are separate entities, which makes it easy to conclude that the mind produces behavior."

"How is that? I don't follow you."

Janice stopped walking as she attempted to summarize a difficult topic. "The body is like a car," she said. "Each part has a job to do, a function. If something goes wrong with your car, if it does not function properly, you don't blame the function, you try to find out which part is not doing its job. The mind is not a part, it is a function. So if you say the function is ill, you are saying that it is impaired; and when you do that, you are blaming the function for the problem, not the part."

"I see what you mean. Like with the car, if a part, like a distributor, is not working right, you blame the malfunction, not the part. And with the mind, like you say, if you say it is ill, you are blaming it for the problem. Going back to he distributor analogy, if you blame the malfunction, you wouldn't even think of checking the distributor, would you? "

"Exactly! And by the same analogy, if you blame the mind, you wouldn't even try to find out why it is 'malfunctioning.' You would just concentrate on trying to find out what is wrong with it."

"Okay, I'm with you. Now, to take this a step farther, what is this 'problem' that we're blaming the mind for?"

"Behavior," replied Janice simply.

"I get it. If a person is not behaving properly, and we believe the mind produces behavior, ergo, there's something wrong with the mind."

The couple strolled lazily on, briefly silent as they drank in the pleasures of the evening. Coming to an inviting park bench, they seated themselves, stretching their legs as they gazed upon the tranquil lake, now dimly lighted by the setting sun.

After a brief silence Michael posed a question: "I'm with you on this: a function can't be sick; but just for the sake of argument, what's wrong with the idea that the mind can be sick? What about those people who do weird things, like they're possessed or something? Wouldn't you say they're sick?"

"When you say sick," Janice inquired, "just what do you mean?"

"Come on, you know what I'm talking about! There must be something haywire inside the person to make him behave that way!"

Janice squeezed Michael's arm playfully, then commented, "Yes, I know, that's the dilemma that most people face."

Michael stated seriously, "Really, I need some answers, if I am to go into that courtroom and face probably one of the most famous psychiatrists in the country. I don't want to look like a fool!"

Janice's face tightened as she contemplated the enormity of Michael's dilemma. She pictured herself, with what she knew, in the same situation, trying to convince a jury that the famous psychiatrist didn't know what he was talking about; and she shuddered at the prospect. It would be like trying to convince the early Greeks that there was not a plurality of gods and goddesses. Then, quite seriously, she faced Michael and asked, "Michael, have you considered what might happen to you if

37

you try what you have in mind?"

"Yes I have; and believe me, it's scary. I know I could lose my job and even be drummed out of the county. Or worse. But I can't stand the idea of Wayland or anyone like him being given a chance to go on committing horrible crimes. They say the mental institution is secure. Maybe--but what about the people running the institution? You haven't talked to Wayland, but I assure you, he looks and acts like a normal, healthy young adult. I can see that after about six months in an institution the brass there could conclude that there's nothing wrong with the guy and turn him loose. Then what are the odds that he wouldn't commit further crimes? Nothing will have changed. He'd still be the same guy that did it the first time."

"I admire you for even considering alternatives in this case," Janice said. "And I'm sure there'll be others who feel the same way."

"Yeah, I suppose there will be. The problem is, they may not be the ones who have the most to say about what happens to me."

"I know." Janice's voice expressed something like resignation, along with a hint of sadness.

After several moments of silent thought, Janice said to Michael, "Just how far do you want to go with this, the psychology and everything? We could get into it pretty deep, and it could be a little hard to handle."

Without hesitation Michael replied, "I want to go the whole nine yards--the full treatment." Then, half teasingly, he added, "How far are you willing to go?"

Janice laughed. "You're testing me, aren't you?"

"Well, yes and no," Michael admitted. "But seriously, if you are willing, I'd really like your help in this thing."

Janice hesitated briefly, then replied, "I'll be glad to help you in any way I can. But I think we'll have to get some help. I'll give that some thought. Now bear in mind, if at any point you change your mind and want to stop, let me know!"

"I will," Michael assured her.

As the couple rose from the bench to continue their walk, Janice said, "It is getting a little late--why don't we get together over dinner, and talk about it later?"

"Great," agreed Michael enthusiastically. "How about Chez Alphonse?"

"Fine."

"Good. I'll drop by about 7:00."

Later at Chez Alphonse Michael and Janice enjoyed a cocktail, then ordered. Throughout their friendship the two had demonstrated quite similar tastes in both food and drink. For cocktails they were partial to martinis, mutually shunning Scotch, commonly held to be the choice of intellectuals. In wine selections the choice depended largely on associated menus, but there was no snobbery here: American wines were as good as French, if not better in many cases, and a good wine, either white or red, need not be expensive. In short their focus was on enjoyment, not showing off. Both were flexible in their food choice, tending toward a balance of red meat, fowl, and seafood, with an abundance of fresh vegetables and fruit.

Michael's choice on this occasion was a spencer steak, medium, with mushrooms, baked potato, and fresh peas in a white sauce. Janice selected a combination seafood plate (called the captain's plate). Both enjoyed the salad bar, a very popular feature at Chez Alphonse.

In contrast to the tensions of recent days, Michael felt relaxed and free from worldly troubles. He felt comfortable with Janice, seeing her as a friend who could be depended on to stand by him through any kind of trouble. Now, as they lingered over after-dinner coffee, he began to feel a closeness to her, a sense of warmth and delight, that transcended such objective attributes as loyalty and trust.

Janice was subtly aware that something was happening here, although she was not yet able to bring that awareness into focus. She sensed the change in Michael's perception of her, and at the same time detected some sort of change in her perceptions of him.

These changes were temporarily obscured as Michael brought up the topic of their earlier discussion, how to proceed in opposing the insanity plea in court. Janice responded almost eagerly to the introduction of the topic, saying, "I've thought about that all evening, and don't feel confident to point out any positive directions for you. But I have an idea: why don't we go and talk to a good friend of mine, Doctor Jefferson Folger? He's a semi-retired GP, but he used to be a psychiatrist. He gave that up after becoming disillusioned about what psychiatry had to offer. OK?"

"Yeah, fine," Michael agreed. "When did you want to see him?"

"I think right now, if you have the time. I'm sure he's home. He won't mind if we drop in on him."

"Good. Let's go!"

CHAPTER THREE

Jefferson Folger, MD, was sixty-five years old but could easily pass for fifty, being in excellent physical condition. He had studied medicine at a prominent eastern college and obtained his degree with a minimum of trouble. At the time he finished his schooling he was fascinated, as were many of his contemporaries, with the burgeoning field of psychoanalysis and psychiatry, following the influence of Sigmund Freud, and decided to specialize in that field. After a couple of years of general internship in a general hospital, as required for all aspiring MD's at the time, he began a three-year internship in psychiatry. For that purpose he was assigned to a large eastern mental hospital.

Folger had expected classes of instruction in the hospital, but there were none. He sat in on conferences, seminars, and diagnostic boards. He visited group treatment sessions. The professional focus in the hospital was Freudian, although much of the diagnostic framework was pre-Freudian.

When Folger first entered the mental hospital he was struck by the visible evidence of so-called mental disorders--individuals sitting in corners, staring at nothing; men and woman with misshapen faces and bodies sitting or moving about, paying little attention to what was happening about them, some occasionally uttering strange noises, cries, or screams. At times an inmate would approach him, smile or grin inappropriately, and utter something quite meaningless. One middle-aged fellow, hardly able to speak, grabbed Folger's clothing and clung desperately to him, until an attendant intervened and got the fellow interested in something else.

The total scene in the hospital was rather disheartening to Folger, as he could see these inmates as being hopelessly lost, beyond the powers of medicine to cure them. Later he learned that many of the inmates were not beyond help, that modern medications were often so effective that many inmates, even some of those most seriously affected, could be sent back to their communities, under the supervision of families or local agencies. All in all, the populations of most mental hospitals, Folger learned, were being rapidly reduced, due largely to modern medicines. It was soon apparent to him that given these

41

miracle drugs, psychiatry was in a position to render a quite worthwhile service to society.

With this encouragement Dr. Jefferson Folger, during his internship, devoted himself energetically to learning the diagnostic categories and numerous medications now available to psychiatists. He also monitored some sessions of psychotherapy, to learn more about the techniques related to that form of treatment. He noted the psychotherapists' calm, reassuring approach to their subjects, including efforts to draw them out and encourage them to talk about their problems.

His internship finished, Folger, MD and now psychiatrist, left the hospital and established a two-room suite of offices in the downtown area. Proudly he watched as the artist lettered his name and occupation on the entrance door. He hired and trained an attractive young woman to be his receptionist and stenographer. Once fully established, he let it be known about town that he was in business and ready to receive referrals.

Referrals were not long in coming. Other psychiatrists in the area were overloaded, and the community was glad to have a new resource.

Dr. Folger began his practice with much confidence and belief that he could make a difference in the world of troubled people. Following the usual practice he scheduled each session at fifty minutes.

It was not long before Dr. Folger began to experience disillusionment, which increased steadily as time went on. He had trouble sleeping at night. He began to feel uncomfortable around people who knew his profession. He was not yet married, and though he had previously sought the company of eligible young women, now he avoided them, finding that romantic sessions often developed into mutual suspicions as to each other's real reasons for doing this or that. He became somewhat distrustful of people he did not even know, picturing the deeper, hostile unconscious motives that, according to Freudian doctrine, most people carry around with them, and fearing that these unconscious hostilities would prevail wherever feasible in social interactions. He had been confident that he could help people, but was rapidly losing that confidence. He began to suffer feelings of inferiority.

Unwilling to accept the changes in himself and his way of

life, Dr. Folger began to take stock of himself and to think about what he should do. As soon as he fully admitted to himself that he was in the wrong profession, he closed his office, acquired a larger suite, hired a registered nurse (keeping his erstwhile office girl), and went into practice as a general practitioner, a move that he never regretted.

Now, semi-retired, Dr. Folger sat in his comfortable living room, pondering the aforesaid developments in his life.

The doorbell rang, and Dr. Folger arose and ambled toward the door. Most people these days, if they cannot see the caller at the front door, will inquire as to who is there before opening the door. Not so Dr. Folger, not any more, at least, since he gave up psychiatry. He boldly opened the door, and was pleased to recognize his good friend, Janice Farley, with a companion. "Come in," he invited graciously. "Have a seat. Want some coffee, wine, anything?"

Janice introduced Michael, then both accepted comfortable seats. They declined anything to eat or drink, saying they had just finished dinner.

"All right," Dr. Folger began, "to what do I owe this pleasant intrusion?"

"We have something a little off the beaten track to talk with you about, if you don't mind," Janice explained.

"That sounds interesting," Dr. Folger beamed. "What is it?

"Better let me field that one," said Michael. As Dr. Folger assumed a listening posture, he began, "I am the district attorney for Mallon County, and I am facing a crisis. It has to do with a difficult case involving a series of murders involving rape--you've no doubt heard of the 'midnight strangler' murders (Dr. Folger nodded). Well, the sheriff, with the help of U.S. Government people, managed to solve the crime, and arrested Daniel Wayland, son of our local oil baron. The case against Wayland is so strong that the defense is not even going to attempt proof of innocence. Instead, they plan to plead not guilty by reason of insanity. I happen to believe that Daniel is too dangerous a person to take a chance going that route. Protection of the public is my chief responsibility. The family wants the insanity ruling, and are willing to generate power to make it happen. They've already hired one of the country's top lawyers from New York, who has now engaged one of the top

43

psychiatrists in New York."

"Which one?" Dr.Folger asked.

"Dr. Sidney Goldman."

"Yes, I know who he is. He has quite a reputation in the courts. Go on."

"Well, I know what I am up against. My professional future could even be on the line. But that's beside the point. I've made my decision to oppose the insanity plea, no matter what. But I'm not sure just how to go about it. Janice said you were once a psychiatrist, and thought if we talked it over with you, you might have some suggestions."

"Yes, I tried psychiatry, but not for long. The profession is not all it's cracked up to be. Now, what would you like to know?"

"All right, to start out, what is your view on the concept of insanity?"

Dr. Folger peered at Michael suspiciously, suspecting a possible ruse to trap him. Then, satisfied that Loudon was sincere, he began to speak.

"On the whole, insanity is a phony concept, invented and used centuries ago because people had no other explanations for strange behavior. The term 'sane' comes from the Latin 'sanus,' meaning healthy. I'm not sure where the word health comes from, probably from the Middle English term 'haelth.' Anyway, ancient people had the notion that someone who behaves strangely is unhealthy. The mind was believed to direct behavior, therefore the person who acted strangely was thought to be sick in the mind. Thus the concept of mental illness, as Janice has probably explained to you, is almost as old as civilization. 'Insane' and 'mentally ill' are broadly synonymous.

"With modern knowledge of the body and how it works we should by now have gotten away from the mental illness idea, but it has never been seriously challenged, because, I think, it is too valuable as a tool for manipulating and controlling people. Someone who believes that the mind, as such, can go haywire, is as vulnerable as someone who believes in evil spirits, and thus susceptible to being manipulated by persons who claim to have knowledge of what goes on in the mind. It is a dangerous tool--labeling someone as 'mentally ill' can have

44

a devastating effect on the person's entire life. It can go on a person's record and be used against him or her in many ways. A person so labeled can be denied employment, or certain privileges such as having a driver's license. A person can be hospitalized and incarcerated in a mental facility without any choice simply because some psychiatrist labeled him or her as mentally ill or incapacitated, possibly on so flimsy a basis as a third party's reports and descriptions of odd behavior. Once that sort of thing is established there is no defense against it. In other words, there is no way a person can 'prove' that he is sane, if influential persons say he isn't; and the harder one tries to do so, the worse it gets. Unfortunately many psychiatrists and clinical psychologists allow themselves to be used for that purpose. You've probably seen a lot of that in the courts, Michael. And when you have a 'body of knowledge' such as psychoanalytic theory and terminology that is made up mostly of false concepts and terms but is not seriously challenged by anyone, the idea of mental illness is difficult to oppose. Nobody listens to you, or worse, they may try to attack or discredit you."

Dr. Folger paused briefly, then went on, "Of course there are those people who are largely incapacitated because of some malfunction in the body, the ones you see in mental hospitals and occasionally in public. But I'm sure there is physical abnormality to account for most of those symptoms. The mind is a function that can be affected by physical disorders, just like any other function, so there can be a diminishing of mental powers in such syndromes; but that by no means indicates that the impairment of mental powers is what is causing the problem. It is just part of the problem. I suppose it is all right to refer to such syndromes as insanity, or the term more commonly used in medicine, psychosis--I don't have too much objection to that, as long as it is understood that the problem is physical, not mental."

Dr. Folger paused again, this time to judge whether his audience, particularly Loudon, was still listening or not. He was soon satisfied that he need have no concerns in that regard. Loudon had never heard anything quite like this before, and was literally hanging on every word. Janice, too, was listening intently, because some of Dr. Folger's revelations were new to her as well.

"But as you know, Michael," Dr. Folger went on, "in the courts they have this idea that a person can be insane part of the time, and perfectly sane at other times. I think that is ridiculous. That's like saying a person can have cancer part of the time, and be perfectly healthy at other times (without treatment, of course). That the ailment can occur off and on, like changes in the weather. Medically speaking, in my opinion insanity, or psychosis, is like diabetes: you can reduce the symptoms with medication, and make it possible for the patient to function more or less normally; but once you have the disease, you have it for life. There is no cure for it. You have to stay on the medication as long as you live, or suffer relapse."

"So what you are saying," offered Michael, " is that where a patient has been diagnosed as psychotic, or insane, if there appears to be a genuine 'cure' the person wasn't psychotic in the first place. Right?"

"That's very astute," agreed Dr. Folger. "In my view, yes."

Michael now leaned forward and remarked earnestly, "If I read you right, if a person who committed a serious crime was found to have been insane at the time the crime was committed, he would have to be incarcerated for the rest of his life, or he would be apt to commit further serious crimes after release. Do I read you correctly?"

"As I see it, yes."

"--Even if the person was put on medication that appeared to result in a cure, and he was thus released--if he did not stay on the medication, he might commit further crimes."

"Yes, indeed."

"But once released, and on his own, he might not continue the medication."

Now a bit excited, Michael continued, "Now if the criminal who was found to have been insane actually was not insane, medication wouldn't do any good, would it?"

Impressed by this unexpected display of logic, Dr. Folger paused a moment or two, then stated, "I hadn't thought about it along those lines, but I think you're quite right. If the person who committed the crime was not actually insane, then his motive for committing the crime was something else, and the medication would not alter that in any way."

46

"So such a person, in a mental hospital, would appear to be quite normal," said Michael.

"I guess he would."

"And if released, medication or no, there would be absolutely nothing to deter the person if he chose to commit further crimes, would there, aside from the possible fear of getting caught, retribution, etc.?"

"Again, that would appear to be correct," Dr. Folger agreed.

As Michael pondered the significance of these latest insights, Janice took advantage of the break to pursue a question of her own:

"There's something I've been wanting to ask you, Dr. Folger. Since I am not a biologist--is it possible for a person, under severe stress due to high levels of fear with no perceivable means to reduce it, to go into a psychotic state?"

"That's a good question," said Dr. Folger. "I do think it is possible for a person in such a state to begin behaving in a manner that appears to be psychotic, but really isn't."

"I get you," Michael broke in. "I've seen films of persons being tortured. They scream, make horrible sounds, struggle against their bonds, and actually go into a frenzied state. I have seen drug addicts in the throes of severe withdrawal, and they behave much the same as that."

"Yes," Janice put in, "a person can understand that sort of behavior if they can see what caused it; but if the torture was inside the person, not visible to others, an observer might think the person was indeed mad."

Suddenly Michael laughed heartily, then related, "I remember a time when I was a kid, I saw a guy running around in an open field, screaming, gesturing wildly, grabbing and tearing at his clothes. Finally he jumped into an open water trough. I was scared, because I thought the guy was plumb crazy, and might take after me. Later I found out that the guy had gotten a bunch of bees inside his shirt and pants."

Janice and Dr. Folger joined heartily in the laughter as they mentally pictured the scene described by Michael.

As the laughter subsided Michael stated, "I've got one more question, if you don't mind."

"Go ahead."

"The defense in the Wayland case is going to base their insanity plea on the apparent fact that Daniel can't remember committing any crimes. What are your views on that?"

"My views on that," echoed Dr. Folger thoughtfully. "I don't think that's an indication of psychosis. I think the fellow doesn't remember simply because he can't reconcile the criminal behavior with the image he tries to maintain with his family. He could remember if he didn't mind being labeled criminal. He's got that strong father figure, who he is undoubtedly scared to death of, and the fear of what might happen if the father found out what he'd done could certainly cause him to deny to himself that he ever did those things. I think most of us do that occasionally, but when it's about behavior that isn't serious it never gets brought out into the open."

At this point Michael had begun to feel that he had some answers he could use, and began to feel more confident. He smiled as he compared his present level of understanding to that of a few hours ago. Considering how clear this all seemed to him now, he wondered why educators were not teaching people such insights. On a sudden impulse he asked Dr. Folger, half teasingly, half seriously, "How does it feel to know all this, knowing that nobody else--figuratively speaking--knows it?"

"Well, that's a good question," replied Dr. Folger, apparently not ready to answer it.

"It makes me wonder how the guy felt who discovered that the earth is round, when everyone else was convinced it was flat," Michael offered.

"I like that analogy," said Janice. "There have been lots of innovators in the world's history, and I've often wondered how they made out while the world was discovering that they were right and the rest of the world was wrong."

"We know two who didn't make it," Dr. Folger added. "Christ was killed on the cross, and Aristotle was forced to drink poison hemlock. Other innovators that we know of, composers, artists, writers, who died penniless or worse because the world was not ready to accept the greatness of their works."

"Which sort of brings it back to me," said Michael. "I didn't think it was a big deal to oppose an insanity plea in court, but

48

what I've learned the last few days, I feel like I'm going against a world that still thinks the earth is flat."

"You might get by with it if you weren't up against some powerful people," opined Dr. Folger. "Now you know what you're up against, do you still want to go ahead with it?"

"Yes, I do," replied Michael firmly. "I've thought it over, and decided that for my own personal peace of mind, it's the only way I can go. The thing now is, do you have any suggestions as to how to go about it?"

"First of all," replied Dr. Folger, "I suggest you go and talk to Dr. James Forsyth at the college. He's basically a biologist, but he also teaches anatomy in pre-med. He can help you get a better understanding of how the living system works. He might have some suggestions, too."

"I know I'll be cross-examining a highly skilled psychiatrist on the stand," Michael said. "Any suggestions as to how to approach him?"

"Get him to define his terms," said Dr. Folger succinctly. With that the doctor indicated that he would like to get on with what he was doing.

Michael and Janice obligingly rose, thanked the doctor profusely, and prepared to leave. Suddenly Michael turned and asked Dr. Folger, "Would you testify if I called on you?"

"Absolutely not," the doctor replied firmly, meanwhile making it clear that the interview was over.

Michael and Janice elected to walk the few blocks to her apartment. They strolled slowly, enjoying the warm air and the pleasant smells of the evening. There was little traffic on the adjoining street. Occasional street lights seemed to give the night a soft glow that added to the charm of the setting. The two acknowledged that the discussion with Dr. Folger had been most interesting, but beyond that they did not seem inclined to elaborate. Instead, their thoughts seemed to be focussed in quite another direction.

After they had walked along quietly for a short while, Michael spoke, "You know, I've always thought of you as a very good friend, but considering everything that has happened lately, somehow I've come to feel closer to you. Not like a sister--it's different. It's a nice feeling. I like it."

Janice stopped, turned and faced Michael. She reached out

and took both of his hands in hers. The warm touch was stimulating, almost exciting. With a low voice she replied, "I'm glad you said that. I've been feeling closer to you, too, and--I like it. Thank you."

The couple walked on silently for a time, now holding hands as naturally as if they had been doing it for years. They were not thinking of anything in particular, content to feel the warmth of the evening and the subdued excitement of this new discovery: that their regard for one another had transcended the mere comfort and security of an agreeable friendship.

Finally they arrived at Janice's apartment. At this point there could have been an awkward moment, but no--they felt as natural and unfettered in their attachment as two puppies. It was late--they felt no obligation to pursue their new discovery at the moment--so Michael supplied the rhetoric to meet the needs of the situation:

"It's quite late, and I think I'd better get ready for a big day tomorrow, trying to digest all I've learned recently."

"Me, too," Janice agreed. "I've got exams tomorrow."

The two were holding hands, and though not really averse to separating, Michael decided to take one more step toward the future. "You know," he said, as he grinned broadly, "It just occurs to me that in all the time we've known each other we've never kissed. Want to give it a try?"

"I like that idea!" agreed Janice enthusiastically, as she threw her arms around Michael's neck and planted her lips firmly on his. Michael matched her enthusiasm in returning the kiss. After a moment Janice extricated herself, laughing, and said, "I guess we'd better--"

"Yes, I guess we'd better," Michael agreed, chuckling. He added, "I like what's happening here. I will sleep like a rock tonight. Good night!"

"Me too," Janice said. "Good night."

Janice then entered her apartment and Michael trudged off to retrieve his car, feeling a wonderment that he had not felt for many years. He was starting to feel that despite all the trouble in the world, there was underneath it all a glory that was nature, dirtied but unadulterated by man's greed, hostility, and destructiveness.

The next day Loudon contacted the college and made an

appointment to meet with Professor Forsyth, as suggested by Dr. Folger. He found the professor to be an average-sized man, probably in his mid fifties, with a small chin beard and no moustache. As many professors do, Loudon had oft noted, the man had a thick head of hair, in this case black with a good mixture of grey.

"I have about ten minutes between classes," Forsyth said. "What can I do for you?"

Loudon identified himself as the DA for Mallon County, and said that he had been referred by Dr. Folger. Then he began, "I have a difficult case to talk to you about. I'm sure you've heard of the Wayland case (Forsyth nodded). Perhaps you've heard also that the defense wants to plead not guilty by reason of insanity. To make a long story short, I intend to oppose that plea, on the grounds that Wayland is too dangerous to be confined in a mental institution. Dr. Folger suggested that you might be able to help me in making my case."

"What for? I don't believe in mental illness--I think it is a myth--but I am not an expert, and my testimony wouldn't be any good to you. They wouldn't accept it."

"I don't need your testimony as a mental health expert. Dr. Folger said you are primarily a biologist, and teach anatomy to pre-med students. Is that correct?"

"Yes, it is," agreed Forsyth. "But how would that fit in?"

"I could use your testimony as to certain aspects of the structure and functioning of the human body," explained Loudon. "Would you be willing to appear in that regard? It wouldn't take very long, maybe a half hour at most."

"It all depends. What sort of questions did you have in mind?"

"I have the questions all written down here." Loudon pulled a piece of paper from his breast pocket and spread it out before Professor Forsyth, who examined the list intently.

"Yes, I think I see what you're getting at," Forsyth remarked, looking up from the list.

"Right," said Loudon. "I want to lay an expert foundation regarding the relationship between body parts and body functions before I start my cross examination of the psychiatrist, defense's chief witness."

"It sounds like you're well prepared for this test," remarked

51

Forsyth.

"I've been doing my homework. I've been talking with Janice Farley--I believe you know her--and Dr. Folger. They've been a big help to me."

"I admire your courage in what you are trying to do," said Forsyth. "I'm sure you are aware that you are bucking a pretty powerful system."

"In more ways than you know," asserted Loudon.

"Well, I'll be glad to do what I can," promised Forsyth. "But I do request that you stick to the questions you have written down here."

"You can be assured of that," said Loudon. "Fine, I'll notify you of the date and time as soon as I can. Thanks very much."

Having secured the testimony of Professor Forsyth, Loudon felt that he had pretty much rounded out his case in the upcoming trial. From this point on he needed only to work out his questions and techniques for cross-examining defense witnesses.

Back in his office, Loudon attended to some routine matters that had accumulated during the last few days while his attention was diverted elsewhere, assigned some new cases to his capable staff, and settled down to prepare for the trial.

It was soon evident, however, that he was not able fully to concentrate on the task, as his mind kept taking him back to what had occurred between him and Janice the previous evening. He was aware of an inner stirring, of a sort to which he had been a stranger for many years. It was not an uncomfortable stirring. On the contrary, it was warm and invigorating. He felt eager to be with Janice again, to tell her how he felt. He found himself dreaming of future hours of pleasure with her, doing and enjoying things together. He was eager for the day to end so that they could take up where they left off last evening. But it was too early to call, so he forced himself to concentrate on his work.

Across town, at the college, Janice Farley was having a similar experience. While actually teaching a class she was able to concentrate, but in her office, with nothing facing her that demanded attention, she found herself thinking about the discoveries of last evening. She smiled secretly as she recalled her enthusiastic acceptance of Michael's kiss proposal, and for the moment felt almost like a school girl again. It was nice, Janice thought. She liked this new feeling. It was like finding the fountain of youth, in a way--a reawakening, a rejuvenation. She winced as for a brief moment she recalled the possible trouble facing Michael after the trial, but that was immediately replaced by a feeling that the trouble did not matter. With this newly discovered joy, she and Michael together could face any kind of difficulty.

After what seemed an eternity the work day ended, and Michael closed his office and left to meet Janice. He had been in contact with her by telephone a few moments ago, and they had agreed to meet in the park for a walk prior to deciding upon arrangements for dinner.

As he walked toward the park Michael began to have uncomfortable thoughts about this new experience. It came on so rapidly--was it love? Infatuation? Escape from worries about the future? Was he about to impose his own need for gratification on a very dear friend, who might not feel the same way about him, but would pretend that she did just to please him? Michael felt a moment of apprehension, but replaced it immediately with a resolve to talk this out with Janice, and above all, to let her make up her own mind as to how she felt and what she wanted.

Michael met Janice at the designated spot, and grinned broadly as he caught sight of her. Janice was ready with her own expressions of pleasure upon seeing him. It was evident to Michael, rather a good student of human behavior, that in Janice's greeting there was no pretense, no restraint, and no other artificial something that might spell misgivings about this relationship.

A big hug and a kiss seemed the most natural thing to do at the moment, and the couple obliged with unfettered sincerity. Following this ardent embrace they began to stroll hand in hand along the path beside the pond. Gone were Michael's questions about what was happening to him. In Janice's arms he knew that this was real, and it was good. He wasn't sure what to call it yet, but then, he thought, what does it matter? We don't have to label everything. Just take it as it is, work it into your life focus, and make the most of it.

53

After they had walked silently for a few moments, enjoying the warm evening and the pleasant smells emanating from the park foliage, Michael decided to express something of what he had felt.

"I was a little surprised at the suddenness of what happened between us," he began. "Where did it come from? And why so suddenly? I found myself wondering if it was because I was worried about the trial, and was seeking solace. I couldn't justify that concern, so when I saw you here today, and I felt your warm body in my embrace, I decided that what I felt must have been there already, and I just never recognized it."

Janice's face was aglow as she responded, "You know, the same things were going through my mind, and I felt the same reassurance as we met this evening. I'm with you: speaking for myself, I think the feeling was there all the time."

They stopped briefly and Janice took both of Michael's hands in hers as she said, "I think we might have been a little afraid to let ourselves go, considering our past experiences with close relationships. After all, we are not the most demonstrative people on earth--a bit conservative in our relationships with other people, I think for a number of reasons. I guess we had to feel this one out for a while before we dared to take a chance with full commitment."

As they resumed strolling hand in hand, Michael responded, "I think you are right. Do you think this upcoming trial and threat of possible disaster had something to do with it?"

"I do," Janice replied. "I think that may have triggered what was already between us, as if we thought we'd better bring this to the surface now, before tragedy strikes, else we might become totally blocked if we wait until the threat becomes a reality."

"Do you feel a threat in your own future?" Michael asked gently.

Janice was ready with a response. "Yes, I do. If you get into trouble, my association with you is bound to cause difficulties, in publicity if nothing else."

"I don't like the sound of that," said Michael. "It makes me wonder if I'm doing the right thing in opposing the insanity plea. I don't want to get you into trouble."

Janice stopped abruptly and faced Michael. She wanted to

reassure him, but avoided a close embrace, which under the circumstances might have seemed artificial. Instead she placed her hands on his chest and said, "Michael, a career to me is not important. It's all right, everything else being equal; but what is important is relationships, and harmony in those relationships. And this relationship matters to me--a lot. I have made my decision. As long as you care for me, that is worth more to me than career, reputation, or anything else. As for what might happen if you buck the system, I think we can handle that kind of trouble. And I happen to think we can do it better together than either of us can do it alone."

Janice's words were most reassuring to Michael. He was vividly impressed. However, he did not respond verbally. There seemed to be nothing he could say that would add anything to what had already been said. His only response, therefore, was a gentle squeeze as he put his arm about Janice's waist; and in that small gesture Janice found everything she wanted to know.

* * * * *

Leonard Burnham, Secretary, Department of Vital Resources, U. S. Government, was in his ornately furnished office in Washington, seated behind his very large, uncluttered desk. Mr. Efficiency, he was known as in resource circles, because he could be depended on to get the job done. The President felt that he had done well in selecting Burnham to keep the incoming flow of oil intact, free of obstacles and encumbrances. Within the Department of Vital Resources itself, Burnham was considered to be a man who would go to extremes if necessary to achieve success in his assigned duties. Some close associates also believed the man to be capable of stepping outside the bounds of propriety, or even the law, to get things done, although he had never been caught in any actual law violation.

The President knew about Burnham's tendency toward extreme measures, but did not interfere. In fact, he liked the way the man got things done, as long as he didn't stray so far from accepted procedure that he would get himself and the President into trouble. It was thought around the capitol that maybe the President leaned a bit over backwards to avoid too close a scrutiny of Burnham's methods, but all such speculation was kept very quiet.

Secy. Burnham was looking at a disturbing memo on his desk. It told him that Franklin Dupree, his trusted assistant, had failed to get a commitment from DA Michael Loudon, Mallon County, Oklahoma, to accept the plan in the Wayland case to plead not guilty by reason of insanity. He immediately got his secretary on the intercom and instructed her to get Dupree in his office at once. In a matter of a few minutes Dupree appeared, looking rather apprehensive. "Yes sir," he said. "You wanted to see me?"

"According to this memo," Burnham said, almost angry, "you didn't get a commitment from the Mallon County DA to go along with our plan in the Wayland case. How come?"

"The man was adamant!" Dupree defended. "He said he thought the defendant was too dangerous to be incarcerated in a mental facility, because it was not safe enough. He definitely had his mind made up!"

"Did you make it clear to him how important this is?"

"I did! I explained to him that MAPS, that does a lot of business for us through Angus Wayland, did not like doing business with criminals, and so on. So to protect our oil supplies, we wanted the Wayland son to be declared insane, instead of being convicted as a criminal. But Loudon, the DA, thought we were perpetrating a scam. He didn't take me seriously at all!"

"Did he get rough with you?"

"No, but it was quite plain that he wasn't a bit flexible in this."

"Well, hold on a second, and I'll check with MAPS and see if they can be flexible in this." Burnham instructed his secretary to get the head man of MAPS on the phone. Within a few seconds she announced that the head man was on the line.

"Hello," Burnham said into the mouthpiece, "is this Ahmed Roshine?"

The voice on the other end replied with a stiff British accent, "Yes, what can I do for you?"

"This is Leonard Burnham, Secretary, Department of Vital Resources, U. S. Government. I wanted to talk to you a bit

56

about this Wayland case. You are acquainted with the case, I understand."

"Yes, I am acquainted with the case."

"Well, as you are aware, Angus Wayland is one of our chief dealers in the acquisition of oil through your cartel. You are aware also that Daniel Wayland, the son, has been arrested and charged with a series of murders. The case against him appears to be quite strong, although the son does not remember committing any such crimes. On that basis the defense plans to plead not guilty by reason of insanity, and we were depending on the DA of Mallon County, Oklahoma, where the case will be tried, to go along with the insanity plea, rather than have the young man convicted of a crime. I understand that your people had concerns about a member of the Wayland family being labeled a criminal--"

Something was said on the other end, to which Burnham listened briefly, then explained, "Yes, I know, I understand that that would cause difficulties. However, we ran into a little snag--the DA refused to go along, and said he was going to oppose the insanity plea."

Burnham again listened briefly, then said, "Yes, Wayland has obtained the best representation, we feel, that money can buy. And they feel there is a very good chance to get the insanity plea accepted in court. In that case, can we depend on your organization to continue our present arrangements, working through Wayland to keep our supplies flowing without interruption?"

Burnham listened briefly, then said, "Yes, but--"

After listening briefly again, Burnham said, "Yes, sir. We'll try to get back to you with some assurances before the trial. Thank you."

Burnham hung up, then, turning to Dupree, said, "They wouldn't give us any slack. Roshine said that unless they have something more definite, they would come back on Wayland with assurances that unless the trial goes the way they want, oil supplies will be cut off. I want you to get back to DA Louden and make it clear that we are not playing games here, it is vitally important that our plan succeed, and there will be severe consequences if the DA continues to try to block us." Burnham stared pointedly at Dupree for a brief moment, then went on,

"You might arrange for a little demonstration before you talk to the man, to convince him that we mean business. You know what to do."

"Yes, sir," Dupree replied, and departed.

* * * * *

After a pleasant evening in the company of Janice Farley, Michael left to return home, intending to get a refreshing night's sleep in preparation for the rigors of the coming day. He felt elated as a result of his newfound romance, and permitted himself, for a moment, to believe that the threatened severe consequences for his failure to cooperate would not materialize, that it was all just a bluff.

As Loudon neared his home his elation and the night's quiet were suddenly shattered by a very noisy explosion. Fearing the worst, Loudon raced the remaining block to his home. He stopped dead as he noted, with shock and dismay, that the entire front of his house was blown out. There was no fire, but the explosion had generated so much heat that wisps of smoke drifted up from the wreckage. Down the street half a block away a black sedan suddenly accelerated with screaming of tires, heading away from the scene. Michael was able to get a partial license number and a rough description of the car before it careened around a corner and disappeared.

It became crushingly evident to Michael that the threatening forces against him were not bluffing. If this explosion, a rather drastic departure from lawful procedures, was any indication, he was facing troubles down the stretch rather worse than anything he had anticipated.

Loudon's official car, parked beside the house, fortunately was not damaged. It was equipped with a cellular phone, so he ran to the car and called the police, providing what he had observed about the escaping black sedan. While the police were on the way he called Janice and told her what had happened. She came at once, arriving shortly behind the advance police contingent.

Janice shared Michael's shock and dismay. Almost crying, she said with tremulous voice, "I tried to think of what they might do, but it never occurred to me that they would do some-

58

thing like this!" Now with sudden alarm she added, "Michael, this is gangster stuff! Who could be behind this sort of thing?"

"I don't know," Michael replied dazedly. "I don't know."

As the two stood and stared at the devastation the police were busy. Within minutes, explosion experts had examined the scene. Police cars explored the neighborhood, and one officer reported that the black sedan described by Loudon had been found abandoned a few blocks away. A quick check with records disclosed that the car had been stolen.

The police chief came and reported to Loudon. "This was strictly professional," he asserted. "Those guys knew what they were doing. The explosive was an ordinary variety, impossible to trace. They apparently knew you were not at home, which indicates that they were spying on you. We'll check the car for prints, but I'm sure we won't find any."

"Do you have any idea who might have done this?" Loudon asked.

"At the moment, no," the chief replied.

"How about the modus operandi? Is it familiar to you?"

"Yes, but it's big city stuff. We never see anything like that here in Mallon City."

"Well," said Loudon, "if you need anything more from me I'll be on hand tomorrow. Just let me know. Thanks a lot."

After posting a police barricade, the police departed, leaving Janice and Michael to contemplate their future.

Michael took Janice in his arms and said reassuringly, "This looks like a great tragedy, but really it is not. The damage is not as extensive as it appears. But there is a problem--now I don't have any place to stay!"

Janice's reply was not unanticipated. "Of course you do! You can stay at my place!"

"Thank you, I'll accept!" Then, teasingly, "How will you explain this to your neighbors?"

"I don't care what the neighbors think!" declared Janice, not without a hint of rancor.

Michael slipped past the barricade to gather up night wear and a change of clothing for the morrow, plus whatever personal articles he would need, and packed them in a small carrying bag. The couple lingered a few more minutes, gazing sadly at the wreckage, then turned and walked slowly away.

The Farley apartment was not a two-bedroom structure. There was just the one bedroom and one bed. There was, however, a rather large couch in the living room. Janice forestalled any discussion of sleeping arrangements by asserting, as she put her arms around Michael's neck, "You know, you don't need to sleep on the couch."

Michael hugged Janice tenderly and said, "Yes, I figured as much, but really, I would not like to take that step under these circumstances. When we do take that important step I would like to be in a frame of mind where I could fully enjoy it. That would indeed be a great joy to me, and I look forward to our first night together with a kind of excitement that I haven't felt for a long time. That is why I would like everything to be just right when it happens."

Janice replied with a firm kiss that said more than could beautiful rhetoric. As she reluctantly detached herself she looked into Michael's eyes briefly, and her face revealed the warmth and ecstasy that she had come to feel the last few days. There was something else, too--a devotion that promised a lifetime of dedication to the role of wife, companion, helper, and comforter. Without further ado she said softly, "I'll bring blankets and pillows. There will be fresh towels in the bathroom." After the couch had been made as comfortable as could be expected, a good night kiss, and then, "I hope you sleep well! Good night!"

The next morning Loudon took time to move his clothing and other needed items from his damaged house to Janice's apartment. After work he would try to find room for his belongings in this already-crowded unit.

Shortly after he arrived at his office Loudon received a phone call. A voice, obviously disguised, asked, "How did you like your little party last night?"

"I didn't enjoy it," Loudon replied gruffly.

"Well," the voice went on, "that was just a message, to let you know that the people who want you to support the defense plan in the Wayland case are not playing games. They are quite serious. If you persist in opposing them, things will happen that you won't like very much!"

"Who the devil are--" But the caller had already hung up.

Loudon sat stunned for a moment, transfixed by the enormity of what had just transpired. As Janice had so aptly put it, this was gangster stuff! What next? The trial was scheduled to start before long--would they keep up this kind of pressure right up to, and including, the course of the trial? He tried to put it out of his mind, at least long enough to ease the burden of work piled up on his desk.

The next phase was not long in coming. Franklin Dupree walked into Loudon's office, planted himself in a chair beside the desk, and said, with some arrogance, "Well, Loudon, what are your plans? Have you reconsidered your position in the Wayland case?"

Loudon turned slowly and deliberately to face the intruder. "No, I haven't changed my plan. I fully intend to oppose the insanity plea with everything within my power. What do you know about the bombing of my house last night? And the threatening phone call I got his morning?"

Dupree tried to look surprised, but not too convincingly. "What bombing? What phone call?" he said. "I don't know anything about that."

"I don't believe you," countered Loudon. "Anyway, what do you plan to do next?"

"I don't know what you're talking about," said Dupree aggressively. "All I came here to do was reiterate my earlier message to you, that powerful people in Washington are very much interested in this case, and very much want you to go along with the insanity plea. It is a matter of national security."

"You didn't say that before."

"Say what?" asked Dupree suspiciously.

"National security. Before you said something about securing the continued flow of oil."

"Well," sputtered Dupree, "it's the same thing, isn't it?"

"I thought this was a scam, and now I'm sure of it. Look, if it's that important, ask the President, or Secretary of State, to get in touch with me. Then I'll listen."

"I can't do that!" Dupree almost shouted. "It's near the end of the week, and you can't get anything going with the President this late in the week! In fact I'm not even sure he's in town!"

"I know you or somebody can get word to the President any time, any place; and if this is as important as you say, he'll send word," declared Loudon. "Now, I have a pile of work here, so would you please let me get at it!"

Dupree glared angrily at Loudon, then snatched his brief-case and stomped out of the office, slamming the door behind him so hard it made the glass pane rattle.

Loudon checked his watch, then got on the phone and dialed the college, asking to be connected with Ms. Farley. In a brief moment Janice answered. "Is that you, Michael?" she asked.

"Yes," Michael replied. "Would it be possible to see you right away? I know you are probably busy, but this is very important."

"It's near the end of the hour, and my next hour is free," said Janice. "Can you meet me in the student lounge in about fifteen minutes?"

"I'll be there!"

Loudon busied himself the next several minutes delegating several jobs that he had intended to do himself, then left the office hurriedly to meet with Janice. She was waiting for him in the student lounge when he arrived.

"What is it, Michael?" she asked, rising to meet him. "You look worried!"

After satisfying himself that nobody was within hearing distance, Michael began, "Janice, Dear, things are beginning to happen. This morning I got a threatening phone call, disguised voice and all, and a little later Franklin Dupree, Ass't to the Secretary of the Federal Department of Vital Resources, or so he said, who was in to see me two or three days ago, came back, reiterating his previous message that it was very important to the U.S. Government that we not oppose the insanity plea. He said he didn't know anything about the bombing, but I didn't believe him. I also believe he knew something about that threatening phone call, and is just too cagy to admit it. So it appears that more unpleasantries are planned for me before the trial, which is set to start before long. Now that I know what they are capable of doing, I'm taking nothing for granted."

"That's terrible!" exclaimed Janice anxiously. "What do you plan to do?"

"I think it would be a good idea for me to get out of town at least for the next few days."

62

"That does sound like a good idea," agreed Janice. "Where would you plan to go?"

Michael stared at the table for a moment, then gazed into Janice's worried eyes as he said, "My dear, this is not how I would prefer to do this, but under the circumstances I think maybe it is the best way. I know you understand the gravity of the present situation, so perhaps you will forgive me. Even on such short notice--will you go with me? And even more--will you marry me? Yes, this is what I want! I have known that for quite a while."

Janice was surprised, but not shocked. She hadn't thought of the plan of going away before the trial, but now that it was on the table, she agreed with it. And would she marry Michael? Yes! Yes! Could she get ready on such short notice? Of course she could. It would just be for a few days. Could they get married on such short notice? If they hurried, yes. Thank heavens the state laws were not restrictive in that regard. She knew of a JP in a nearby town who was available on short notice any day of the week to perform ceremonies. Where to go after the wedding? Well, that would take some discussion.

Janice aired her thoughts to Michael, who was delighted beyond his wildest dreams. He volunteered to get the license today. As to where they would go after the wedding, he suggested a resort high up in the neighboring Ozarks, a sylvan retreat that would be available this time of year on short notice. He would call them. Packing? No problem for either of them. Each agreed to clear the afternoon, and to meet at Janice's apartment at 4:00 pm. They embraced briefly, then hurriedly went their separate ways.

Loudon met with his staff and informed them that he would be out of town for several days. He appointed his most capable assistant, Randy Cole, to fill in for him.

Getting a marriage license on short notice was no problem. Loudon was acquainted with the license clerk, who was glad to oblige, and delighted to hear the news. "Who is she?" the clerk wanted to know.

"Janice Farley," Loudon replied. "She's a psychology professor at the college."

"Well, I'm real happy for you," said the clerk, a not unattractive lady of thirty-odd years. "You know, I was starting to worry about you. I thought it was about time you found yourself a nice lady. I would have applied for the job myself if I wasn't already tied up! When is this going to happen?"

"Very soon," Loudon replied.

"Wow, you do work fast!" commented the clerk jokingly. "I wish you all the happiness in the world. Janice must be a wonderful person, and I do know she's lucky. Please let me know when the ceremony is completed."

"I will," promised Loudon with a big smile.

One phone call and the JP was alerted. Another and a reservation at the Forest Dell Lodge was assured. Another call to Janice, who had been busy finding a substitute for the rest of the week and the entire following week. One of her advanced students was well qualified for the substitution.

His calls completed, Michael went to Janice's apartment, his home for now, to pack. Finished, he drove to his house. He had hired a handy man to clean up the front of his house and board it up, and this was underway. From a special box on his dresser he retrieved a small gold wedding ring that had been his grandmother's, and slipped it into a small velvet-lined case that he stowed in his pocket. He then hurried to meet Janice.

Janice had encountered no difficulties in packing and otherwise getting prepared for the momentous days ahead, so at the appointed time she was ready and waiting. When Michael pulled to a stop she climbed in, smiling broadly. A brief kiss and they were on their way.

It was about a half hour drive to the JP, who was ready. It was a simple but dignified ceremony. Michael placed his grandmother's wedding ring on Janice's finger, after which they kissed briefly but ardently. Michael met the monetary obligations, and they were on their way--husband and wife, embarking on a limited but fulfilling honeymoon!

Arriving at the beautiful lodge that would be their home for the next several days, the couple checked in and were escorted to their quarters, in this event the bridal suite, the extra consideration with the compliments of the management. It was lovely, roomy, and had a striking view of the idyllic setting.

Michael and Janice then blended together in body and spirit as naturally and gracefully as a pair of swans on a placid lake.

CHAPTER FOUR

For the next few days the newlyweds relaxed in their secluded retreat, putting back-home reality behind them. Thoughts of past troubles were suppressed in the joy of their newly-found romance and the exhilaration stimulated by the balmy air and the quiet beauty of their surroundings. They took long walks in the woods, learned to identify trees--pine, larch, red gum, hackberry, box elder, buckeye, and hickory; and birds--crowned kinglets, canyon wrens, painted bunting, pileated woodpeckers, red breasted nuthatch, and even an occasional bald eagle. They swam in the warm waters of the large lake. They read books and magazines borrowed from the lodge's well-stocked library, and watched some of their favorite shows on television, cabled up from distant urban centers.

Eventually, however, back-home reality began to seep through the screen of tranquility, as it became obvious to them that inescapable problems would shortly be reaching the crisis stage if they were not on hand to take care of them. With heavy sighs, therefore, as they permitted themselves brief sojourns into wishes that things could be better, they packed their belongings and began the trip home.

Janice's apartment was the logical choice for their current occupation, because Michael's house was still in disrepair, and in the haste of their departure he hadn't had time to engage a carpenter. It was late afternoon when they arrived, so little could be done except to unpack and arrange for their evening meal. As Janice set about cooking the meal, Michael telephoned his assistant, Randy Cole, at his home, to report their return, in the event that there was some urgency needing his attention.

Cole reported that after he, Loudon, had left, several individuals contacted the DA's office, expressing anxiety about the DA's absence. Some of them appeared, according to Cole, a bit suspicious, suspecting that there was some secret maneuvering going on that they didn't know about. Who were these individuals? Cole named Dupree for one, Jacobs for another, a few reporters (evidently sensing that they were missing a story), and even Angus Wayland. They all tried to pump Cole for information, but he, Cole, refused to say anything, or even spill the news of Loudon's hasty wedding. How did they know that he, Loudon, was absent? Cole did not know.

Michael thanked his assistant and said he would be in the office first thing in the morning. He was a bit shaken by the news that reporters knew he was out of town. If they knew that, they must have known about the wedding as well, although Cole had implied that they did not. There has got to be a leak, Loudon thought. He recalled previous evidence of leaks, and now with this latest evidence he decided it was time to take it seriously. No great harm had resulted from the leaks as yet, but something could go awry unless the source was identified and something done to stop the leak. He decided that tomorrow for sure he would check for bugs in his office.

After they had finished dinner, and since it was not yet dark, Michael and Janice strolled over to Michael's house to see if there had been any change. They noted that the damaged area was now fully boarded up, and that the police tapes were still in place, indicating that some investigation might still be going on. Other than that, everything looked the same.

As they stood observing the damaged house Michael commented, "I wonder if the house is worth repairing. It was adequate for me, but would it be what we would want for us? What do you think?"

Janice hesitated briefly before replying, "That could be something of a problem for us, considering the uncertainty of our future. Why don't we put off doing anything about it, and just stay at my place, until we know what is going to happen? Could you be comfortable with that?"

"You know," Michael admitted, putting his arm around Janice's slim waist, "for a moment I forgot about that. You're right--it would be a mistake to make any major moves just yet. It really shouldn't be for long," he added, "because the trial is only a few days away, and it should be of short duration. Yes, I could be comfortable living at your--our--apartment. Considering the time element it really wouldn't be worthwhile looking for another apartment at this time."

"I think you're right, " Janice agreed. After a last sad look at the stricken house, the couple returned home.

As they rested comfortably in easy chairs that evening Michael commented jokingly, "You know, we've been married

66

for several days now and we haven't had our first fight yet. How about that?"

Janice looked at Michael with mock seriousness, "Do you think we should have one, so we can say we are completely married?"

"No way," Michael responded, chuckling. "No way. I think we can consider ourselves completely married--we don't need that!" Then he asked with feigned gravity, in the manner of an afterthought, "Do we?"

Janice came over and planted a big kiss on Michael's forehead, then replied, "No, Dear, we don't need that."

Michael and Janice could joke about such a matter with no hint of submerged anxiety, because in their long acquaintance they had found strong similarity in their views about marital fighting. While some people believed that marital fighting was natural and thus inevitable, Michael and Janice were convinced that such fighting is not natural, and amounts to a power struggle between the spouses. They recognized that fights could break out when the partners were under severe stress, but if there was no power struggle, such fights would soon be terminated, as being totally non-productive. In line with these beliefs the couple also believed, contrary to popular misconceptions, that married couples do not fight about some-thing, such as money, in-laws, or how to treat the kids--their fights are the power struggle, no more, no less. Without the power struggle, other problems are simply worked out, using methods that work. Fighting never solves anything, and is never intended to, despite pretenses to the contrary, of that they were sure. On this particular day it did not occur to Mr. and Mrs. Michael Loudon that the time would not be far off when their views on such matters would help to see them through some very difficult times.

The next day Loudon checked in at his office and began reviewing the work that had been done while he was gone. He called in Randy Cole, intending to go over cases that had come up and their disposition. After almost three hours of confer-ence with Cole he was satisfied that everything was under control, and there was no residue of dangling crises. Cole had done a good job, as had other members of the staff. Loudon was thankful for that, because the Wayland trial was only a few days away, and there was still need for preparation, including a thorough review of Loudon's "game plan."

Dismissing Cole, Loudon obtained from the sheriff's office an electronic device for locating bugs, and began scanning his office for concealed eavesdropping mechanisms. He searched in, under, and around desks, files, and all other pieces of furniture, in potted plants, behind pictures, and in every crack or crevice that could serve as a hiding place for a tiny device no larger, possibly, than a pencil eraser. He was unsuccessful, until he turned a file cabinet completely over. There, hidden in a small space under the cabinet bottom was a tiny sophisticated device that proved to be both a microphone and a radio transmitter.

Loudon went to see Sheriff Lerner and told him privately of the find. Lerner went to the office to see for himself. In his years as sheriff Lerner had become acquainted with most varieties of eavesdropping devices, but had never seen one quite like this one. He calculated that this device could pick up any sound within a radius of thirty feet, and would transmit to a distance of several blocks, at least. The two men went into the lavatory and turned on the water, so their conversation could not be detected by the bug.

"Of course you don't have any idea where the receiver is," Lerner commented.

"No, I haven't the foggiest," Loudon replied.

"What do you want to do with the bug?"

"I think for the time being at least we'd better leave it right where it is. What we have to do, if we can, is find out where the receiver is and who planted this thing. If we take it out now we'll never know. I'll just have to be careful what I say until we get it solved. You'll stay on this, won't you?"

"You bet I will," Lerner agreed. "We have some electronic tracking equipment, so if we can hone in on the signal we might be able to track it down. But this might take a while, so be careful. I'll keep in touch."

Lerner departed, saying nothing of any consequence to an eavesdropper. Success was not long in coming. Sheriff Lerner's electronics expert managed to connect with the radio signal emanating from the eavesdropping device, and tracked it to a van located in a garage just a block away. The receiver was being monitored by one man, who was arrested. An effort was made to get the man to say who had hired him to do this surveillance, but to no avail. Obviously the man was much too frightened to reveal anything.

The van was confiscated, and Loudon was informed that the bug could now be removed. "However," Lerner advised, "we still don't know who's behind this. The equipment operator won't talk. So we'll have to conduct a thorough investigation. It should be possible to trace some of the equipment back to the purchaser. The van might tell us something, too, but I doubt it. It was stolen in Tulsa six months ago and transported here. Anyway, we'll stay on it."

Loudon was relieved that the bugging equipment had been found, but he knew he would not rest easy until he found out who put it there.

*   *   *   *   *

Jacobs, recently back from a return trip to New York, was busy. Dr. Goldman had been there for a couple of days with his team, a clinical psychologist and a psychiatric social worker, interviewing the subject, his family, and key people who had known and possibly related to the subject over the years. Jacobs went over Dr. Goldman's report rather thoroughly, discussing with the Doctor what material needed to be presented in evidence and what factors to emphasize. Jacobs had also secured the services of a back-up psychiatrist, Dr. Isaac Benfield, who did not bring a team, but who did conduct a thorough interview with the subject. Jacobs took great pains to see that the two psychiatrists had no chance to compare notes before the trial. In fact, all that either of them knew was that the other was in town and would testify at the trial.

The afternoon before the trial Jacobs contacted Loudon and asked if there had been any change in his plan for the trial. Loudon assured him that there had been no change, that he would indeed oppose the insanity plea, if defense intended to go ahead with that strategy.

"We are going ahead with it," Jacobs said.

"Well," said Loudon, "I won't pump you about what you

plan to do. But I would like to know how much detail you are going to require that we read into the record about the investigation. Do we have to go all the way, or will you let us leave out some of the gory details?"

"By all means, leave out the gruesome details. We won't give you any trouble on that. I trust you will make the record include all the clinchers."

"Will do," agreed Loudon. "Lerner is making up the report, and I'll instruct him to meet your requirements on this."

The two men shook hands, and parted with "See you in court."

Loudon paid a visit to Judge Philip Montgomery, who would be presiding at the Wayland trial, to alert the judge as to what he intended to do.

"Judge Montgomery," Loudon said, "I thought I'd better let you know ahead of time what I intend to do tomorrow, because it may look and sound a little strange. I'm sure that defense will change its plea to not guilty by reason of insanity, and they have brought in some highly touted psychiatrists to testify for them. I don't wish to talk about the case--I only want to say that I intend to fight the insanity plea, mainly by attacking the testimony of their chief witness, Dr. Goldman. Maybe it will work, maybe not, but I feel that I have to give it a try. I thought if you knew ahead of time what is happening, it would make it easier for you."

"Well, I appreciate that," replied Judge Montgomery. "While I am not unsympathetic with what you are trying to do, I must warn you--I will require that you stay within the bounds of procedure. If you get out of line, if defense doesn't object, I will." The judge stared at Loudon for a minute, then added, "I personally think you are treading on dangerous soil, and stepping on some powerful toes, so don't be surprised if some of those toes give you a good kick in the butt."

"I think I know what I am up against," returned Loudon. "I am not a crusader. I merely have to consider what I can live with and what I can't. Thanks, Judge, see you in court."

As Loudon left the judge's chambers he met Jacobs in the hall. Apparently Jacobs had heard about this visit and came to check. Accosting Loudon he asked, "I see you were in talking to the judge--were you talking about the Wayland case?"

"No," replied Loudon, "we weren't talking about the case. All I did was let the judge know what my main procedure will be, just so he'll be on board, because it may look and sound a bit unorthodox. If you think we were talking behind your back, go on in and ask the judge. I've known the judge for years, and I know he wouldn't let me talk about the case unless you were present, even if I wanted to. He's very strict about that."

"What is your 'main procedure' going to be?" asked Jacobs sourly.

"Come on, counselor, you know better than that," Loudon retorted, and walked away.

That evening Michael and Janice sat down at the kitchen table and spent a couple of hours going over Michael's plans for tomorrow. The best strategy, they agreed, was to follow Dr. Folger's advice: concentrate on getting Dr. Goldman to define his terms. Michael calculated that since reading the prosecution's investigative report into the record would take up quite a bit of time, the testimony of defense's witnesses would take up the rest of the day. That way he, Loudon, could defer his cross-examination until the next day. If there was time left at the end of the day and the judge didn't want to shorten the day that much, he could fill in with his first witness.

Just as the couple was starting to think about retiring, there came a screeching of tires in the street, followed by the crash of breaking glass, and then the sound of a car departing at high speed. Michael saw at once that a large rock, with something tied to it, had been thrown through their front window. While Janice hurriedly called the police, Michael picked up the rock and read the attached note, "This is your last warning. Do not oppose the insanity plea, or you'll wish you were dead!"

The police arrived in minutes. After examining the scene carefully, they determined that the perpetrators had been quite skillful, leaving nothing by which one could establish their identity. Would the Loudons like them to have a squad car stand by the rest of the night? No, thank you. Michael doubted that there would be any more incidents tonight. After the police departed, the Loudons tacked a blanket over the window and prepared for bed.

Although the incident was shocking, it did not have as great an impact as it might have had several days earlier, thus

71

the Loudons managed to get a fair amount of sleep that night.

The next morning the Mallon County Courthouse was abuzz with anticipation of the highly-publicized Wayland trial. Henry Jacobs arrived early, his huge figure quite prominent as he strode about getting acquainted with the court personnel. His loud voice was outstanding as he chatted and laughed with first one person and then another. He seemed cheerful, confident. Loudon, with his assistant Cole, arrived soon after.

The spectator section of the courtroom was filled. The Wayland family, including the two daughters, occupied a position on the front row. Several relatives of victims were seated near the front. Most of the remaining seats were occupied by the curious. At the last minute Janice and Dr. Folger slipped in and took seats in the back row. Present also were Dr. Goldman, with his team, and the other defense witness, Dr. Benfield.

There was a subdued buzzing of whispered conversations throughout the audience. The facial expressions of all present were serious, no doubt due to recollections of recent violent happenings associated with the case.

The bailiff entered, requesting that all rise. Shortly the presiding judge entered and was seated, whereupon the bailiff intoned, "The Mallon County Court is now in session, Judge Philip Montgomery presiding." The judge was a man of dignified appearance, fifty-five years of age, with a good crop of greying hair. He had a solid reputation for being stern but fair, and was quite well respected in widespread legal circles. At one time he had been asked to accept a Federal judgeship, but declined, asserting that he was content to remain on the local scene, amongst those who knew him well and liked him.

All members of the jury were in the mid-range of age, all white, and about evenly balanced between male and female. There had been much difficulty in selecting a a jury, due to existing prejudices relating to insanity, the defendant's guilt, and the famous Wayland family and rumors about how Wayland got his wealth. Jacobs had tried in a special hearing to get a change of venue due to local press coverage of the case, but that was denied.

Judge Montgomery rapped his gavel and intoned that the case at hand was that of Daniel Wayland. Upon his request the bailiff read the slate of charges against the defendant, six counts of murder and as many counts of rape. Upon completion of this routine procedure Attorney Jacobs rose and begged the court's indulgence. Upon receiving a nod from the judge he announced, "Your Honor, at this time the defense, in order to avoid a possibly long and bitter trial that could be most damaging to all parties involved, will stipulate that the defendant did commit the crimes of which he is charged. The defense also wishes to change its plea to not guilty by reason of insanity."

"Very well," Judge Montgomery agreed. "Is counsel ready?"

Both attorneys stated that they were ready.

"Then you may proceed."

Before proceeding, Loudon addressed the bench, "With the permission of the court, prosecution would like to change the order of procedure--"

"In what way?" asked the judge.

"We would like to proceed with the investigative report now, after defense's opening statement, as scheduled, to enter key evidence into the record. Then instead of proceeding with prosecution's case, we would like to wait until defense has rested before presenting our opening statement and calling our first witness, and before beginning cross-examination."

"Does defense have any objection?" the judge inquired.

"Defense fails to see the reason for this, but, no objection."

"Very well, proceed."

Attorney Henry Jacobs rose, stood to his full height, strode to a position before the jury, and after acknowledging the judge, began his opening statement. "Your Honor, Ladies and Gentlemen. We have before us today the case of Daniel Wayland--" Jacobs gestured toward the defendant, who was dressed in a plain but well-pressed blue suit, well-groomed, and looking rather handsome. Jacobs continued, "--who is before you accused of a series of rape-murder crimes." Jacobs again gestured toward the defendant, saying, "Observe this handsome young man. Does he look like a vicious criminal? As you gaze upon this young man, can you picture him in his right mind committing the kind of crimes of which he is accused? Not only is he of good appearance, he has a very pleasing personality, is well liked by everyone who knows him, and has no criminal record. He has never been a troublemaker. Further-more, young Wayland has absolutely no recollection of having committed the alleged crimes, and was genuinely puzzled and concerned when said crimes were brought to his attention. Ladies and Gentlemen, we have stipulated that the defendant did commit the crimes in question, to avoid a lengthy trial that could be extremely detrimental to the defendant and his family, and instead will attempt to show beyond any reasonable doubt that at the time of the commission of the crimes the defendant was hopelessly insane, the innocent victim of internal circumstances completely beyond his control, and therefore that at the time the crimes were committed he did not and could not have known the difference between right and wrong. We pro-pose that the defendant must be viewed, not as a vicious criminal, but as a very sick person, with an ailment that with proper treatment can possibly be cured. Thank you."

With an air of supreme confidence Jacobs returned to his seat.

Loudon rose and stated, "I call Sheriff Ed Lerner to the stand." Lerner was sworn in, and his credentials entered into the record. When prompted by Loudon, Lerner began to read a prepared report of the investigative findings relating to the six cases featured in the charges against the defendant. Although, as agreed, some of the most forbidding descriptive material was omitted, all evidence essential to support a guilty verdict was included. Defense waived cross examination. The judge admonished the jury that this was not to determine guilt or innocence, because guilt has already been stipulated, but was being read into the record in case of future need to review the entire case.

Upon completion of this lengthy report it was almost noon, so the judge declared a recess until 2:00 p.m.

After the noon recess all parties who had been present for the morning session returned. The Wayland family and families of the victims were eager to hear the defense testi-mony, and mainly to learn what was going to happen to young Wayland. The curious wanted to hear what the psychiatrists had to say, to learn what this alleged serial killer was like, and what went on in his mind.

At this point Jacobs rose and addressed the bench, "Your

74

Honor, before calling my first witness, I request that the court exclude Dr. Benfield from the courtroom, as he will be a corroborating witness and it would be advisable that he not hear the testimony of my key witness."

The judge issued instructions to the bailiff, who then escorted Dr. Benfield to an anteroom.

Jacobs continued, "Also, Your Honor, due to the rather sensitive nature of my first witness's testimony, the family of the defendant might wish to withdraw."

"What exactly do you mean?" the judge wanted to know.

"Well, Your Honor, in order to complete a thorough study of the case and prepare a comprehensive interpretation of the nature and causes of the defendant's mental state, some factors have had to be brought out that could prove embarrassing for members of the family. I know this is a very delicate issue, but I did feel compelled to bring it out, so that key persons could exercise a choice."

"I think I get your point," the judge stated. "All right, the court will recess for five minutes to allow family or anyone else to leave for the reasons stated. There will be accommodations in the anteroom for those who would like to wait."

Five minutes elapsed and nobody left the room. The Wayland family members were apprehensive, but their curiosity outweighed their misgivings. As for families of the victims, they were ready and eager to hear the worst.

"Court is now in session. Proceed."

Jacobs rose and announced, "I call Dr. Sidney Goldman to the stand."

Dr. Goldman obligingly took the stand and was duly sworn in.

"What is your full name and title," Jacobs began.

"Sidney H. Goldman, MD."

"And your occupation?"

"Physician and psychiatrist. I am a full-time practicing psychiatrist."

Attorney Loudon interposed, "Prosecution is willing to stipulate that Dr. Goldman is an expert in his field."

"Thank you," said Jacobs. Then, "Dr. Goldman, have you had an opportunity to examine the defendant in this case, Daniel Wayland?"

75

"Yes, my team and I have conducted a thorough study of the case."

"Your team--who is on the team beside yourself?"

"A clinical psychologist, Dr. Ward Blakely, and Emma Riley, social worker. I take full responsibility for their contributions, and I myself formulated the entire diagnostic report."

"And what are your findings?"

In appearance Dr. Sidney Goldman fit the stereotype of eastern U.S. psychiatrists, which seemed to imitate the Freudian image. He was of average height, slightly obese, with dark hair and closely-trimmed beard and moustache that were dark with traces of gray. He wore dark-rimmed glasses with thick lenses that gave him almost an owlish look. His voice was pitched slightly higher than average, and intonation was slightly clipped. He had a slight accent that suggested a Jewish background.

"I had almost a two-hour session with the subject. In addition, I and my team interviewed all members of his family, and a few persons who played key roles in the subject's life. From this we have compiled this rather voluminous document--" Dr. Goldman showed the court a thick bundle of papers, bound on one side with a sturdy metal fastener.

"That is indeed an extensive document," Jacobs agreed. "However, with the court's consent, I do not think we need to read it all into the record. If you can give us a summary of your findings--"

There being no objection from the prosecution, the judge gave the order to proceed.

Dr. Goldman put the thick binder aside and took out a sheaf of notes, from which he read the following summary statement:

"The Wayland family consists of father, mother, two older girls, and subject as the youngest. It appears that the mother, Cheryl, had always been somewhat dominated by her husband, Angus, an ambitious, driving man, who routinely demanded, and usually got, his own way. The mother, in turn, compensated by dominating her two daughters. The father was too involved in his own pursuits to give heed to his son's needs. The mother, then, sought to relieve some of her own anxieties by smothering the boy with solicitous attention. This created a

76

dual problem. Whenever the father attempted to play the father role by disciplining the boy, the mother would intervene in the boy's defense. This angered the father; but he found it safer to take out his wrath and frustration on the boy, instead of on the mother, resulting therefore in a circular causation cycle. At the same time the older daughters, envious of the mother's solicitation toward the boy, also vented their frustration by picking on the boy. They would tease the lad, calling him a mama's boy and 'privileged character,' meaning one who could manipulate the mother by use of such tactics as whining, temper tantrums, playing sick, and telling on his sisters. The girls would try to get him into trouble by messing up his room, breaking things and blaming it on him, and otherwise accusing him of things he did not do.

"As a result of these various assaults on him there developed in the boy a chronic fear of the father, but more importantly, a chronic hostility toward the female members of the family: toward his sisters for their hostility toward him, and toward his mother for getting him into trouble with other members of the family. The problem was, he could not relieve his stress by striking back in effective ways--whatever he tried only brought more stress--so he bottled it up and developed compensations through fantasy. As a result he became shy, quiet, and preferred to stay by himself. When he started to school the other boys soon saw Daniel as one who could be dominated, teased, and bullied, which of course only made matters worse.

"At around age five Daniel had acquired sufficient mobility to permit him to go off by himself for extended periods of time, such as two, maybe three hours at a time, without being missed. He attempted to forestall efforts to come looking for him by keeping his sojourns away from home limited to these shorter periods, and it generally worked. The father was too busy to notice what the boy was doing, and the mother was content to let him go as long as he got back within a reasonable time.

"At around school age Daniel began developing erotic fantasies toward his mother, in which he would imagine himself embracing and kissing her, just as the father did. These fantasies aroused in him a great fear of his father, who he believed would know what he was thinking and would punish him dreadfully. This dilemma resulted in his further withdrawal, including more and longer sojourns away from home.

"During these short trips away, Daniel would go to secluded areas in the surrounding woods and do some solitary role playing, acting out these erotic fantasies, apparently in an effort to get rid of them. It is most interesting that these wooded retreats corresponded almost exactly with the areas where the murder victims were later found.

"No really serious problems developed for Daniel until he entered puberty, and began to feel actual physical sexual cravings. At this time the chronic hostility that he had constantly carried with him became equated in his unconscious perceptions with the physical sexual urges. Frightened as he was of his earlier erotic feelings toward his mother, these increased physical urges became even more frightening, to the point where he had to do something to gain relief, or risk disintegration of personality. Because of the association of these fears with his hostility toward his mother, he began actually to fantasize physical assaults upon her, which in turn caused dramatic increases in his fears of what his father might do.

"Daniel bore this terrible burden without recourse until he became old enough to attract girls. In his unconscious perceptions this provided a solution: substitute vulnerable girls, preferably ones who would probably not be missed by anyone, for his mother, and act out his fantasies on them, through both sexual and physical assault. He would take the girls to the same secret spots in the woods where earlier he would do his role playing. This amounted essentially to choosing the lesser of two evils: it was safer to act out his fantasies toward the girls than to take the risk that his fantasies toward his mother might be discovered. In order to accomplish this, however, he could not allow himself to be consciously aware of the assaults."

Dr. Goldman paused as he searched his folder for another piece of paper. Finding it, he continued, "In my examination of the subject I found him to be a very pleasant and agreeable young man. He was quite cooperative, readily answering all questions. The examination began with general questions about ordinary, everyday matters, that as such provided no trauma. The examination gradually progressed to more personal

78

matters. As we got into the area of family relationships there were indications of increased tension.

"As I urged Daniel to tell me more about his early relationships with his family, there appeared increased signs of intense anxiety and suppressed hostility, apparently more toward the female members of his family than toward the father. The history bore this out, as indicated earlier. Failure to resolve these early conflicts evidently resulted in an emotional disorder often referred to as hysteria."

Dr. Goldman paused to take a sip of water from a glass provided by the bailiff. The entire court was completely silent, with not even a stir of activity, as though all persons present were spellbound. Mrs. Wayland and the two daughters seemed to be shocked and disbelieving of what they had been hearing. Mr. Wayland, on the other hand, seemed pleased at what he was hearing, evidently feeling that this testimony was succeeding in convincing listeners that his son really was insane, at least while the crimes were being committed. The deathly quiet continued as the witness went on:

"The violent nature of his revengeful acts was itself very frightening to the subject, so much so that he suffered a state known as dissociation, or fugue (commonly known as amnesia), in which he could neither admit nor remember that he had committed the acts of violence. A disorder of that dimension constitutes a serious mental illness."

As it appeared that Dr. Goldman was through talking for the moment, Jacobs asked, "Is it your opinion, Dr. Goldman, that during those periods of dissociation, or fugue, the defendant was insane? That he did not, or could not, at that time, know the difference between right and wrong?"

"Yes," replied Dr. Goldman, "the intensity of the trauma at the time each wrongful act was committed indicates that the subject was at that time indeed insane and unable to ascertain that he was doing wrong. The fact that he returned to an apparently normal state following each episode indicates that the periods of insanity were temporary."

Jacobs asked, "Then would you say, Dr. Goldman, that with proper treatment Daniel Wayland could be cured of the mental illness you described?"

"Objection," shouted Loudon. "Irrelevant! Whether or not

the defendant is amenable to treatment is not an issue here."

"Sustained."

"That is all. Cross examine." Jacobs returned to his table looking quite satisfied.

Loudon stood and addressed the bench. "Your Honor, as agreed earlier, prosecution would like to defer cross-examination of this witness until after defense has completed its case."

"Very well. Is defense ready to continue?"

"Yes, Your Honor," replied Jacobs. "I call Dr. Isaac Benfield to the stand." He indicated to the bailiff that the witness was probably in the anteroom.

Dr. Benfield appeared shortly and took the stand and was sworn in. He was a middle-aged man of medium height and slight build, with brown hair, beard, and moustache, dressed in a plain grey business suit.

Approaching the witness, Jacobs began, "Your name and occupation, sir?"

"Isaac Benfield, MD, psychiatrist."

"Are you acquainted with the defendant, Daniel Wayland?"

"Yes, I examined him at your request."

"Have you heard testimony in this regard today in this court?"

"No, sir, I have not."

"Do you have knowledge of such testimony?"

"No, sir, I am not at all familiar with previous testimony."

"From your examination of the defendant," queried Jacobs, "what was your impression of his mental state?"

Dr. Benfield cleared his throat and began, "First of all, I was impressed by the young man's good bearing and demeanor. I expected to find arrogance and defiance, which is commonly exhibited by young men, even young women, who have committed acts of violence, but no such traits were evident. The subject was quite cooperative and agreeable. I had been informed by you, Mr. Jacobs, that according to the evidence young Wayland had indeed committed the crimes of which he is charged, but I could not elicit any signs from the subject that he remembered committing them, or even knew, besides having been told, that he had committed them. This did

80

not appear to be simple denial. I tested him in several ways to see if there was any sign of recall, and there was none. There were indications of trauma when we talked about his family, especially the female members--" (At this point Mrs. Wayland bowed her head, covered her face with her hands, and remained in this posture for several minutes as Dr. Benfield continued.) "--and I suspect something of a sexual nature, perhaps sexual fantasies that frightened the subject and triggered intense denial. The exact nature of the early trauma could possibly be ascertained after an extended period of psychoanalysis, which of course is not possible at the present time. The extreme denial, accompanied by acts of violence toward young women, amounts to severe mental illness."

"In your expert--"

"Objection," said Loudon. "The expert status of the witness has not yet been established."

"Sustained."

"In your opinion, then," said Jacobs, "was the defendant insane at the time he committed the crimes, and therefore unable to distinguish right from wrong?"

"In my opinion, yes, the subject was suffering from extreme states of dissociation and was insane at the time the crimes were committed. The fact that he now appears to be, and evidently has in the past appeared to be, normal, indicates that the psychotic episodes were transient."

"Thank you," said Jacobs, returning to his table. "Your Honor, the defense rests."

Since the afternoon was getting late, Loudon petitioned the court to grant a recess until tomorrow morning.

"Court is recessed until tomorrow morning at 9:00 a.m.," declared the judge, banging his gavel.

As the Loudons left the courthouse and walked toward home Janice remarked, "That was a rather impressive report by Dr. Goldman. He and his team certainly were thorough."

"Did it sound right to you?" Michael wanted to know. "I mean, was it psychologically sound, and all that?"

"Yes, I think so. The analysis was defensible. I just think the psychiatric diagnosis was open to question--that based on the data Dr. Goldman presented, other conclusions were possible."

81

"Like what?"

"Like simple selective amnesia. We all fail at times to remember something we did or failed to do. I remember one time I was scheduled to appear at a meeting where one person whom I hated with a passion was going to be present. I forgot about the meeting, and it never entered my mind again until another professor asked me why I didn't show up--and that was two days later! If I hadn't been reminded of that, I may never have remembered it."

"Do you think the analytic report was convincing enough to make people accept the shaky diagnosis?"

"Unfortunately, I believe so."

"Well, then, I guess I've got my work cut out for me. I took some notes on Goldman's testimony, some of the terms he used, and if you'd like, maybe we can go over these tonight. Is that okay?"

"Yes, indeed. I'd be happy to!"

As the Loudons were preparing to have dinner at home, Angus Wayland, Henry Jacobs, and Dr. Goldman had gathered in Jacobs' hotel suite and were in a jovial mood, celebrating the anticipated victory in court tomorrow. Jacobs had ordered a magnum of champagne, and they were drinking a toast to Dr. Goldman's expert testimony. "What a magnificent job you did, Dr. Goldman," said Jacobs, holding his champagne glass on high. "I don't think our country boy, Loudon, has got what it takes to cancel out what you did. What do you say, Angus?"

Angus smiled and replied, "Well, you sure laid it on us, Dr. Goldman, but if that's what it took to do the job, I'm with you. You had those jury members eating out of your hand. They were sitting there hanging on every word you said. So, it looks like we've got it made, doesn't it?"

Dr. Goldman himself, although smiling, was not actually contributing to the celebration, choosing to remain on the conservative side. Perhaps he had recollections of previous court appearances in which the jury did not perform as expected.

After finishing the magnum the trio departed to enjoy a sumptuous feast at Chez Alphonse. There they met Dr. Benfield, who congratulated Dr. Goldman on his work on the Wayland case. The four of them took a table, where the upbeat mood continued. After completing their meal the visitors retired to their respective quarters and Angus Wayland returned home. Mrs. Wayland and the girls had returned earlier, but they were not celebrating. In fact their mood was quite somber. After Angus arrived there was no discussion amongst them regarding what they had heard that day. After performing essential duties they went straight to bed.

The Loudons, after dinner was over and the dishes washed, sat down to discuss today's testimony and decide what to do tomorrow. After hearing the testimony of Dr. Isaac Benfield they decided that there was no essential difference between his analysis and that of Dr. Goldman, so they concentrated solely on the latter's contributions. Janice thought the analysis of family interactions and Daniel's internal conflicts and compensatory activities was sound, but she believed that when Dr. Goldman got into the medical terminology he was not on solid ground at all, and in that area was vulnerable.

The first term that Janice pointed to was anxiety. "I think I would challenge him on that," she said. "It's not very significant, but I would think it's a good place to start, and go after the more important ones later."

"What's wrong with anxiety?" Michael wanted to know

"Nothing, really--it's just another term for fear. But for some reason psychiatrists avoid using the term fear in their diagnoses, perhaps because it's too mundane, too common-place--something that people associate with everyday living, whereas anxiety can sound more like a medical condition. Getting Dr. Goldman to admit that anxiety is nothing but fear can help set the stage for later challenges."

"Okay." Michael made a notation. "What next?"

"Well, next we have 'emotional disorder.' We can pass emotional, but 'disorder' needs to be challenged. Disorder of what? And so on."

"Yes, I get the picture. I suppose the next term to look at is 'hysteria'."

"I think," Janice suggested, "that you are going to be dealing with several terms that are merely references to behavior. Hysteria is one of them. I would think that an effective approach would be to touch on each, to the point of getting the witness to admit that the term in question is merely a

83

reference to some kind of behavior."

"I'm with you," agreed Michael. "Don't try to make a case on just one point. Touch on each, leave it and then bring it all together in summary. Good strategy! You should have been a lawyer!"

"No, thank you!" returned Janice, laughing.

"Okay, now," Michael went on. "What about dissociation and fugue?"

"No, those are simply fancy terms for forgetting. They do not refer to behavior."

"All right. I guess the only one left is 'insane.' But we've covered that. Now, what do I do about memory? A lot hinges on that."

"I think you can get around the memory thing simply by pointing out that we all forget things we don't like. I think when it is brought out that defense's entire case rests on something so commonplace as failure to remember unpleasantness, the jury will be convinced. They should be."

"What about this idea that the criminal might not know the difference between right and wrong?"

"Why don't we call Dr. Folger on that?" Janice suggested. He probably has some cogent thoughts about that."

"Fine! Let's do that!" Michael picked up the phone and dialed Dr. Folger's number. Dr. Folger answered almost immediately. "Hello?"

"Dr. Folger," Michael began, "this is Michael Loudon. How are you?"

"I'm fine. What's on your mind?"

"First of all, I very much enjoyed talking with you the other night. I feel that I learned a lot. Second, you probably haven't heard--Janice and I were married a few days ago. I thought you'd like to know."

"That's great! Congratulations to you both. I hope you will be very happy."

Janice, on the extension, thanked Dr. Folger warmly.

"But I do have something else to ask you about, if you don't mind," said Michael. With Dr. Folger's consent he continued, "I'm involved in the Wayland trial. Janice and I have been discussing some of the key points, but on this one she suggested that I get your thinking on it: the question, in a con-

84

sideration of a criminal's sanity, whether or not the criminal knew the difference between right and wrong at the time of committing the crime. Do you have some ideas on that topic?"

"Yes, I've thought about that a lot," Dr. Folger replied without hesitation. "I think it is important. Seeing those inmates in the mental hospital, I can agree that some of them function on about the same level as an animal, and may instinctively attack if they think their safety or security, or that of a loved one, is threatened. The same can be said in cases of severe retardation. But the main point, I think, is this: that while there are predators, in both animals and humans, who will attack without being threatened or attacked, they do so for a reason, usually to obtain food, defend themselves, or defend a territory or their possessions. In cases of diminished capacity, like the retarded person or the true psychotic, the individual is essentially operating on an instinctive level. I know there are cases of animals that somehow go berserk and wantonly destroy other creatures for no apparent reason, and I'm sure the same can be said about some humans; but in such cases you'll observe that the destruction is general and indiscriminate. Powerful creatures on a rampage destroy everything that gets in their way. If such a condition exists in a human, you will see the same indiscriminate destructiveness. Another thing, too, a human in such a state will employ crude methods, using whatever means are readily available."

"If I read you right," Janice interpreted, "you are saying that if a human, in killing other humans, selects a particular kind of victim and employs distinctive methods and equipment in doing so, he or she is not acting on an instinctive level, but rather is acting rationally, and thus is not retarded or psychotic."

"Absolutely," agreed Dr. Folger. "Just like war. In fact the person who goes on such a killing spree is in effect waging war, his or her own personal war, against what he or she believes to be his or her personal enemies."

"Whether or not he or she appears to be aware of what is happening?" asked Michael.

"Yes. I don't think awareness has anything to do with it. Take sleep walking for example. The somnambulist is capable of sophisticated, even physically demanding, performance, and still be totally unaware of it."

"Thanks a lot, Doctor, I think that just about does it. I appreciate it very much." With that Michael and Janice hung up.

"Very interesting," mused Michael. "We are seeing indications of how deeply our legal system is rooted in age-old myths, misconceptions, and illusions. I guess it will take some time to pull ourselves entirely out of the dark ages."

Suddenly the phone rang, and Janice answered.

"This is Cole. Is Michael there?"

Michael took the phone. "Cole? What's up?"

"Have you heard about the latest Supreme Court ruling about insanity in legal procedures?"

"No, I haven't."

"It was a small item buried on the third page of today's Herald. The ruling was that people acquitted of crimes by reason of insanity may not, after, quote, 'returning to sanity,' end quote, be detained in mental institutions on the grounds that they may still be dangerous. I thought you'd like to know."

"You bet I like to know! Thanks a lot, Randy. I appreciate it!"

Michael repeated the message to Janice and commented, "That makes it even worse. A killer like Wayland, who acts normal most of the time anyway, could easily be declared 'cured' after a year or so and released."

The next morning the courtroom was again filled to capacity. All of those present on the previous day were back, plus a few more, necessitating setting up a few portable chairs on the lateral perimeters. The defendant was ushered in. Henry Jacobs shook hands with the young man and said something encouraging to him. Michael Loudon was ready, looking probably more relaxed than he felt, as he faced one of the most challenging undertakings of his career. Waiting for the court to be officially opened, Loudon pondered briefly what impact his performance today might have on the future of jurisprudence.

Following the routine opening procedures, the court was in session. The judge asked if counsel was ready, and counsel responded affirmatively.

Michael Loudon rose and faced the bench and the jury, stating, "Your Honor, Ladies and Gentlemen of the jury, as you know we have before us today the case of Daniel Wayland, accused of six counts each of rape and murder. The defense, you will recall, has stipulated that the defendant did commit the crimes in question, so that is not an issue here today. Instead, the defense has entered a plea of not guilty by reason of insanity. It is the prosecution's belief and contention that the defendant was not insane at the time the crimes were committed, and that at that time he did know the difference between right and wrong, and we will endeavor to prove that here today. Thank you."

Loudon turned and announced, "I call Dr. James Forsyth to the stand."

Jacobs looked surprised as Professor James Forsyth rose and approached the witness stand. When the witness was seated, Loudon called for him to give, for the record, his full name and occupation. "James Forsyth, PhD, professor of biology and pre-med at the local college."

Loudon asked, "Then you could be considered an expert in your field, biology and pre-med anatomy, could you not?"

"That has been established on previous occasions, yes."

Defense grudgingly stipulated that Forsyth was an expert in his field.

"All right," Loudon began, "since you are an expert in the structure and function of the human body, how would you differentiate between function and tangible body parts?"

"Objection," roared Jacobs, jumping to his feet. "I fail to see the relevance of this line of questioning!"

Loudon turned to face the bench. "Your Honor," he said calmly, "I am merely trying to lay a foundation for my cross-examination of defense's key witness. This witness's testimony is important for the prosecution's case."

"Overruled," said the judge. "Continue."

Jacobs looked as though he was going to protest further, but sat down with an air of disdain.

"Well," said Forsyth, "the body is made up, as you know, of tissue, bone, cartilage, and so on. These are tangible body parts, many of them going to make up what we call the organs. Each part, organ or otherwise, has a job to do in the total package. These jobs are functions. All of the functions together constitute what we call life."

"So there cannot be a function without a part. Is that what you are saying?"

"That is correct. It is impossible for the life package to contain a function that is not related to, or as we say, springs from, some tangible body part."

"What about behavior?" Loudon asked. "Can that occur separately from any body part?"

Jacobs again roared his objection. "Your Honor, I protest. I strictly fail to see where this line of questioning is going!"

"Overruled!" the judge announced firmly.

Forsyth went on, "Behavior, as you imply, is a function. While it can be infinitely varied, it cannot exist in a vacuum. Strictly speaking, behavior is what the individual does in relation to his environment, and is the activity of those body parts that we call our equipment--equipment that we use in dealing with the environment."

"What if a body function is impaired, so that it is not doing its job? I know you are not a practicing physician, but you teach medical students, so from your knowledge, what would a physician do about an impaired function?"

"Well, if the function was important, so that something needed to be done about it, the doctor would examine the body part that produces that function, to see what was wrong with it."

"What was wrong with the part."

"Yes, with the part--not the function. Fix the damaged part, and the function will be revived."

"All right, now," continued Loudon, "in layman's terms, what is a disease?"

"A disease is a damaging process in the body, especially important where it damages body parts that are crucial to sustaining the life process."

"And illness?"

"Just another term for disease."

"Then what you are saying," interpreted Loudon, "is that there cannot be an illness of a function--only of the part that produces the function?"

"That is correct."

"Thank you. That is all. Cross-examine."

Jacobs looked disgusted. He started to rise, as though to question the witness, but instead sat down and growled, "No

88

questions." The witness was excused.

"I call Dr. Sidney Goldman," announced Loudon.

What had been a hush in the courtroom was now a deadly silence as Dr. Goldman rose and approached the witness stand. He was advised by the judge that he was still under oath. The doctor appeared to be confident. Behind the beard one could detect a slight smile, an impression that could be supported by a faint twinkle in the eyes.

"Good morning, Dr. Goldman. That was a very impressive analysis that you reported yesterday in this case. Very thorough. Now," said Loudon with a disarming smile, "as you know, we are dealing with a very crucial case here, and it is important that these good people here--" (gesturing toward the jury) "--understand what we are talking about. Do you agree?"

"Yes, of course, very much so," responded Dr. Goldman, smiling.

"Then as I review your testimony of yesterday, there are a few terms that the jury might not be fully familiar with. For example, you used the term 'anxiety.' What exactly do you mean by that?"

It was apparent to Jacobs immediately what Loudon was starting to do. He jumped to his feet and roared, "Objection! Prosecution is nit picking! Dr. Goldman is an expert witness, and there is no need for him to waste our time defining all the terms he has used. The witness has given his expert opinion, and that is all the court requires!"

"The court will decide what the court requires," returned Judge Montgomery dryly. "I see no reason why the witness cannot be required to define his terms. Objection overruled."

Jacobs sat down so hard that one might have concerns about the safety of his chair. He was angry, fists clenched, eyes glowering. But he remained silent.

Dr. Goldman, no longer smiling, hesitated briefly, then replied glumly, "Anxiety is fear, but--!"

"Thank you, Dr. Goldman! Now," Loudon continued, consulting notes he held in his hand, "in your previous testimony you used the terms 'hysteria,' 'dissociation,' and 'fugue' in reference to the defendant's inability to remember committing the crimes of which he has been charged, or even that the acts had taken place. Is that correct?"

"Yes, that is correct."

"In layman's terms, what is hysteria?"

"It is a form of psychoneurosis in which the individual suffers extreme anxiety."

"And what exactly is psychoneurosis?--"

Steadily and persistently Loudon required that each psychological or psychiatric term used by Dr. Goldman be defined. As he expected, the terms he asked to be defined were at best uncertain as to true meaning, and at worst outright distortions; and it was soon evident that as Dr. Goldman tried to define them, he resorted to other terms that were equally as unreliable.

At first the witness appeared to be getting angry, but then he apparently decided that such would be detrimental to his credibility, because the signs of anger disappeared. However, as Loudon pressed on, the anger signs were replaced by signs of uneasiness. In a vain effort to ease his witness's discomfort, Jacobs frequently jumped up, roaring objections, despite being consistently thwarted by the judge.

As the cross- examination continued it was becoming more and more evident to all present that a close inspection of Dr. Goldman's terms led one back to common, ordinary mechanisms that everybody uses at times, a point that Loudon brought into focus now and then, as with a comment such as this (to Dr. Goldman), "It does seem to me you are saying that if the bad thing one does is serious, forgetting it indicates 'mental illness,' but if it is not serious, forgetting it is just normal behavior," a comment to which Dr. Goldman did not respond.

After the cross-examination had continued for nearly an hour the earlier quiet of the courtroom began to be punctured here and there by slight sounds indicating uneasiness amongst both spectators and participants, possibly a reaction to the now evident discomfort of Dr. Goldman. On the faces of some spectators appeared signs of concern for the welfare of the witness.

Shortly thereafter Loudon began moving toward his final strategy. He asked the witness what he sees when examining a subject. Trying to keep from getting himself pinned down in specifics, Dr. Goldman replied that basically, what he sees is what the subject is doing, including stance and expression. "In other words, behavior," Loudon said.

90

"Yes, behavior," Goldman admitted, now looking very nervous. Loudon referred to the topic of mental illness and disorders of the mind, asking Dr. Goldman how can he, simply by observing a subject's behavior, conclude that there is something wrong with the subject's mind, arguing, "Doesn't the diagnosis that there's something wrong with the subject's mind amount to a judgment of the subject's behavior?" Loudon pursued the matter, pointing out that if the observer cannot know the reasons for a subject's behavior, how can he assume that there is a disorder? Furthermore, he went on, the mind is a function, not a tangible body part, and did he (the witness) disagree with earlier expert testimony that there cannot be an illness of a function?

Dr. Goldman was becoming reluctant to respond to Loudon's queries, and flatly refused to answer the last question. But on insistence by the court that he answer, Goldman finally replied that he did not disagree.

Dr. Goldman tried to escape by protesting that the whole area of mental disorders is extremely subjective, and cannot be reduced to black and white. Loudon countered with a question, is a damaged heart or liver subjective? Is a woman's pregnancy subjective? In cases of extreme trauma, what can we do with subjective? And isn't that just a fancy word for guessing?

At that point there was a distinct murmer throughout the courtroom, that occasioned a rapping of the gavel and a warning by the judge. Loudon continued with the question, doesn't the continued focus on the mind as a source of wrong behavior lead us away from effective action? Upon Jacobs' objection that the question calls for speculation, Loudon withdrew the question.

During the last several minutes of Loudon's cross-examination Dr. Goldman became increasingly nervous, to the point finally where he was becoming visibly distraught. He had tried to stress the point that psychiatry has to be subjective, supported somewhat by Jacobs' frequently jumping up and shouting objections, but now he refused to answer any more questions and appeared almost at the point of a breakdown. The courtroom became very quiet as everyone viewed the witness's disturbed condition.

Seeing that his work was done, Loudon stated that he had

91

no further questions, and the witness was dismissed. Dr. Goldman, head bowed, a defeated man, walked slowly out of the courtroom and disappeared. No one tried to intercept him.

Since there was no further testimony on either side, Loudon faced the jury and began his closing summation. "Ladies and Gentlemen of the jury," he began, "what we have witnessed here today has been a tragedy growing out of the perpetuation of a myth--the myth of mental illness, from which many have reaped great benefits for themselves in terms of both power and material wealth, at the expense of hapless citizens who are unable to defend themselves against disparagements by individuals or groups seeking such benefits. Also, due to the misuse of power afforded by general acceptance of that myth, many dangerous criminals have been freed from appropriate restraints because they were deemed to be insane, or as it is sometimes called, psychotic. Certainly some persons are clearly psychotic. One need only visit a mental hospital to see that. But Ladies and Gentlemen, those persons are not psychotic just now and then--they are psychotic today, tomorrow, next week, next month, and year after year. Some may be in remission due to effective medication, but contrary to frequent claims and popular belief, they are not cured. They are not cured until the underlying cause, whatever that may be, is corrected, and medication itself does not do that--it only alleviates the symptoms.

"Here we are dealing with a dangerous person, who killed and raped at least nineteen young women (although only charged with six). Defense has attempted to establish that the defendant was insane at the time he committed the crimes. Ladies and Gentlemen, defense has failed to prove their case. They have submitted no evidence that the defendant was ever insane. Defense's claim was based on the apparent fact that the defendant could not remember committing the crimes, and supposedly was never aware that he did commit them. If failing to remember something we did was evidence of insanity, Ladies and Gentlemen, I'm afraid we would all be candidates for a mental hospital.

"Our objective here is to protect the public from dangerous persons. The defendant is clearly a dangerous person. If the court should find that he was insane and thus not responsible

92

for his actions, he would have to be incarcerated in a mental hospital, until it was clear that he was no longer insane. Now, defense does not claim that the defendant is presently insane-- only that he was so at the time the crimes were committed. In that case, if the defendant was committed to a mental facility, he would, by admission, be sane at the time of entry. Isn't it likely, therefore, that after the minimum required stay in the facility the defendant would be released as being non-psychotic? In that case, what guarantee do we have that he would not again commit vicious crimes? If he has the ability to block out awareness of such deleterious crimes, how, then, could he even restrain himself from committing them? If the defendant was free, then there would be no control at all--either community control or self control.

"It is up to you, Ladies and Gentlemen, to provide the guarantee that the defendant will not be able to commit further serious crimes, by finding that he was not insane at the time he commited the crimes in question. Thank you."

Following Loudon's impassioned argument Jacobs slowly approached the jury and began a brief summation. Mainly he repeated the major points in his opening statement. He pleaded with the jury to think of Daniel Wayland as a man who, with proper hospitalization, care, and treatment, could be saved. Jacobs made no mention of what had happened to his chief witness, and did not attempt to refute Loudon's strong point that the mental hospital could not guarantee security.

The summations completed, the jury filed out. In anticipation of what the jury would decide, the courtroom remained silent, and nobody departed.

In less than thirty minutes the jury filed back in and were seated in the jury box. As the judge asked if they had reached a verdict, the foreman slowly rose, looking as though he was obliged to do something most distasteful to him. "We the jury," he said slowly, "find that the defendant is guilty as charged, and that he was not insane at the time the crimes were committed." (Interviewed later, the foreman explained that jury members were shocked at what had happened to poor Dr. Goldman, but the DA's final arguments persuaded them to vote in favor of protecting the public. They saw little difference between confinement, as such, in prison or in a mental hospital. The difference was the possibility that the subject could legally get out of the mental hospital, without assurance that he would not commit further crimes, and they preferred not to take that chance.)

As soon as the verdict was heard reporters raced toward the telephones. Attorney Jacobs stuffed papers into a briefcase and stalked out, saying nothing to anyone. The defendant was ushered out of the room by two burly deputies. Some spectators remained quietly seated for a moment or two, seemingly shocked at what they had witnessed here today and not fully comprehending what had happened. Finally, with the exception of Janice and the Wayland family, all rose and filed out. Janice waited for Loudon to gather up his papers. Angus Wayland sat stonily, staring straight ahead, his expression etched in hard lines. When the spectators were gone Angus rose, gathered his coat and his family, and exited the courtroom. A close observer could have seen in Angus' eyes a gathering of dark clouds that boded unpleasant futures for somebody.

Finally Michael and Janice stepped into the now empty hallway and closed the courtroom doors firmly behind them. Janice quietly congratulated Michael on his accomplishment, but neither felt like rejoicing.

In less than two hours the evening newspapers appeared on the street, the editors evidently having saved key space until the Wayland verdict was heard. Headlines screamed, WAYLAND FOUND SANE AT TIME OF MURDERS, or DA WINS IN SANITY TRIAL. There was no editorializing in these reports.

CHAPTER FIVE

Leonard Burnham secluded himself in his office at the end of the day to await a call regarding the outcome of the Wayland trial. He had already made elaborate arrangements to activate several channels of action in case the insanity plea failed. He had his assistant, Franklin Dupree, standing by ready to push buttons. Now there was nothing to do but wait. After what seemed an interminable time the telephone on his desk jangled with an ominous ring. Burnham grabbed the receiver and said, "Burnham here."

On the other end of the line Angus Wayland replied brusquely, "Len, bad news. We lost the trial, and Dan has to go to prison. We thought we had it made when our chief witness, Dr. Goldman, came up with a crackerjack report and diagnosis, but then today that s.o.b. Loudon got up there and made an ass out of Goldman, would you believe this, just by making him define his terms! Loudon must have gotten some pretty smart coaching from somebody, because I don't think he's that smart.

"We'll appeal, of course, but I think the damage is already done. Even if we manage to get a new trial, I'm sure MAPS will already have Dan written off as a criminal. They probably have the news by now, because I'm sure they had their ears on, waiting to see how this came out. So you might as well go ahead with whatever you had in mind."

"I'm sorry to hear the news," said Burnham. "Anyway, we're ready. Dupree is standing by, ready to start the ball rolling. All our people have been alerted and are just waiting for the go-ahead. It may take a few days for everything to jell, but then one thing you can take to the bank: that asshole Loudon is going to wish he'd never been born!"

"OK, I'll leave everything up to you. I've started the ball rolling by getting the editor of the CHRONICLE--he's in my pocket, you know--to write an editorial that ought to scorch Loudon's pants off. I'll see you get a copy of tomorrow's paper. Let me know if there's anything more I can do."

"All right, Angus. Again, sorry things worked out this way. We'll get together later to map out our strategy for the road ahead. I think we're going to have to bite the bullet for a little while. Once we get Loudon out of the way, it may be that

MAPS can be persuaded to ease up a little. It's worth a try. OK. Thanks for filling me in."

Burnham hung up, then immediately pushed an electronic button that summoned Dupree.

"Dupree," Burnham announced with tension in his voice, "We didn't make it. The sanity plea failed, and Daniel Wayland will have to go to prison. Now all hell is going to break loose!"

"Well, we did all we could," said Dupree consolingly.

"Anyway, it wasn't enough," growled Burnham. "Now we have work to do. We have to try to salvage what we can out of this, and see if we can't keep MAPS from cutting us off. The first step is to show them that we are trying to set things right. We have to get rid of Loudon--get him out of there, destroy him. Maybe that will convince Roshine that we have the power to set things right, and maybe get a retrial and get the court's decision reversed."

Burnham rose from his chair and pointed a finger at Dupree. "You know what to do. Notify all our people, and get things moving! Now!"

Dupree lost no time exiting Burnham's office. In his own office, a few doors away, he hastily dialed a long distance call to Mallon City.

George Faulkner, a clerk in Sheriff Lerner's office, was at home lounging in an easy chair, waiting for a crucial telephone call from Washington. It was nearly seven o'clock when the phone beside him jangled. He answered readily. "Hello?"

"George, this is Dupree. Operation Dog is on. Follow Plan A, according to the special message sent to you day before yesterday. There's no slack in this. You must succeed in your assignment. Let me know when you are finished. Meanwhile, I'll be in contact with The Shaker."

"Right, Chief. I'll get back to you."

The Shaker in this case was Randy Cole, ass't DA, waiting at his home for Dupree's call, which came through shortly after seven. "Randy, Operation Dog is on. Now here's the scoop:--" As Dupree outlined his plan, Cole made noises indicating that he understood. When finished, Dupree said, "You'll be getting another call tomorrow, from someone higher up, maybe Burnham. Meanwhile, plan A is being activated, so be alert for developments. Got it?"

Cole said he understood, and hung up. Since there was nothing further to do tonight, he ate his dinner and after watching a show or two on television, prepared for bed.

Attorney Randy Cole, born and educated in Texas, was a rather quiet man in his late thirties, studious, and fond of detective stories. Married, with two children, he had been assistant DA for five years, having been hired personally by Michael Loudon when an increase in caseload warranted an additional staff member. He was average height, about five nine, and slender, weighing about one hundred sixty pounds. His countenance featured a rather large nose, perched atop thin lips and a slack chin, and a receding hair line. Randy's wife, Rachel, was a rather mousy little woman with an abundance of thick brown hair. She was not well, suffering from a chronic ailment similar to muscular dystrophy, not as debilitating, but still requiring regular treatment and medication. She was able to care for her husband and children, but was limited in endurance and subject to occasional dizzy spells. Her children were healthy enough, but were so vulnerable that they caught everything going around, thus necessitating additional medication and trips to the doctor. Randy himself required occasional treatment and medication for a bad back. The Coles had purchased a house of medium price, which, being rather old and in frequent need of repairs, was an additional drain on a limited budget. The same could be said of an automobile that had seen better days.

This night, as he considered what he had agreed to do, Cole struggled with feelings of guilt. He had to weigh his conscience against the dread reality of his being deeply in debt, to the extent that he was in danger of losing his home, perhaps even his car. The money offer he had received--exactly from whom he wasn't sure (the message had been delivered by special messenger)--was substantial, enough to cover all of his debts and leave him with a respectable balance in the bank. The money was to be deposited to his account upon completion of his assignment. Furthermore, he had been assured, again from an anonymous source, that the future was going to be somewhat brighter than he theretofore had any reason to expect. Cole did not rest easily that night, but upon reviewing his dilemma he concluded that he had no choice.

Satisfied that all of the planned exercises of Operation Dog were initiated, Franklin Dupree sent the appropriate signal to Leonard Burnham. Their work done, even though it was past midnight, the two men took a cab to their favorite late-night restaurant and had a scrumptious meal, complete with the best wine, to celebrate the machine they had just launched. There were no misgivings here. Both men were simply, in their estimation, doing a disagreeable but totally necessary job.

In Mallon City, the next day, THE DAILY TRIBUNE and THE MALLON CHRONICLE carried highly critical editorials regarding Loudon's performance in yesterday's trial. The CHRONICLE editor was most scathing in the following diatribe:

> The citizens of Mallon County yesterday witnessed a desecration that is unmatched in the county's history. In the Daniel Wayland sanity trial the District Attorney, employing trickery and deceipt that could not have been anticipated by the defense, made a mockery of the time-honored legal system for granting clemency to unfortunate persons suffering from severe mental disorders. In his rabid hunger for power, the DA has sought to deny even the existence of such debilitating mental disorders, thus sweeping aside accumulated knowledge and wisdom in several highly respected fields, including socio-biology, economics, the medical sciences, and well-established schools of psychology from Freud to Jung to Adler to Maslowe. In making this bold power play, the DA elected to destroy the credibility of one of the finest psychiatrists in the country, and not only that, to destroy all possible chances for a fine young man, Daniel Wayland, to obtain treatment that could salvage his life and allow him to fulfill his potential to become, like his father, one of our more respected citizens. It was brought out in the testimony of not one, but two eminent psychiatrists that with proper treatment, young Wayland has a good chance to overcome the problems that led

him into serious trouble.

In our opinion the DA, Michael Loudon, should resign his post immediately, and should be permanently enjoined from holding office of any kind in Mallon County. It is our further opinion that Loudon's conduct constitutes a breach of legal ethics so serious that he should be disbarred and no longer allowed to practice law anywhere in the United States. To demonstrate our sincerity in this regard we will begin at once to contact key people and extend our recommendations in the above vein.

Beyond our profound revulsion at Loudon's conduct, our only regret is that there is no criminal law under which the man could be sent to prison for what he did.

About two hours after the newspapers hit the stands, Zachary Brooks, editor of the CHRONICLE, slipped out the side door of the CHRONICLE offices and drove to the Wayland home, where the gate was open and ready for his arrival. He was met at the entrance by Angus Wayland, and the two entered the house without saying a word. Once in the drawing room, Brooks handed Wayland a copy of the newspaper containing today's editorial. Wayland read the editorial eagerly. Brooks watched Wayland's expression intently for signs of approval. When Wayland seemed to be satisfied, Brooks allowed his face to break into something resembling a smile.

"It's OK," Wayland said. "It's pretty much what we had worked out yesterday."

"I'm glad you like it. If it's all right with you, I'd like to have my money now."

"All right," Wayland growled. "You've earned it. How much was it?"

"Five thousand."

Wayland crossed the room to his wall safe, pulled out a sheaf of bills and handed it to Brooks, who thanked him with a somewhat obsequious demeanor, then hurriedly departed.

* * * * *

99

Upon leaving the courthouse after the trial Janice returned home and Michael went to his office to tie up loose ends and to reflect on what had taken place this last day of the Wayland trial. He was alone in the office when Sheriff Lerner knocked on his door.

"Come in."

Lerner entered, closing the door behind him.

"What's on your mind, Ed?"

Noting that Loudon was alone, Lerner stepped closer and took a chair beside Loudon's desk. He looked strange, and was quiet for a few seconds, as Loudon waited to hear what he had to say.

Finally Lerner spoke, in a tone that suggested mild shock and disbelief. "I found out who was behind that bug in your office."

Loudon had a sort of sinking feeling, and refrained from comment. His mind raced as he tried to imagine just who the culprit might be. He could not pinpoint anyone with whom he was well acquainted, so he gave up and asked, "Ok, Ed, who was it?"

"It was George Faulkner, you know, a clerk in my office."

"How did you find that out?" Loudon knew the fellow, but not well.

"Well, like I said before, we traced some of the eavesdropping equipment back to where it was purchased. The store owner had a record of the purchase, but I figured the name on it was phony; then it so happened that the store owner remembered the guy and gave me a good description. With that lead we were able to do some more checking and found out it was George. We lucked out, really."

"Have you talked with the man about this?"

"No, I haven't said a word to him. I doubt that he knows we're onto him. What do you think we should do?"

"Nothing right now." Loudon thought a moment, then commented, "I wonder who he's tied in with? Forget it--I think I know. He's evidently part of a sophisticated undercover team, and I don't think Wayland would go in for that sort of thing himself. He's more a direct, out-in-the-open type of operator. No, I think Dupree is behind this."

"Who's Dupree?"

100

"I think I may have mentioned him before. He's an assistant to the Secretary, Department of Vital Resources, U.S. Government. He came here a couple of times trying to browbeat me into not opposing the Wayland insanity plea."

"Did he threaten you?"

"Not directly, in terms of exactly what would happen to me if I didn't play ball with them, but he did make reference to possible unpleasant outcomes. It wouldn't take a genius to figure out what he was talking about."

"Do you think Wayland is in with them?"

"I'm sure he is. I'm not sure just how, but I do suspect a mutual arrangement of some kind."

Reflecting on what he had been hearing, Lerner tried to fit the sheriff's department into the scene just described, but he came up empty. The idea of messing with the U.S. Government conjured up visions of heavy-handed manipulations by power-hungry bureaucrats, influencing local officials and that sort of thing, with threats of conforming to their demands or else. Bold as he was, Lerner was not an activist. He actually felt that you'd get more done by playing along than by fighting them, especially when the odds were so heavy in the other guy's favor. But the burly, down-home sheriff was also fiercely loyal; so he said to Loudon, "I'm not real sure just how I fit into this picture, so I'll leave it to you to do whatever you think needs doing, and let me know what I can do."

"You're right, Ed," said Loudon. "This isn't something for you to get mixed up in. You just do your job like you know how, and let things develop however they will. And while we're on the subject, Ed, I'd like to mention that sooner or later there's going to be things happening around here that won't be very pleasant, and it may be that you'll be called upon to take certain actions that will twist your guts. Now I want you to promise, if and when that time comes you'll do what your job calls for you to do, regardless of your own personal feelings."

"I'm not exactly sure what you're talking about," responded Lerner apprehensively.

"When the time comes, you'll know. Now run along, I've got work to do."

Lerner obligingly, albeit reluctantly, removed his large frame from the chair and walked slowly toward the door, looking backward just once as he stepped out and closed the door behind him.

Shortly thereafter Loudon closed his desk, locked the office, and went home. That evening he and Janice had little to direct their conversation, so they confined themselves to small talk, and later, after a pleasant dinner, went for a long walk. Uppermost in their minds, but unspoken, were reflections on what might happen to them in the near future, what sorts of things the vindictive power seekers might have in store for them. Because of the trial outcome, the threats now loomed so much closer to possible reality. Michael and Janice did not verbalize their anticipations, lest doing so would make dread reality seem that much closer. They did not deem it necessary to verbalize their commitment to mutual loyalty and support through whatever difficulties they would face. They felt that this was understood, and that verbalizing it might somehow suggest a weakness, a flaw, in it.

Unverbalized also, but still foremost in both their minds, was the determination that whatever trouble came their way as a result of this trial, they would accept it without complaint, self-pity, or blame.

At his office the next day Loudon detected a slight uneasiness amongst members of his staff. He thought this might ease up as the day went on, but it did not, so he asked his secretary, Madge, about it.

"Madge, everybody seems so uneasy or uncomfortable around me today. What's going on?"

Madge, a very nice older lady, a little on the heavy side but not noticeably so, and with an engaging personality, replied, "Everybody is worried about you, Chief! They know you've been told that bad things are going to happen if you win that sanity trial, which you did, and now they don't know what to say."

"Oh, is that it? Well I'll tell you and you can pass it on, both Janice and I knew what we were getting into. We acted on principle, and are ready to cope with whatever happens. And we are not worried or scared. We feel that we are in the right, and if God decrees that we shall be punished for that, then there must be a good reason for it--a reason that we may not know about for quite some time."

102

"Chief, I admire your faith, and with that going for you I'm sure that everything will work out right in the long run. And I will pass that on, you can depend on it."

"Thanks, Madge," said Loudon, smiling.

Across town at the college Janice was having a somewhat similar experience, not with the students, who were not fully aware of all that the Wayland trial meant to her, but with the staff members with whom she regularly associated. Like Michael, she finally decided to ask someone about it. At lunch she approached a fellow psychology professor, who explained that some rumors had been going around to the effect that she, Janice, was about to be called on the carpet. No, the rumors were not explicit as to why she was in trouble, but the concensus had to do with something she was believed to be teaching her students.

"You've got to be kidding!" Janice exclaimed.

"No, not kidding. Somebody apparently overheard a couple of the deans talking about you. This person, whoever it was, wasn't sure just what the deans were saying, but seemed to be of the impression that said mentors were not proposing to offer you a commendation. Rumor has it they were very much put out."

"Well, I'm really not surprised," said Janice, lapsing into a philosophical frame of mind. "In fact I've been anticipating trouble, but coming face to face with it is still a bit of a shock. I'm just curious as to what they are going to throw at me! Anyway, thanks for filling me in. I really appreciate it."

The rest of the day went rather smoothly for Michael and Janice, until the afternoon papers hit the stands and they saw the scathing editorials in the Tribune and the Chronicle, especially the latter.

"I don't believe this!" Michael protested vehemently. "How can those people write that kind of stuff?" He tossed the Tribune aside, concentrating on the Chronicle editorial, compared to which the Tribune blast was tame, and passed the paper over to Janice.

Janice was shocked, and for a moment said nothing. Michael stared at her, watching her reaction. Finally she commented, "I can't believe this! I know both the Tribune and the Chronicle are conservative, but this--(pointing to the offending

103

diatribe)--is far out! I get the impression that this editor is out to get you, and will say or do anything he has to, to do it."

Janice dialed Dr. Folger's number, and when he answered asked him if he had read the Chronicle editorial. He had, and so she asked, "What did you make of that?"

"Well, first off, that kind of hostility suggests an axe to grind that has very little to do with the reality of the situation. The editor is just using the Wayland trial as an excuse to get rid of your husband. My guess is that he was paid to write that editorial, and you might know who I guess did the paying."

"Yes, of course, the person who most wants revenge for losing the trial! Well, that makes me feel better. Thanks, Dr. Folger!"

After hanging up Janice told Michael what Dr. Folger had said. Michael replied, "That's it! It has to be! Well, I guess we've witnessed the first volley. But, I can handle that. What disturbs me is that a lot of people around here are going to agree with that editorial."

"I got some disturbing news at the college today," said Janice. "Rumors are going around that I will be called on the carpet for, would you believe it, something I am supposed to be teaching my students! They don't even know what I've been teaching! One of the deans monitored my class one time, and that was last year! If these rumors turn out to be true, we are going to get an important lesson in how the power struggle works!"

The next couple of days passed without incident, and the Loudons began to experience a faint hope that maybe--just maybe--the worst was over.

But that hope was short lived. Michael was in his office when he heard a fire engine racing nearby with sirens blaring. He thought nothing of that, until he received a phone call. An excited neighbor told him, "Your house is on fire!"

Michael dropped everything and went to look. When he arrived he saw his entire house engulfed in flames. The fire fighters had stopped trying to save the house and were trying valiantly to keep the fire from spreading to neighboring proper-ties. The fire chief, seeing Loudon standing there, came over to talk to him. "Loudon," he said, "it was already too far gone when we got here. I never saw a fire spread so quickly through

104

a house."

"Do you think it was arson?"

"Too early to tell for sure, but spreading that fast it almost had to be. We won't know until we get it out. I'll let you know as soon as I have anything."

While Michael was watching helplessly, Janice showed up, having heard about it at the college.

"That's terrible!" Janice exclaimed breathlessly, having run a good part of the way. "What happened?"

"I don't know," Michael replied. "The entire house was ablaze when I got here. The chief said he'd never seen a fire spread so rapidly through a house. He suspects arson, but he won't know until the fire is out."

"Do you have insurance?"

"Oh, yes, I have fire insurance, which I believe is adequate to cover the loss, so since we aren't living in the house, that's not too bad."

Later, after the fire was completely out and the embers cooled enough to permit inspection, the chief conducted his customary search for the cause. Since it was now late in the day, nothing was done further until the next morning, when Michael got hold of the chief and asked what he had found.

"Well," said the chief, "it's hard to tell just what did cause the blaze. We searched the place thoroughly, and found nothing conclusive." He made a noise that sounded like clearing his throat, but over the telephone it was hard to tell.

"What do you mean, you found nothing?" Loudon protested. "You seemed pretty sure yesterday that it was arson."

"Well, yes, I know," the chief replied lamely, "but it was just so hard to tell. If it was arson it was done by someone who really knew what he was doing."

Loudon was stunned at this turn of events. He was pretty sure the chief was waffling about it, evidently covering up for somebody. Knowing the chief as well as he did--they'd been friends for years--he was sure the man had gotten the word from some official to enter a false report, or else.

Anyway, small matter, Loudon thought. It wasn't any skin off of his back. He got on the telephone and called his insurance company to report the blaze and arrange to collect on his policy.

"What policy are you talking about?" the agent asked.

"My fire insurance policy on my house. I have the policy right here!"

The agent replied, "I think you'd better come in to the office. There is some irregularity here."

"Fine," said Loudon, feeling a thrust of apprehension, "I'll be right over."

In the agent's office, the agent pulled the file and spread it out on the counter so Loudon could see it. "According to this file," he said, "you don't even own the property in question. It belongs to the Federal Government."

"What!?" Loudon exclaimed. "What the devil are you talking about?"

The agent pointed to a certain provision in the file. "It says so right here. In fact there's no record that you ever owned that property."

Convinced, Loudon was dumbfounded. Dazed, he returned to his office to study this amazing turn of events. On an impulse he called a local office of the Federal Government that had records of government property in the area and asked for a check of the house and lot he considered to be his. The clerk pulled the file in question and announced, "The property in question was confiscated by Federal drug enforcement agents day before yesterday after finding a controlled substance in the house."

Loudon hung up, shaking his head. How could they move that fast, he wondered. Obviously somebody higher up was on the phone orchestrating this whole scenario. In a matter of hours, it seemed, insurance records were altered, and government records changed. And a controlled substance in the house? How come nobody had told him about this yet?

Loudon decided to say nothing to Janice until they got home that evening. Then she would have to know--they were keeping no secrets from one another. When they were both home together Michael related the fiasco about the house and the insurance. "This sounds like something right out of a horror movie!" Janice exclaimed. "Is there anything we can do about it?"

"No, I'm afraid not," Michael replied. "I know how the government works, because I've seen it before. They change

106

records in secret, at night, and make key officials toe the line under threat of personal and financial ruin. In this case I just don't know how they did it so fast. And I will have to admit I was taken by surprise."

"You're not saying that the government itself works that way, are you?" asked Janice.

"Well, no. I should qualify that. It's just that certain individuals with a lot of power and few restraints decide to take things into their own hands, and go by the principle, the end justifies the means. They convince themselves that they are acting in a really good cause, and therefore any means to that 'good' end is justified. Then they get defensive, expecting people to try to defeat them, and develop certain techniques for yanking the rug out from under anyone who tries it."

"Well," said Janice, "I guess the bottom line now is that we can expect more trouble, big trouble, and that it won't be long in coming. In that case maybe we'd better salvage some of our resources before they all become government property."

"Yes!" agreed Michael. "If it isn't too late already! We still have our separate bank accounts--tomorrow morning I'll go down and close out my account, and maybe you can do the same. Then maybe together we can garner enough cash to get us through a few rough spots."

As soon as the bank opened next morning Loudon went in and asked to close out his account. The teller went to check, and was accosted by a supervisor. After casting a quick glance in Loudon's direction, the supervisor engaged in a whispered conversation with the teller. The supervisor then came to the window and said to Loudon, "I'm sorry, sir. The IRS has put a levy on your account, and we cannot grant your withdrawal request. I'm very sorry."

Shocked, Loudon demand to know, "When did that happen?"

"I really don't know, sir. I didn't know about it until this morning. There was no problem when we closed yesterday, so it apparently was quite recent. I'm really sorry, sir. I wish I could help you."

As Loudon left the bank he was still somewhat dazed by the speed and thoroughness of these government actions. Back at the office he called the college and demanded to speak to

Janice, saying, "This is an emergency!"

Within a few minutes Janice answered, excited, "What's wrong, Dear?"

Michael told her about his experience at the bank, and advised her to get down and close out her account immediately, in case they got after her too.

"I will," Janice replied, then added apologetically, "I'm sorry, Dear, I should have told you, I can't contribute very much. I just have a small amount in the bank, because of helping out my parents. I'll take out what I have, right away."

"That's OK," said Michael reassuringly. "Talk to you later."

Janice found that her account had not been levied, so she closed it out. As she had said, there wasn't much, only two hundred dollars, which seemed alarmingly little now that Michael's account was frozen.

Janice's mother, Alicia, had taken seriously ill last year, requiring extensive surgery. She then had to be hospitalized for weeks, with extensive and very costly treatments. Total cost of her medical care had run well over eighty thousand dollars. Much of this had been covered by the parents' savings, and some by insurance and Medicare; but in order to avoid her parents' going deeply into debt, Janice agreed to meet the balance of the medical costs, partly because her father, Harold, nowadays was employed only part time due to his advanced age. In recent weeks Alicia was able to remain at home and live a normal life, so even with reduced income she and Harold could manage on their own. But it had cost Janice all of her savings and most of her last pay check. Janice thought, what unfortunate timing, that these huge costs should be incurred so close to her and Michael's current troubles. But then, she reminded herself, it was fortunate that her parents were no longer dependent on her. Janice was pensive as she returned to her class.

An hour or so later Loudon received a telephone call from a party identifying himself as Clark Bennett, IRS Agent. "I'm sorry, Mr. Loudon, but a recent audit of your account discloses an error of considerable magnitude in your return of two years ago. In view of the seriousness of this matter we have placed a levy on your account at the bank."

108

"I know that. I was just there."

"Yes. If your house had not already been confiscated by the drug people, we would have put a lien on that too. You are in a lot of trouble, Mr. Loudon."

Curious, Loudon asked, "Just when did your people discover this 'error' in my return of two years ago?"

"I really can't say, sir. I was informed just late yesterday, and was ordered to take the levy action at the bank, which I did."

"All right," said Loudon dryly, "What do I have to do to get out of 'a lot of trouble'?"

"I am not at liberty to say at this time, sir. I was just told to secure your assets, then to put you on notice. You will be contacted later by one of the officials, who will discuss your options with you. Good day, sir."

Discuss my options? Loudon thought. "I'll bet I know the way out of this one."

That evening, as the Loudons were sitting quietly at home, there came a knock at the door. Michael opened the door and saw two Mallon City policemen standing there.

"What's this about?" he asked.

"I'm very sorry, sir," one of the officers said, "we have a warrant for your arrest, for violation of the controlled substance laws. You have a right to remain silent--" The officer continued reading Loudon his rights, and then said, "You'll have to come along with us, sir."

Michael said goodbye to Janice, who promised to be in to see him in the morning. Arriving at the city jail, he was promptly fingerprinted and booked.

The next morning Dupree came to visit Loudon at the jail. At his request Loudon was escorted to an interviewing room. A guard stood ready in the adjoining hall.

"Well, what a surprise to see you here," commented Loudon derisively.

Dupree ignored the comment, and stated, "It looks like you've gotten yourself into a bit of trouble."

"And what business is that of yours?" Loudon asked.

"I thought you might like to know that your chair is being filled by your able assistant, Randy Cole."

"All right, Dupree, just what do you have in mind?"

"I just dropped in to see how you were doing. I'll be around again in a day or so after you've had a chance to think about your situation."

"Do you have any suggestions?" asked Loudon.

"Eat right and save your strength. You might need it." Dupree signalled the guard that he was through, and departed.

Loudon was escorted back to his cell, where he amused himself by reading a magazine that had been left in the cell by a previous occupant. He wondered how Janice was doing, and hoped she was all right. That she had not yet come to visit was an occasion for some concern, but he would not push the panic button at least until he had some word from her.

That same morning Janice decided to go to the college and take care of a few crucial details before going to visit Michael at the jail. She was barely inside the door before she was summoned to the office of the Dean of Instruction. Awaiting her there were three gentlemen, seated like as many Buddhas, and looking very uncomfortable. On the left was Professor James, head of the psychology department. Next to him was the Dean of Instruction, Harry Ginsberg. On the right was the Dean of Students, Walter Peabody. The atmosphere in the room was very somber.

"Please be seated, Janice," said Professor James.

"You fellows look like you've just been to a funeral," Janice commented. "What's this all about?"

There was some shuffling as the three officials shifted uneasily in their chairs. After a brief interval Professor James cleared his throat and said, "Um, we have a matter to take up with you--" He could not look directly into Janice's eyes, but kept his gaze focussed on the area of her chin.

"This looks like a wake," Janice interrupted. "Am I being disciplined?"

Again there was some uneasy shifting. The three gentlemen were having trouble deciding what to look at, and could not even look at each other. Apparently Professor James was the appointed spokesman. He cleared his throat again, and even took out a handkerchief to blow his nose, as the other two gentlemen remained stonily silent.

"First of all," began Professor James, "we want you to know that we here are acting under the authority of the Board

110

of Regents. We have to be honest with you, this is not our doing."

"What is not your doing?" Janice demanded to know

"I hate to do this, Janice," said James apologetically. "I guess we just have to come right out and say it--you are being discharged from the college staff, effective immediately."

"And you three got stuck with the hatchet job," said Janice with genuine sympathy. "I wouldn't want to be in your shoes for anything."

The men relaxed somewhat after Janice's acknowledgement of their predicament. "We're real sorry about this," James said sincerely. The other two men nodded in agreement.

"All right, now that it is out in the open, let's see what this is all about," said Janice. "What is the complaint?"

"It isn't our complaint," countered James. "The Board of Regents told us that you have been teaching some things of which the college cannot approve."

"Like what, for heaven's sake?"

"Well, to be specific," said James, "they heard that you do not believe in mental illness, neurosis, and other well-established concepts in the fields of psychology and psychiatry, holding that such concepts are myths, concocted for use by persons seeking power and wealth. They felt that was a pretty damning repudiation of the entire mental health field, and that if you continued to, as they put it, poison the minds of your students with such blasphemy it could be extremely disruptive and possibly quite damaging."

"But I have not been teaching such things," Janice protested. "What evidence do they have?"

"Well, it seems that some students came to the college president and complained that you were teaching such things. These students were interviewed by some board members at length, and reportedly they were quite convincing."

"Which students were they?"

"We are not at liberty to say."

"Were they in one of my classes?"

"Yes, of course they were. We checked on that."

"Don't I have a right to face my accusers?"

"I'm sorry, Janice. We have no latitude here. We cannot discuss the matter further. You are expected to remove your belongings from your office today. You will receive a check in the mail for salary due you. Please leave now, and don't make this any more difficult than it is."

"I think I understand. Sorry you fellows got stuck with this."

Janice rose from her chair and stepped toward the door. As she grasped the knob she turned and faced the three unwilling agents of her detractors. In a firm, unshaken voice she said, "I'm sure you gentlemen know as well as I do what is happening here, and I'm just as sure that you are appalled that this sort of thing can happen in our enlightened democracy. And I think you feel helpless to do anything about it, because your own careers are on the line. 'You can't fight city hall,' I think the word is. Gentlemen, I think the answer is not in fighting city hall. I think the answer is in education, especially at the college level, because that is where it begins. What is taught in college trickles down to high school and elementary schools. The answer, if you please, is in what we teach our children. In short, gentlemen, you are not helpless. You have the highest power of all: the power to teach. In that regard your influence stretches far and wide. Please, fellows, I hope you will give that some serious thought.

"Don't worry about me. I am merely the victim of this outrage, and though there will be small problems here and there, my conscience is clear. I'm sure none of you will be able to say the same. I hope some day you will be able to resolve that dilemma. Good bye. Maybe I'll see you later."

As Janice departed the three messengers sat motionless and speechless.

Outside the Dean's office Janice began to realize that she was not as emotionless as she had appeared to be a few moments ago. A feeling of anger began to rise within her, anger that such flagrant misuse of power could go unchallenged even in the hallowed halls of higher education, which, theoretically at least, should be immune to such dictatorial barbarity. Her anger momentarily became so strong that she had to seek refuge in a supply closet to compose herself. When a feeling of self pity began to assert itself, she resolutely refused to permit such a useless emotion to gain a foothold. She replaced it with a realization that things were not as bad as

112

they could be--in some other countries dissidents were commonly flogged, tortured, and even summarily executed. She also refused to permit any thoughts of revengeful actions.

Feeling better, Janice left the supply closet and returned to her office, only to be confronted with another abomination--her office, her desk, and her chair, were occupied by a total stranger. Her books and other belongings had been boxed and stored in the hall. This must have happened during the night, Janice thought. And the strange woman in her chair--who was she? She decided to find out.

"Hello, I am Janice Loudon. I am not surprised to find someone else occupying my office and my desk, but--well, to start with, who are you?"

The newcomer, an efficient-looking woman of perhaps thirty years, rose and introduced herself. "I am Mildred Wallace. I'm sorry, I didn't know this was your office--they didn't tell me." The young woman looked genuinely disturbed at this turn of events.

"Out of curiosity, just what did happen?" Janice inquired.

"Well, it's real strange," Miss Wallace responded. "I live in Tulsa. I have been teaching psychology there on a temporary basis for the past two years, temporary because I haven't completed all the requirements for permanent status. Last night about nine o'clock I got a call from some man saying he was with the Federal Government, telling me there was an opening for a full assistant professorship in Mallon City, and they wanted me to take it."

"What did you do?"

"Well, I was flabbergasted. I didn't know what to do. I told the man, he gave me a name but I can't remember it now, that I did not meet all the requirements for a full assistant professorship, but he said that didn't matter. Then he said he wanted me to be there--here--by eight o'clock this morning and report to a Professor James. I couldn't see how I could make it that soon, with my apartment, my belongings, and all that, but the man said I could come back later and take care of moving. He said Professor James would see that I got settled in at Mallon City all right. So here I am, and I feel terrible about all this, getting lied to and putting you out and all." Miss Wallace seemed almost at the point of tears.

113

Now that her anger was gone, Janice seemed almost amused with the whole scenario. It was almost like a scene from a James Bond movie. She asked Miss Wallace, "Did you get the feeling, when talking to this government man, that you didn't have a choice?"

"Yes, I did!" replied Miss Wallace. "Of course it was a much better deal than I had at Tulsa, so I didn't mind too much. But if I had known--"

Janice smiled. "Think nothing of it, Mildred. Before long you'll know the whole story, then you'll understand. You may not like it, but at least you'll know. So don't feel bad about replacing me, especially under these conditions. It's all part of a very large and very sordid story. Just relax and enjoy the opportunity. I may be around for a few days yet, so if there is anything I can do to help, let me know. Here's my address and phone number." Janice wrote the information on a small notepad and placed it on the desk.

"I really appreciate your being so kind," said Miss Wallace gratefully. "I'm not sure I could be so forgiving under such circumstances."

"Thank you," smiled Janice. "Believe me, I am pleased that I can be so forgiving. But be assured this does not apply to you--you had nothing to do with it. You are just as much a victim in this case as I am. Good bye, and good luck!"

Janice left Miss Wallace staring at her desk in consternation and dismay, and hoped that the young woman would soon adjust, forget the circumstances, and go on with her new teaching opportunity.

After making arrangements to have her belongings picked up at the college, Janice made her way to the city jail to see Michael. She found him in a somber mood, and hesitated to burden him further with her misfortunes, but she decided the best approach was to be straightforward about it.

"How are you doing?" she inquired of Michael.

"Not too bad, considering," he replied. "How about you?"

"I could be better, too. But as you say, not too bad considering the circumstances."

"What about the circumstances?" queried Michael, sensing that something had happened.

"I was fired this morning. When I got to the college I was

114

met by a trio of deans, who gave me the bad news."

"How do you feel about that?" asked Michael, his voice showing concern.

"Well, it was a surprise, but I think I was ready for it. I was angry for a while, but got over it. Then I got a further shock when I went to my office and found someone else in my place, and all my things moved out into the hall. I was astounded that the college would let them do something like that, but when I saw the looks on those deans' faces as they confronted me, I could understand. Never in my life did I ever suspect that I would witness something like what is happening to us. If someone had told me it could happen, I guess I wouldn't even have believed it. Now that it has become a reality, I'm not sure what I am going to do with it."

"I know exactly what you mean," responded Michael. "But I keep reminding myself that it isn't over yet--there is still the matter of what they are going to do to me on this trumped-up narcotics charge. They could send me to prison for a long time. However, I think they might be afraid to go that far. I still have a few friends with influence. So I think they'll probably offer me a deal, like they'll drop the charges if I will resign and get out of town. Which may be why they got you fired--if you were staying here, I might be hard to get rid of. Anyway, I'll know more about that when our new DA comes around."

"Who is this new DA?" Janice asked.

"Who else? Randy Cole."

"Is he mixed up in this?"

"He must be. I know he's been having financial troubles, and he's a little on the weak side. I presume they've made him an offer he can't refuse. Don't get me wrong, I think Randy is basically honest, but susceptible. If he is mixed up in this, he's probably going through all kinds of hell. In that case I would really feel sorry for the guy."

"When do you think he'll be around?"

"Probably some time this afternoon."

"Well," said Janice, "I'll go on home and start getting things organized, ready for whatever. Let me know as soon as you have anything." She kissed her husband ardently and departed.

True to Loudon's prediction, early that afternoon Randy Cole appeared at the city jail and arranged an interview with Loudon in the jail's interrogating room. Loudon noted that Cole's face was drawn and peaked, indicating that he had been under considerable strain lately. Loudon waited for Cole to speak.

"Hi, Mike," Cole began, his voice sounding unnatural. "You don't seem to be surprised to see me."

"I'm not surprised. Dupree was in and told me you were in my seat."

Cole struggled with an urge to apologize to Loudon, to try to explain why he did what he did; but he decided not to do that. Instead he decided to play the game the way it was written on Dupree's "cue cards," and steeled himself for what he had to do.

"I was sorry to hear that you got yourself into this trouble," he said to Loudon. "Surprised, too. I didn't think you would do something like that."

My God, Loudon thought--can you believe this guy, pretending that the drug bust was on the up and up? Loudon looked around for hidden mikes, being sure that such a performance was being recorded. He decided to go along with the sham.

"Well, Randy," he said, "you know how things are. Sometimes a guy gets desperate for cash, and the drug scene is good for a buck now and then."

"You know you don't have to tell me anything without your attorney being present," Cole reminded.

"Do I need an attorney?" Loudon asked.

"Maybe not," said Cole. "You have a pretty good record here, and so far as I know have been clean up to now, so I don't want to jeopardize your future when you don't really deserve it. So I'm sure the citizens of Mallon County will not hold it against me if I offer you a way to avoid serious trouble. And I'm sure you understand that it is within my power to throw the book at you, because we do have an airtight case for drug possession, and could possibly make a case for dealing. No doubt some witnesses could be found who would swear they had bought narcotics from you, if you decide to fight this."

"I understand that," replied Loudon dryly, "and I appreciate

116

your concern about my welfare. What did you have in mind?"

"All right," said Cole, breathing slightly easier. "Here's the layout. All charges will be set aside, if you forthwith resign as district attorney, forfeit all rights and accrued salaries and entitlements commensurate thereto, and leave Mallon County immediately, with a promise under oath that you will never return here, or in fact never hereafter engage in any negotiations or business dealings with any person or organization residing or established in Mallon County." Cole produced a document setting forth the above provisions and added, "All you have to do is sign this, and you are free to go."

"And what if I sign, then later return or have 'dealings' with someone in Mallon County?"

"Then of course you will be cited for violation of your contract, and/or depending on the circumstances, be again charged and tried for the narcotics violation."

"Then what about the 'error' on my income tax return, the levy on my bank account, the confiscation of my house, and insurance on my house?"

Cole's entire being tightened up as he replied, "If you sign, you will not face criminal charges for your transgression on your tax return, but confiscation of your property will stand, and your bank account will be forfeited and revert to the Federal Government. If other holdings of worth are discovered, they too will be confiscated."

"What about my clothes and other personal belongings?"

"Come on, Mike, this isn't a joke. You know as well as I do that your personal belongings cannot be confiscated."

"All right, what about my car?"

"Well, in view of the fact that you have no money and so no other way to get out of the county, we will leave you your car with a tank full of gas."

"How nice. Thank God for small favors. Okay, I'll sign your document."

When the signing was completed, Loudon asked, "How soon do I have to leave?"

"Since it is now getting late in the day, tomorrow morning will be fine."

Cole gathered up his papers, and as he turned to leave, he paused and offered this final comment: "And Mike, I hope that

117

Janice will be going with you, because if she stays, according to your contract, you can have no further visits with her."

With that Cole departed, looking for all the world like a weary old man.

CHAPTER SIX

Within minutes after Cole's departure Loudon was released, and the jail door clanged shut behind him.

Michael hurried home and related to Janice all that had transpired during his visit with Randy Cole. She was astounded at the thoroughness of the agreement that Michael had to sign, but she accepted. With no time to waste, they began at once to make plans for closing the apartment and notifying suppliers of utilities and services. Michael checked with his bank, and true to Cole's statement, his account had been closed, with all funds reverting to the Federal Government. An apology by the bank official seemed weak and insincere. And the packing--they could not possibly carry all of their belongings in one vehicle, so what should they do? They decided to take what they would have to have for the next couple of weeks, then box up the rest and prevail upon the landlord to ship the cartons to Michael's parents in Norman.

The Loudons considered the possibility of living with either his or her parents until they could find gainful employment, but as one they decided against it. True, either family would be happy to accommodate them, at least for a while, but the idea simply did not appeal to these truly independent individuals. In fact they decided not even to tell their parents what had happened, beyond telling them they were moving, until they got settled somewhere. Of course their parents would need to know sooner or later, and hopefully it would be sooner. But for now the news of their offsprings' "disgrace" would simply upset the parents, when there was nothing they could do about it.

Then, where to go? The only thing certain thus far was that they had to get out of Mallon County. South? North? East? West? Did any realm have special advantages or appeal to them? The most important consideration at the moment, considering that they had only two hundred dollars to their name, was cost. And even the two hundred was dwindling as they paid in advance the cost of shipping their belongings. Credit cards? They carried Visa and Master Card, but a quick check revealed what Michael had suspected: their cards had been cancelled, obviously by direct order from a governmental source.

Forwarding of mail could be a problem. The landlord was willing to take care of that, but Michael thought there could be danger associated with any future effort to contact the landlord, so they decided that their first stop would be a motel they knew about in Kansas, and to use that as a forwarding address until they had time and opportunity to notify correspondents. Officials might block incoming mail, but surely they could not or would not try to block mail that was being forwarded by the landlord. A telephone call to the said motel secured a reservation for the following night.

With packing and other essentials completed or taken care of to their satisfaction, Michael and Janice brought out a bottle of vintage Cabernet to relax and ponder their current status.

"Well, here's looking at you," toasted Michael, as they raised their glasses.

"And you," echoed Janice.

After a thoughtful pause Michael commented, "There really isn't much to say, is there? In spite of our anticipating everything that happened, it still seems almost like a nightmare, and we will soon wake up to the realization that nothing has changed after all."

The couple proceeded to finish the bottle, sipping slowly to make this precious moment--the last ticking seconds of their once-secure life--last as long as they could. They felt that as they drained the last savory drops of wine from their glasses the coach and horses of their erstwhile promise would turn into a pumpkin, and henceforth their lot would be a corner near a dingy fireplace in a mansion, belonging to another world, to which they were denied access.

That night the Loudons slept easily, with no nightmares. An alarm clock assured them that they would not oversleep, and have to be awakened by rude pounding on their door.

Despite their awareness of coming hardships, the Loudons were not really prepared for a harsh ordeal. Neither Janice nor Michael had ever felt the burden of severe deprivation, as had millions during the great depression of the thirties. Their wants and needs had always been supplied by parents who were both willing, and to the necessary extent, able, to do so. They could sleep well this night because they could not fully anticipate the hardships they might encounter, with little or no money, and little or no chance to obtain gainful employment suitable to their credentials, and before very long, to be sure, increasing difficulty in just getting enough to eat and getting from one place to another. In case of health problems they could not afford proper care, as the health insurance previously furnished by their employers was no longer in effect. They would have no credit and no chance of getting any. Soon they would be living from hand to mouth, ever wondering where the next meal was coming from, or the next comfortable bed to sleep in. No, they were not yet able to comprehend what troubles might lie ahead.

However, people differ in their ability to cope with adversity. Some are more clever than others, more ingenious in detecting and utilizing available resources, and just as important, less given to wallowing in self pity and blaming others for their troubles. The days to come would test the Loudons' "pioneer spirit," that remarkable ability displayed by early settlers, as in the old West, in utilizing materials at hand to get by and even thrive. The fact that so many thousands of people left the security of homes and jobs for a new life in a mostly unsettled and often uncharted land spoke of the appeal of a chance to find and build something better, even at the expense of initial hardships.

One might wonder, then, if the Loudons' willingness to abandon the security of their own situation on the basis of principle meant that down underneath, unknown to them, they welcomed the chance to trek into the wilderness to find and build something more compatible with their basic instincts. One might guess that somehow in the next few days the true purpose of their voluntary exile might be revealed in how they coped with difficulties.

The next morning the Loudons were shocked to find a police car stationed in front of their apartment, obviously there to make certain that the couple departed without delay. Almost amused at such audacity, Michael dressed and went out to assure the waiting policeman that they were packed and ready to hit the road. Was the policeman also going to follow them, to make certain that they did in fact leave Mallon County? The policeman, who was looking rather uncomfortable in this ridiculous assignment, assured Michael that they would not be followed (although Michael was certain they would be followed, but by an unmarked government car).

The final step was to pack all the groceries that would keep or would be eaten before the summer heat could take its toll. It took two medium-sized boxes to pack it all. The box carrying non-perishable staples could go in first. The second, with some food that would be consumed right away, would go on top, as would other items that they would need today and in the immediate future. Records and miscellaneous items of intrinsic or sentimental value were carefully stowed in little strong boxes, for now at the very bottom of the load. Janice's fine camera, a gift from her parents, was placed in the front compartment, ready for use.

The last box required a bit of rearranging to find a comfortable niche for it. That done, Mr. and Mrs. Michael Loudon wedged themselves into the automobile, checked the time, waved to the police monitor, and were on their way.

As Cole had promised, the car's gas tank was full. Michael was driving, largely because he knew the area quite well. He drove at moderate speed to conserve fuel, and because there was no need for haste to reach their destination before evening.

It was not far to the Kansas border, and they crossed it before noon. Janice commented that she had never been in Kansas. In a humorous vein Janice asked Michael, "How many states have you been in?" That led to a search of Michael's memory. Soon he replied, "Ten--ten states, I think." He then listed the states, as Janice kept count. Then Michael posed the same question for Janice, who had to admit that she had been in only seven states, most of those in the new England area. The greatest distance that she had ever traveled was from Maine to Mallon City, Oklahoma. "You've never been to Florida? I thought all New Englanders went to Florida."

At noon they stopped briefly for lunch, nice egg-salad sandwiches packed by Janice that morning, with coffee from their vacuum bottle. They had found an agreeable spot near a smooth lake, where they watched large numbers of water fowl going and coming. The lunch consumed and the vacuum bottle empty, they were soon on their way again. They arrived late afternoon at their destination, a nice-looking motel on the outskirts of Salina (pronounced Sal-eye-na).

122

Roger Harrison, the motel manager, greeted them cordially. As they were signing in, Roger, a pleasant-looking, middle-aged fellow, commented, "I heard what happened to you folks. It was on the morning news here, and I think on the network news, too. Everyone around here thinks you folks really got shafted just for standing up for your principles. We feel real bad about it, and want to try to make you as comfortable as we can."

"We sincerely thank you," Michael replied, as Janice smiled concurrence. "We'll talk to you later, after we get settled in."

The room, with a small kitchenette, was forty dollars, not bad in this day and age, Michael commented. In the room, Michael counted the remaining money: one hundred and twenty dollars. He carefully stowed the money back in his wallet, with grave questions about how long this amount would last.

A local paper contained a brief account of the Mallon City debacle, with a brief editorial about what "politics" is coming to. As Michael read, Janice prepared a scant but tasty repast on the tiny stove, using groceries they had salvaged from their Mallon City home. Afterward they watched a televison network news program, where indeed the Mallon City/County incident was covered in some detail, including the information that the Loudon family had, as agreed, left Mallon County, with their present whereabouts unknown.

Shutting off the television, the Loudons discussed plans. They agreed that they could afford one more night at the motel, which would give them time to consolidate and figure out how to get more money.

Suddenly Michael said excitedly, "I have an idea. When I was a young man I often went around door to door looking for odd jobs when I needed money, and I almost always found some. People have a hard time finding someone to do odd jobs because not many guys are willing to do that. Why don't we sign up for one more night here, and tomorrow I'll hit the streets. How about it?"

"Well, if you can do that, so can I," Janice agreed. "There may be a lot of homeowners who could use a few hours of help doing housework. In a pinch I can do laundry, even a bit of

123

ironing. I'm with you! Let's do it!"

Before retiring, Michael signed up for one more night, then had a talk with Roger, asking if he would be willing to receive and forward their mail, explaining that they were not allowed to have dealings with any person or organization in Mallon County. After again expressing his opinion about the Loudons' raw deal, Roger readily agreed to serve as their "post office." "Just keep in touch, let me know where you are and how long you are staying, and I'll see that you get your mail. Glad to do it! If there's any way we can help you, let us know!"

The next morning Janice prepared a hearty breakfast, using up the last of their eggs and sausage. Both Michael and Janice then dressed in sturdy work clothing and began a house-to-house canvass, each taking a different part of what appeared to be a reasonably prosperous part of town. They approached homeowners with a prepared opening statement, that they were professional people (lawyer, teacher) who had positions secured in a different part of the country, but at a future date, and meanwhile they were unemployed and needed money to cover living and travel expenses. They asked only for minimum wage, because higher wage demands might discourage some who might otherwise be willing to engage them. The idea, they agreed, was to get work, not to get rich.

Michael was astounded at the response. There was yard work--weeding, making new flower beds, planting and hoeing vegetable gardens, even putting in a new lawn. Just about every third home was glad to have a healthy younger man to do a few things that were badly needed. Some homes even had plumbing and minor household repair requirements. For jobs that could not be completed this day, appointments were made for the following day (especially the new lawn job). All of the homeowners paid at once upon completion of a job, and seemed happy to do it. At the end of the first day Michael had worked about seven hours at what he believed to be minimum wage, and collected twenty-five dollars.

Wearily he trudged back to the motel. Janice was already there. "How did you do?" she inquired.

Michael proudly announced his success, emphasizing commitments for work at least the following day, and perhaps successive days. "And how did you do?" he inquired of Janice.

124

"I'm sorry," Janice replied sadly. "I didn't do well at all. I went to at least twenty houses, told the ladies what I wanted, and got nothing. It seemed almost like they were afraid of me. I don't know. It's hard to explain." She put her hands to her face and sighed with discouragement.

"Don't worry about it!" said Michael encouragingly. "It looks like I will be getting work every day, probably even weekends. So we're going to make out all right!"

Janice smiled in an effort to appear more cheerful. "I know, Dear. It's just that I had hopes of finding some work too, and it sort of sets you back when you draw a complete blank."

"OK, but I will say this--since it looks like I will be able to earn only about twenty-five or thirty dollars a day, we can't afford to keep this motel room. We've got to find something cheaper. I think I'll go and talk to Roger, explain our circum-stances--I know he'll understand--and get his advice. There's got to be cheaper accommodations around somewhere, and he ought to know where they are."

"Another thing, too," Janice added, "we will have to go grocery shopping. We haven't much left for either dinner or breakfast, and almost nothing for your lunch tomorrow. I can get by tonight by going strong on starch, potatoes and pasta. We have some canned tuna that will do for tonight. Why don't you go and talk to Roger while I fix dinner, and then after dinner we can go shopping. OK?"

Michael found Roger at the desk, proceeded to explain their need to find cheaper lodgings, and asked where they might find some. Roger asserted that he understood, and indeed had been expecting them to make other arrangements. He did have a suggestion: "Over on the old highway into town there are a few of the old motels, built back in the thirties. In those days they mostly built cottages, separated by carports. I think there's about three left, but two of them, I believe, are being used for storage. There is one that is still being rented out, called the Bide-a-Wee. It isn't much, but it is cheap. It's being run by the owner, an old fellow named Bill Parkinson. I'm sure each cottage has a kitchenette, and I know people do cook in there."

"Do you know how much they charge?" Michael wanted to know.

125

"I'm not too sure, but I believe about fifteen dollars a night, maybe a little less if you stay a week or more."

"That's awfully cheap," Michael commented. "Are you sure the place is liveable?"

"Oh, I'm sure it is," replied Roger. "People do rent those cottages, I know."

"Well, thanks a lot. We'll look into that tomorrow. Good night!"

When Michael returned dinner was well underway. As Janice finished the preparations Michael explained about the cheaper cottages.

"It doesn't sound like much," Janice commented, "but I guess we don't have much choice. Why don't we go over tomorrow morning and check it out."

"Fine," Michael replied. "I have a couple of small jobs scheduled in the early morning, but I'll be free around ten. Suppose I pick you up then and we'll go over."

Janice agreed. After they finished dinner they went to a nearby grocery store to replenish their larder. They were careful to choose foods that would not need continued refrigeration, considering the uncertainty of what would be available to them in new accommodations, but did make sure that they would be adequately fed for the next several days. For now they would have to be satisfied with a less-than-ideal diet, but perhaps after getting settled they could do better. As it was, they spent most of Michael's earnings that day.

As planned, the next morning, after Michael satisfied two job commitments, the couple went in search of the Bide-a-Wee motel. Following Roger's directions, they had little trouble locating the structure, situated amongst a number of ramshackle buildings, the remnants of what had once been thriving business establishments along the old, once-busy highway into town. The motel was as Roger had described, frame cottages separated by roofed carports, six cottages in all. The carport floors were unpaved. The units needed paint, but appeared to be sound. Beyond the gravelled traffic area of the motel was a patch of waist-high weeds, almost obscuring the rusting hulk of a 1938 Buick. Beyond that, with high weeds growing up all around, was the remains of an old machine shop, with rusted gears, shafts, and other equipment reminiscent of a by-gone

126

era. A seedy-looking mongrel dog was busily sniffing through the area, seeking God knows what.

Parked near one of the middle cottages was an old Chrysler, badly in need of paint and body repair. A few car parts and pieces of defunct kitchen equipment near the entrance door suggested that the cottage was occupied, probably on a permanent basis. Recent car tracks near an adjoining cottage indicated a possible tenant there as well. The other units appeared to be unoccupied.

Bill Parkinson, owner-manager, a grizzled old fellow who could barely get around even with the aid of a cane, was on hand as the couple arrived. Yes, he did have a cottage available, fifteen dollars a night, twelve if they stayed a week or longer. Taking a key from a wall rack, Parkinson led the couple down a dusty path to the end cottage, unlocked and opened the door. Janice paused briefly as she noticed a small flower bed near the entrance stoop, boasting a row of varicolored petunias bravely challenging the summer heat. The bed was free of weeds, and had been recently watered.

As the Loudons entered the cottage they were struck immediately with intense heat, with a slight musty odor, that hit them like a blast from a hot oven. The cottage had been completely closed, probably for several days, and the summer heat had caused the interior temperature to rise to what seemed to be even higher than the external heat of the sun. Both Janice and Michael were accustomed to the hot summer temperatures of the area, but had never experienced such a heat buildup as greeted them here. Somewhat taken aback, the couple silently pondered what they should do. Obviously they could not go back to the other motel. Parkinson, apparently unaware of the heat buildup as a possible problem, stood silently by, waiting for the pair to make up their minds.

The cottage was fairly roomy, with a small bedroom and connecting bath adjoining the living area. The bed looked comfortable, and was covered by an attractive bed spread. The bathroom, with linoleum floor, had a custom built shower stall, toilet and small sink, over which was hung a metal medicine cabinet with several rust spots. (The room looked added on, and Michael guessed that when the units were built the "bath" was an outhouse.) Upon close inspection the bathroom seemed

127

to be reasonably clean.

Both the bedroom and living area were carpeted, although the carpet was badly worn and faded and almost worn through in spots. To the extreme right was a small kitchenette, that appeared to be adequately furnished with cheap but serviceable utensils and dishes. A small, two-burner gas stove was set in a small alcove. Nearby was a small, apartment-size refrigerator. There were two worn but comfortable chairs in the living area. Nearby was a table that apparently served for both kitchen preparations and dining, complete with two straight-back chairs that appeared to have received at least a half-dozen coats of paint through the years. There was no television. The walls were paneled with cheap, faded, plywood paneling, stained here and there by past splashes and spills. On two walls were small, fairly attractive pictures in worn frames, bearing modest religious symbols.

Parting the shabby lace curtains that offered privacy in the tiny bedroom, Michael looked out, to see a right-of-way strip, covered with maturing weeds, bordering the old highway.

All in all, the cottage showed its age and the wear and tear of years of service, but it looked clean, and showed reasonable care in making it attractive to prospective tenants.

After several minutes of cautious deliberation Janice took Michael to one side, apart from the waiting manager, where they engaged in whispered conference. "I think we can manage with this," Janice commented. "If we open up all the windows and the door, we can probably get it cooled down a bit by bed time. The windows and door are screened, so we won't get plagued with flies and mosquitoes. It isn't much, but it does look clean, and God knows we can't afford anything better."

"Yeah, it isn't the Waldorf, but I agree--I think we can manage. We could look around, but I'm sure we couldn't do any better for the price, and I do have to get back to work."

The couple told Parkinson they would take the cottage, whereupon the old man led them back to his hole-in-the-wall office to sign the register. To assure the cheaper rate, Michael paid the manager eighty-four dollars plus tax for a week's rent, and received a brace of keys plus the information that there would be daily newspapers available, and there was a pay telephone just inside the office.

Janice drove Michael to his next job, then went to move their belongings out of the motel to their new quarters. She thanked Roger for telling them about the Bide-a-Wee, and indicated that they planned to stay there for at least a week, in case they got any mail. She then returned to their new home and unloaded the car, stacking belongings in corners and on the bed until they could sort them out. With windows and door open, she hoped to generate some breeze to cool the unit down. She discovered a small thermometer on a wall near a small heater (Kansas can get quite cold in the winter!) and read the temperature: one hundred and fifteen degrees! No wonder! The outdoor temperature at that time, she had heard on the car radio, was merely eighty-five degrees. She then busied herself storing groceries in the small kitchenette and making preparations for cooking.

About six p.m. Parkinson came to the door with the message that Michael had called and wanted to be picked up. Thanking the old man, Janice drove at once to the address provided. She found her husband very tired, but smiling. He had collected twenty-eight dollars that day, which would bring their cash holdings to just over fifty dollars, free and clear for the moment.

Back at the cottage Janice brought out a surprise. When she was out earlier she had obtained a six-pack of beer, using the little money she had stashed in her purse. With a big smile she now served her hard-working husband this bit of cheer, an ice-cold bottle of Kansas beer, which he accepted with fervent thanks. She related her findings about the indoor temperature, which news elicited a surprised "Wow!"

Janice had learned that afternoon of a special at a fried chicken convenience establishment, an eleven-piece chicken dinner complete with four rolls, butter, mashed potatoes and gravy, and cole slaw, for just twelve dollars; so, partly to avoid adding heat by cooking, she got money from Michael and drove to pick up this bargain while Michael savored his beer. While Janice got the food ready, Michael showered to rid himself of the day's grime and changed into his regular clothes. They fully enjoyed the tasty meal, and found that they had enough food left over for another meal.

129

After dinner it was still a hundred degrees in the cottage, so Michael and Janice went for a stroll. Beyond the cluster of old buildings were broad fields of wheat, barley, and corn. Following an inviting lane between two fields, the couple wandered down to the nearby Smoky Hill river. There in the shade of huge shade trees bordering the stream it was cool, with the soothing quiet broken only by the murmuring of the flowing water and an occasional cackle of a bobwhite. The couple sat down on a convenient log and watched the stream, noting an occasional fish jumping out of the water to nab a juicy insect. At this moment they felt that the most serious of their burdens had been lifted. They were settled in a cottage that they could afford, and enough earnings were assured to meet their needs of the moment. Of course there would be demands and problems down the road, but they felt adequate to cope with whatever came up. In fact they admitted that they were beginning to enjoy this freedom from the constant demands and pressures of their previous employment.

After almost an hour of drinking in the pleasures of the setting, Michael rose, hands in pockets, stretched, and gazed out over the flourishing fields. As he did so he began to sense a sort of longing for the open country, with its peace and quiet and freedom from the hustle and bustle of the city, with its traffic, its incessant noise, and the intense competitions of its masses. Even a smaller community such as Mallon City could have its problems in that regard.

Michael gave Janice a hand to arise from the log, and the two wandered back to the cottage, to face the heat and try to get some sleep, as Michael had a big day lined up for tomorrow. They took cold showers to cool off as much as they could. Leaving windows and door hooked but wide open, they retired, and after a little bit of trouble getting to sleep, did manage several hours of much-needed rest.

The next morning Janice drove Michael to his next work site and then pursued an idea that had come to her yesterday after learning that Salina boasted two colleges, Kansas Wesleyan University (Methodist Episcopal) and Marymount college for girls (Catholic). It was summer, but most colleges do stay open at least administratively during the summer, and so, she thought, it would do no harm to see if there might be a teaching position available to her in the fall. She tried Kansas Wesleyan first, because she wasn't sure if a Catholic college would hire a non-Catholic teacher. Entering the business office she asked to speak to the executive in charge of hiring, and was referred to a nearby office, where she met the head of the school, Dr. Joyce Billingsley. "Have a seat," invited Dr. Billingsley, smiling. Then, "What can I do for you?"

Janice stated her purpose, she had been teaching psychology for some years but had terminated her last position and was now looking for a permanent job elsewhere. When asked she gave the name of the eastern college where she had obtained her PhD. Dr. Billingsley appeared interested, and asked for a few other details, nodding her head with each disclosure. Finally she came to the question that Janice had been dreading:

"And just where was your last teaching position?"

"The college at Mallon City, Oklahoma," Janice replied.

Upon hearing "Mallon City" the expression on the administrator's face changed slightly but quite noticeably.

"I see," Dr. Billingsley replied. "That is a very good school. Now let me see--" She moved a few papers on her desk, supposedly looking for something, then looked up and stated, "I really do thank you for coming. We are always interested in keeping names of qualified candidates on file for when a position becomes vacated, however there is no position open at the moment. We do hope you will keep in touch and let us know where you will be in case we need you."

I know, Janice thought, don't call us, we'll call you. She rose, cordially thanked Dr. Billingsley for her kind attention, and left.

The next stop was Marymount college, where again the head of the school appeared interested until Mallon City was mentioned, with the same result.

Janice had half expected this rejection, believing that she probably had indeed been blackballed, at least in this south central part of the country, probably under threat of severe consequences to any school that would hire her, such as loss of federal aid. But half expecting it did not make her feel any better. She felt sick at her stomach, and felt again the rising anger at such gross injustice. To ease her discomfort she reminded herself that she had asked for it. She had received

131

adequate warning, at least indirectly.

Returning home, Janice again donned work clothing and went looking for odd jobs. The result was the same--no house-wife wanted to hire her, for what reason she could only guess. At least, she presumed, it had nothing to do with the Mallon City fiasco. So until time to pick up Michael, Janice occupied herself trying to make their new home look just a bit more like home.

Michael again proudly brought home twenty-seven dollars and promises of continued work, and was rewarded with a warm kiss and a cold beer. Janice told of her lack of success at the two colleges, whereupon Michael attempted to ease her concern by predicting that they were going to do just fine finan-cially. Looking ahead, Michael thought that when they had enough money to take a little time off, he could look for a better job, perhaps with the city or a local law firm. If he worked over the weekend, he thought, they might have enough to do this before their week at the Bide-a-Wee was up. Once situated in a good job, they might be able to establish enough credit to get by until the first pay check. Janice remembered that she still had some money coming from her teaching job at Mallon City, not much, she thought, because she had been fired only a few days after the last pay day, but it would help. With this assurance they relaxed and enjoyed the remainder of yes-terday's chicken dinner.

After these days of unaccustomed physical labor Michael suffered many aches and pains, but he felt good. He could tell that his muscles were beginning to toughen up, and he was getting stronger. He now had more energy, he had a better appetite, and he slept more soundly, in spite of the heat. Before being ousted from the DA job he did exercise some, but the physical benefits of those meager efforts were not nearly as great as those he was now experiencing. He was physically tired at the end of the day, but it was a good tired: not the ex-hausting, debilitating tiredness after a day of coping with the stress of the DA's office. He intended to seek a position in his field, because the pay was so much better, but if that did not pan out, he was not averse to finding regular work involving physical labor. Some labor jobs did pay fairly well, better than what he was doing now, and surely the government had not

132

blackballed him from that type of employment.

Two days later, when he had a couple of hours not committed to odd jobs, Loudon paid a visit to the city manager, Fred Lyle. He wasn't quite sure how to go about this, but decided that it would be best to find out up front whether or not the city had been told not to hire him.

Lyle shook hands with Loudon and invited him to have a chair, then asked, "What can I do for you?"

Loudon began, "My name is Michael Loudon. Is that name familiar to you?"

"Should it be?" Lyle asked, appearing to be somewhat evasive.

"I don't know. I am a lawyer, looking for a job, as a lawyer or something else where I can earn an honest living."

"Are you a resident of Salina?"

"Well, not really, I guess--I've only been here a few days."

"Where do you come from?"

"Mallon City, Oklahoma."

As soon as he heard "Mallon City" the manager's expression changed, as the name cued off a recollection of something that had passed over his desk a few days ago. He had paid little attention to it at the time. As he recalled, it was a simple memo professing to be from the sheriff of Mallon County, to "whom it may concern," giving the name of Michael Loudon and relating that the subject was a fugitive from justice. The message advised all concerned parties not to employ this fugitive in any capacity whatsoever. Lyle pulled the memo out from under a pile of papers and showed it to Loudon, commenting, "I don't know what this is all about. If you are a fugitive from justice, how come they don't want you back? I heard on the news that you had been ordered to leave the county."

"I was ordered to leave the county," Loudon replied. "This memo is a phony. It didn't come from the sheriff's office at all. Evidently it was intended to give any and all a good reason not to hire me."

"How did you get yourself in that mess?" the manager wanted to know.

Loudon did not feel like talking about that right now, so he stated simply, "I stood on a principle and got the wrong people mad at me. I knew it was going to happen, so I have nothing to

133

complain about. They definitely gave me a choice, but I had to go with what I believed was right."

Lyle was impressed, and said so. He leaned back in his swivel chair and added, "Well, whatever the principle was is not important. We could use someone of your caliber in Salina. Unfortunately I can't offer you a job, at least not now. You're a hot item, Loudon, and we'd get in all kinds of hot water if we failed to recognize that. The Commission would never go for it. I'll tell them about it, of course, but I know how they'd vote. If you're broke I could possibly arrange a small loan based on future--"

"No, thanks," Loudon interrupted. "In the first place I don't think you could do it, and in the second place I wouldn't want that burden hanging over my head, considering how hard it is going to be for me to find a job."

As he rose to leave, Loudon thanked the manager for his compassion, and said that some day, after the stigma was gone, he might consider making Salina his permanent residence.

Loudon felt no negative emotions as he left the manager's office. After all, this was fully expected. Rather, he felt slightly encouraged by Lyle's forthright acknowledgment that he was not the villain they were trying to paint him. If Lyle was not taken in by such efforts, then maybe a lot of others would look at it the same way.

With a little time left before his next job, Loudon decided to drop in to see one of the local attorney groups. He chose Baker, Ledbetter, and Finch since it wasn't far from city hall. The secretary indicated that Ledbetter was the head man. Yes, he was in, and would see him. Loudon entered the rather un-pretentious office, and faced a slightly balding, middle-aged man with horn-rimmed glasses, who rose and extended his hand. Loudon shook hands, then came right to the point.

"My name is Michael Loudon," he said. "I'm looking for a job."

"I presume you are an attorney," offered Ledbetter.

"Yes, I was in private practice for a while, then was a district attorney for several years." Loudon studied Ledbetter's expression for some sign that the man recognized who he was. He saw no sign of such recognition; however, that was mislead-ing, because Ledbetter said right out, "You're that DA who was

134

forced to leave Mallon County, down in Oklahoma, aren't you?"

"Yes, I am."

"Well, to be truthful with you, I think you'll have a hard time finding a job in this part of the country. I used to work for the U.S. Government, and I know that when they get after you they get pretty determined. You've been blackballed around here. I wouldn't mind hiring you myself, but I'm afraid it would backfire on us. Anyway, we don't have an opening right now, so the question is academic. I don't mind saying that I hope you beat this."

Loudon thanked Ledbetter warmly, then walked out feeling even more encouraged.

Loudon went back to his odd job commitments. Word of his availability and capabilities had gotten around, so several jobs awaited him for the next couple of days at least. Loudon thought this could work out quite well if the pay wasn't so meagre. However, he didn't feel justified in charging more, because these were not wealthy people he was doing jobs for. He decided to try for a regular job with one of the mills in the area. Flour milling, he had learned from Roger, was the chief industry of Salina. There was even one mill, built in 1868, that was still operating and still using the original water turbines.

When Loudon returned to their cottage home that evening he told Janice of his lack of success with the city and a law firm.

"Are you discouraged, Dear?" Janice asked softly.

"No, not at all," Michael replied, sipping the cold beer that Janice had supplied. "I suppose I could be, but no--I've got jobs lined up already for the next two days, and more coming, I'm sure. If we don't run into any major expenses we should do all right. However, I'm going to take a little time each day to look for a regular job. Tomorrow I guess I'll try one of the mills. I hear they hire quite a few people. At least I can get my name on a list or two." Then, "How about you, Dear? How do you feel about all this by now?"

"I find this very interesting," Janice replied with a smile. "I've lived a kind of sheltered life, and this is all new to me, living in a cheap old motel, watching every penny, doing things for us that I used to pay others to do. I used to send out most

135

laundry, but now, like tomorrow, I've got to try to find a laundromat. I wouldn't deliberately choose this kind of life, but since this is how it is, I believe some good can come of it. I'm even learning how to bake bread, using Mr. Parkinson's oven that you put on top of the gas burners. I think I'll be learning a lot before this is over!"

Janice stood up and walked over to the narrow front window and looked out over the gravelled traffic area. Michael walked to her side, gave her a big hug, and kissed her on the cheek. As she responded with an arm snugly around his waist he said, "You know, the best part of all this is that we have each other, and we love each other. I wouldn't trade that for all the wealth and power in the world."

"That goes for me, too," Janice replied, squeezing Michael's waist more tightly. Together they stood quietly, looking out beyond the gravel, the weeds, and the shabby buildings to a world of peace, contentment, and good will.

CHAPTER SEVEN

Michael went to two of the local mills and applied for jobs. No jobs were available at this time, but he did get his name on the lists for future employment. Meanwhile he continued doing odd jobs. To save gas, wear and tear on the car, and wear and tear on Janice getting him back and forth to his work, he bought a used bicycle for fifteen dollars. After groceries and other necessities were purchased, there was still enough cash on hand to pay Parkinson for another week at the motel.

The money situation improved substantially when Janice received her salary check in the mail, forwarded by the Mallon City landlord and then by Roger. It was for six hundred dollars, which amount formerly would have seemed rather puny, but now looked almost like a small fortune. After she and Michael rejoiced in this together, Janice decided to take some of the money and try to bring into their current life something that she, at least, had been missing a lot: music. She adored classical music, which had been part of her life ever since she was ten years old; but she also liked any sort of music that had good melody and rendition. When packing to leave Mallon City she had tucked a small collection of tapes and CD's into one of the sturdier boxes. Now, while Michael was at work, she went shopping to find a used stereo tape deck, and with luck, perhaps a used CD player that could be attached to it.

Her first stop was a Salvation Army store where donated items were sold to the public. Good fortune! There was a fine looking stereo set, much used but still working, suitable for playing audio tapes. The store manager obliged by plugging in the set and furnishing a tape for demonstration. The speakers were surprisingly good, and must have been expensive when new. Janice bought the set, priced at only twenty- five dollars. Unfortunately the store did not have a CD player, but the manager referred Janice to a privately-owned used goods store not far away. There she did find a somewhat battered CD player that still worked, as guaranteed by the store owner. The set was priced at twenty dollars, but due to the shabby appearance of the machine, the owner accepted Janice's offer of fifteen dollars.

Janice took her new-found treasures home and installed

them at once, attaching the CD player to the stereo with the cable provided. Inserting one of her most prized CD's, a Mozart collection, she sank into one of the comfortable chairs and listened with pleasure, ignoring the almost imperceptible squawks that crept in now and then.

When Michael came riding in on his bicycle that evening, Janice showed her acquisitions with pride, and put on a tape that she knew Michael would like. Michael grinned with pleasure as the mellow tones filled the room. After listening for several minutes, he commented, "That was a great find, Dear. I didn't realize how much I missed music. I used to listen to FM on the radio a lot, the easy-listening stations, but those stations have all switched to other kinds of music, mostly country-western and rock. Thank you for making this good music a part of our lives now!"

"You're welcome," returned Janice, looking pleased as punch.

They enjoyed music all through dinner and the ritual of washing dishes in the tiny sink.

Afterward the couple took one of their evening walks through the fields and down to the river, where they sat in the shade of the huge trees and held hands as they watched the gently-flowing water and occasional antics of fish leaping for insects. They had little to say, as by now it seemed that words would add little to the calm comfort they felt in being free of financial concerns, at least for now. The future that had a few days ago, despite their efforts to console themselves, seemed somewhat threatening, now took on a more benign appearance. They now permitted themselves to dream a little, and talk of better jobs, a nice house to live in, and maybe--just maybe-- even a family. As they dreamed they allowed themselves to mention some possibilities, although being careful not to lose sight of current drawbacks. As the sun sank low in the northwest they ambled back to their cottage, and after their customary cold showers, retired to face the morrow with re- newed vigor.

Three days passed, during which Michael rode off on his bicycle early in the morning, carrying his lunch in a brown paper bag, and came home late, bringing the money he had earned during the day. With Janice's money to help, they now started to save a little, to build up a cash reserve. They felt eager as children as they watched two, three, even five, dollars go into the plastic bag that they called their piggy bank.

The morning of the fourth day was no different from any other to start with. Michael took off on his bicycle, carrying his lunch and whistling cheerfully. But after he had worked about four hours it happened. He stepped into a concealed hole about a foot and a half deep. He sat down and extricated his leg from the hole, but when he tried to stand, his leg gave way and he fell, this time unable to get up. As he yelled for help his employer, an elderly woman, Eliza Brown, emerged from her kitchen door to see what was wrong. When it was clear that Michael could not get up, she called the motel and asked Parkinson to tell Janice to come at once.

Within minutes Janice arrived, and dashed to Michael's side to see what was the matter. As soon as she saw the twisted and swollen ankle she knew that Michael could not walk. She enlisted the aid of a man who was passing by, and between them they managed to get Michael to the car, as Mrs. Brown stood helplessly by, wringing her hands and looking like she was going to be sick.

Michael was in extreme pain. Janice did not hesitate. Learning from her assistant the location of the nearest clinic, she drove her husband to the emergency entrance, and called for help to get him inside. Two stout young men helped get Michael out of the car and onto an examination table. A doctor was on the scene almost at once. Without hesitation he ordered an X-ray.

"How did this happen?" the doctor asked Janice.

"He stepped into a concealed hole, a deep one, almost two feet deep, and twisted the ankle," Janice related.

"OK, we'll wait a minute to see what the X-ray shows. The ankle may be fractured, but we hope not."

While they waited the registration clerk brought forms and took all the pertinent information, name, address, next of kin-- all the usual stuff--including, "Do you have insurance?"

"We have no insurance," Janice replied.

The clerk then asked, "And how is this going to be paid?"

"It will be paid in cash," Janice replied, a bit defensively.

The X-ray now in his hand, the doctor studied it with care.

"Well, I don't see any fracture," he related to Janice. "There is some torn ligament, but not bad enough to need surgery." Putting the X-ray down, the doctor continued, speaking to both Michael and Janice, "What we have here is a bad sprain. I'll put on a supporting bandage." Taking a hypodermic needle from a waiting nurse, the doctor injected a pain-killing medicine. "Here's something to ease the pain, until you can get home and into bed." When the doctor had finished wrapping the ankle tightly he continued, "And here's a prescription for further pain medication. Now here's the routine, which is very important if you want to get over this as soon as possible: put an ice pack on the ankle for twenty four hours, to help reduce the swelling. Keep the foot elevated, except when exercising the limb or soaking it. Soaking the sprain in warm water several times a day can help. After a day or so start exercising the limb as much as possible, but do not put your weight on it. Here's a chart that shows you what to do." The nurse handed a printed sheet to Janice. "No need to come back, unless the sprain gets worse. Follow these instructions carefully, and there should be no problem."

The doctor then left to look after another patient. The clerk handed Janice the bill as the two young men helped get Michael back to the car. "Can you pay this now?" she asked. Janice was shocked and disturbed as she noted the amount--two hundred and fifty dollars! How could that be? She said to the clerk, "I don't have any money with me now. I'll bring it as soon as I can."

As she drove toward home Janice wondered, speaking to Michael, "How am I going to get you into the house?"

Michael spoke up, "Gosh, Hon, I'm sorry about all this! This is a terrible thing to happen, just when it looked like we might be out of the woods. I feel just awful!"

"We will manage," said Janice reassuringly. "We'll do just fine."

On the way Janice had an idea. "I know--we'll stop off and get you some crutches!"

"I've never used crutches before."

"I haven't either, but it looks easy enough."

Janice stopped at a drug store and rented some crutches, then continued on to their cottage. As Michael slid out of the

140

car, standing on his good foot, Janice handed him the crutches and steadied him as he tried to get the hang of using them. Not as easy as it looks, he soon learned. But he did manage to get inside and into an easy chair. "I know the doctor said bed," he commented, "but here I can still keep the foot elevated, and also soak it." Janice thought that seemed reasonable. She brought a straight-back chair with a cushion on which to rest the damaged limb. She obtained some ice cubes, which she wrapped in a towel to make an ice pack for the ankle. The rest of the day she and Michael together worked out routines by which he could manage both to get around as necessary and provide for himself, because it appeared that Janice would have to be gone much of the time.

The next morning Janice recruited a neighborhood boy to go along with her and pick up Michael's bicycle, and promised to give him a dollar for doing so. She took along the clinic bill to pay it; but she also had hopes of getting Eliza Brown's insurance company to pay the entire amount, plus compensation for loss of gainful employment.

Arriving at Mrs. Brown's home, Janice got the boy under way with the bicycle. She then knocked on Mrs. Brown's door. When the lady responded she looked terrible, as if she had not slept since yesterday.

"I know why you are here," Eliza said, her voice sounding weak and strained. "I am so sorry about what happened to your husband. I wish I could help, but I can't."

Janice showed Eliza the clinic bill, and pointed out, "Because you had a hazardous situation on your property, a concealed hole, you are technically liable for damages. If you will give me the name of your insurance company, I will--"

Mrs. Brown interrupted, saying sadly, "I have no insurance. I can't afford it." The lady seemed almost to shrink in size as she talked.

Janice was taken aback. No insurance? This is awful! After contemplating this for a moment she asked, "Could you help pay for this bill?"

"No, I'm sorry," Mrs. Brown replied sadly. "I have no money. I live on a small pension, and it is gone. I have had to do without so much--I keep a telephone only because I live alone and I'm old and need to get hold of someone if I get ill."

141

"Don't you have children, or relatives?"

"No, ma'am. I had a son, he was killed in the war. My husband died five years ago, he was ill for a long time. I had a sister in Memphis, but she died two years ago. Now I have nobody."

Janice wondered why the woman didn't shed any tears as she told this sad story, and suspected that she might be lying. Nevertheless, it appeared that there was no chance of collecting any money from her. But the pay--

"How long did my husband work for you before he was hurt?"

"About an hour."

"Did you plan to pay for his work?" Janice asked suspiciously.

"Oh, yes, I forgot--I did have some money put aside. Here is five dollars." Mrs. Brown reached into an apron pocket and produced the money.

Janice thanked her and left, wondering what the woman would have done if Michael had worked several hours. She went directly to the clinic and paid their bill in full.

This left her with just about two hundred dollars from her six hundred, and with maybe thirty dollars left from Michael's earnings; and that was all they had left to go on.

Janice related to Michael all that had happened this day, and gave him a full accounting of what money they had left. Michael expressed his thanks that they had Janice's pay check to back them up; but it did appear that to avoid a financial crisis they would have to find some way to come up with more money, because he obviously was going to be laid up for quite some time.

Together the couple wrote down expected expenses for the foreseeable future, rent, groceries, medicine perhaps, a few incidentals. It appeared that they could make out for maybe two weeks, but then they would be strapped.

Janice tried again to find some odd jobs, but again with no success.

Just when it was time to pay another week's rent, disaster struck again. Old Mr. Pinkerton suffered a severe heart attack and was considered to be permanently disabled, and since he had no relatives or heirs to run the property, the city came in

142

and shut it down, telling tenants they would have to move.

By this time Michael's ankle was better, to the point where he could get around quite well with his crutches. He could get in and out of the car. Knowing this, he could plan with much more latitude.

As they were starting to make their plans to move, Michael said to Janice, "Dear, I have a confession to make."

"Yes," responded Janice, smiling. "And what is that?"

"I was thinking, since we have no place to go here, it might be better for us to go farther north, like to South Dakota, where living is said to be a lot cheaper."

"That's a confession? Come on, give!"

"All right. I have been thinking, I would like to learn something about ranching. Cattle ranching. Up there in South Dakota I could get a job on a ranch. I don't know much about it, but I could learn. I'm sure I could do it. By the time we got there and got settled, I'm sure my ankle would be healed enough so I could manage to do light work or ride a horse. What do you think of that?"

Janice grinned and replied, "You've been keeping that from me, haven't you--about wanting to try cattle ranching. You know what? I have my own little secret--I've sort of wanted to try that myself."

"You have?"

"Yes, I have! Ever since I was a little girl I have had a fascination for the wide open spaces, working with animals and other creatures one sees on farms or ranches, and just being out there, being your own person instead of bending to other people's whims. Now that you've told me what you want, I'm starting to get excited!"

As Michael beamed his delight, Janice added, "But how are we going to do that, without money?"

"I have another idea," said Michael earnestly. "We have a good, late-model car, more than we need, really. The other day I passed a used car lot and saw an old Volkswagen bus, that still looked in pretty good shape, and it was for sale, for just three hundred dollars. Why don't we sell the good car, and buy cheaper transportation? That way we would have enough money to travel and get set up in another location."

"That seems a little risky," Janice admitted. "But it is a

possibility, and we certainly don't have too many options right now. Shall we go and look at the bus?"

They drove to the used car lot, and saw that the bus was still there. Michael asked the car lot owner if the bus was in good running order, and was assured that it was.

"Can we try it?"

"Yes, of course. Here's the key--take it out and see what you think."

The vehicle started readily, indicating that the battery and starting mechanism were in good order. The engine sputtered a bit at first, then began idling smoothly. The odometer showed moderate mileage, but Michael could not be sure that it had not been turned back. Michael checked for smoke from the exhaust, an indication of oil use and need for repair. There was no visible smoke.

Because the bus was the gear shift variety, Michael could not drive it himself, so Janice agreed to put it through its paces. She wasn't very familiar with gear shift operations, but with a bit of coaching from Michael she soon caught on.

As Janice drove the vehicle around for a few minutes, Michael watched the temperature gauge for indications of over-heating. A quick rise to a high temperature would spell in-adequate cooling and trouble on a trip. Fortunately the gauge rose slowly and rested at a low temperature. Michael was sur-prised that such an obviously old vehicle could be in that good shape. He presumed that the previous owner probably loved the bus, and was financially able to keep it in good condition.

Satisfied, they returned the bus to the lot, indicating that they were interested in buying. Michael asked the lot owner what he would pay for their late model car. Testing the car, the salesman noted its low mileage and like-new functioning. He wanted it, envisioning featuring it on his lot as "driven by a little old lady only on Sunday."

The salesman asked the Loudons, "Why are you willing to sell that late model and buy an old bus? You don't look like paupers."

Michael replied, "We are going up into ranch country, where it is a bit more rugged, and we want something that will take some abuse without spoiling its looks. A real nice car up there would stand out like a sore thumb."

"Where is 'up there'?" the salesman asked, just curious.

"Western South Dakota, maybe Wyoming. We're not sure yet."

"I get your point. OK, I'll tell you what I'll do. I'll give you blue book on the sedan, and fifteen hundred dollars difference between that and the bus."

"Not enough," Michael replied. "The sedan is worth at least three thousand, and you have the bus priced at three hundred. We ought to get at least twenty-seven hundred difference."

"Make it two thousand difference. That's all I can do."

"We'll be back," said Michael, and they left.

They checked with two other used car lots, and received offers of twenty-five hundred and twenty-eight hundred for their car. They sold the car at the latter figure, then took a taxi back to the first lot, where they paid cash for the Volkswagen bus, and drove it home twenty-five hundred dollars richer, leaving behind a salesman kicking himself for having finagled himself out of a good deal.

Janice remembered that the crutches had been rented, so she stopped by the drug store and paid for them, the selling price less anything paid for rental.

The next stop was Roger's, to see if they had any mail, and to tell him that they were moving. Roger was delighted to see them. "What happened to your foot?" he asked of Michael, who told him briefly what had happened.

"I really admire you folks. You came here with nothing, and you made out real good. Not too many folks could have done as well as you. Now what are your plans?"

Michael told of their desire to get into ranching. What kind of ranching? Well, cattle, if possible.

"You ought to see our new vehicle," Janice said.

When he saw the bus Roger said, "Wow--aren't you a little afraid to take that on a trip?"

"Not at all," Michael replied. "I checked it out pretty thoroughly. The engine seems tight, and it runs smoothly. Doesn't burn oil. I think it will do just fine. Anyway, it isn't all that far to where we plan to go."

"Where is that?"

"Well, far enough up in South Dakota to get into ranching

145

country. The southern part of the state, we understand, is pretty much into farming. About the middle there's farming, but still a lot of space devoted to cattle ranching. I guess we'll sort of play it by ear as we go along. We'll write to you after we get settled somewhere, give you an address and let you in on what we're doing."

"Thanks, I would appreciate that," smiled Roger. "Well, you folks have a good trip. Wish you all the best!"

"It has been good knowing you," said Janice. "We appreciate knowing someone as honest and understanding as you have been."

Roger showed his appreciation with a wide grin. They shook hands, then the Loudons took their mail and left.

There was one letter, from Michael's mother, delayed because of an error in addressing the envelope. Michael had wondered if his parents had heard of his predicament on the news. Evidently they had. Mrs. Loudon was inquiring a bit frantically as to what had become of them.

Not having heard from her own parents, Janice presumed that they had not heard the news. She decided to leave it at that. Michael, on the other hand, hastily scrawled a note to his parents indicating that they were all right, and were not in any trouble, and he would write soon to tell them the whole story. He took the letter straight to the postoffice to make sure it was not lost elsewhere.

The next stop was home. They began immediately to load up the bus. Michael couldn't do much, but Janice was able to handle everything, except that she needed Michael's help to get the bicycle strapped to the front of the bus. They were pleased that with the extra room in the bus they could take their new stereo and CD equipment.

By the time they finished loading it was getting late in the afternoon. The city had given them until tomorrow to be out, so they had the use of their bed that night.

The next morning they were up early. Janice fixed a good breakfast of ham, eggs, and toast, after which she finished packing all the food and last-minute items.

They had the bus packed and on their way in record time, eager to seek the new life, now that they had money in their pockets.

146

CHAPTER EIGHT

Janice had obtained a road map from Roger. She stopped for a moment to allow her and Michael to study the map and determine what highway to travel. The interstate went north a little distance out of Salina, but beyond that, it appeared, it would become Highway 81. Typical of central U.S., the road went straight as a string, almost, in this case clear to the middle of Nebraska. It ended at Highway 92, an east-west artery coming straight out of Omaha. Since their objective was westerly, they decided to jump over to St. Paul and take 281 north. That would take them to Huron, South Dakota, which was on Highway 14, a major route toward Pierre (pronounced peer), the state capitol. That route looked like it might lead them into ranch country. On the way they could study the character of the countryside and decide where to stop for further reconnaissance.

Michael folded the map and stored it in the glove compartment, as Janice put the bus into gear and headed north.

There was little talk during the first several miles, because Janice had to concentrate on her driving. She hadn't had much experience in city driving, and she still had a little difficulty with the stick shift. Once out in open country, however, she began to relax. The road was straight and clear, and there was little traffic.

Janice drove at a moderate pace, to reduce strain on the vehicle, which had yet to be tested beyond a few trips around the block. For the first ten miles or so both she and Michael sort of held their breath, hoping that nothing would go wrong. However, the vehicle continued to perk along smoothly, with no odd sounds or smells that could indicate trouble.

It was only about sixty-five miles to the Nebraska border, and they were there easily before noon. Neither of them had ever been in Nebraska, and they wondered what it would be like. They soon remarked that if you didn't know you had left Kansas and entered Nebraska, you sure couldn't tell from the look of the country. For the first twenty miles or so, at least, the two states were like two peas in a pod--rolling countryside, with patches of woods here and there, but mostly fields, big ones, small ones, green ones, brown ones, with fences in between, and an occasional hedgerow as a divider.

The sun beat down with little mercy, and the Loudons, sans air-conditioning, traveled mostly with the windows down. It made their hair fly every which way, but what the heck? They weren't going to any social function.

Around noon they stopped along the roadside, under some low trees, to eat lunch, sandwiches that Janice had prepared before they left. Traffic was very light--only an occasional car roared by to disturb their tranquility. After a few sips of coffee from the vacuum bottle, they were off again.

As the hours went slowly by, with there being little of interest in the countryside, boredom started to be a bit of a problem. To handle that they played games, like Tom Swifties, twenty questions, or playing poker with license plates. When such games became tiresome, they sang songs, mostly the songs they had learned as children, the songs of Stephen Foster, classic pop tunes from the twenties, thirties, and forties. The bus was equipped with a radio, but reception, except close to a sizeable town, was extremely poor, and even strong signals faded out in just a few miles. So they soon gave up trying to find diversion by that means.

It was getting late afternoon when they came to the junction with Highway 92. According to the map it was about forty miles to St. Paul, with no towns in between, so they decided to chance it. They arrived in St. Paul early evening, and found it to be, by Nebraska standards, a fairly sizeable little town that appeared to be rather accommodating. Right away there was an attractive little motel showing a vacancy sign, so with Michael's agreement Janice pulled in and inquired. The room was adequate and the rate reasonable, so they signed in for the night, paying cash in advance. They asked the manager if there was a good restaurant nearby, and he recommended a diner just three blocks away.

The motel unit was pretty standard, double bed, dresser with television set on top, rack for hanging clothes, a small table with two straight-back chairs, and bath with tub and shower. The Loudons were surprised to find that the unit also had a combination heater and air-conditioner. Michael studied the machine to learn how to operate it. Soon he set a certain gauge and pushed a certain button, whereupon a high-speed

148

fan began whirring and a flood of cool air surged through the room, promising an evening somewhat cooler than the outdoors, and, if one could tolerate the noise, a reasonably cool night's sleep.

As Michael rested his foot, putting it on the bed to elevate it, Janice took the small bucket placed there for the purpose and went looking for ice. She found a dispenser just outside the office door. After getting the ice she asked the manager if cold beer could be obtained in the vicinity. Unfortunately not. So Janice returned to the unit, reached deep into her clothing bag, and pulled out a martini mix that she had brought all the way from Mallon City, and surprised Michael with a diluted but cold and very welcome martini.

After enjoying their rest and drink the Loudons drove to the recommended restaurant. They found what they would later learn was a fairly typical type of cafe in smaller farm country towns--cheap construction, worn furniture, and makeshift utilities, but clean, and with lots of good, wholesome food, including fresh vegetables, much fresher than one could ever get in the city. The Loudons were beginning to learn what fresh vegetables, right out of the field or garden, can taste like. And gravy! You don't get that in the big city, either--not that kind of gravy.

Feeling well fed, and relaxed, the Loudons returned to their unit, Michael still hobbling on his crutches but by now becoming quite expert with them. They spent the evening watching a travelogue, a game show, and a Rex Stout mystery on the television. The reception was rather good, indicating that this community must have cable, a rather uncommon innovation in the farm country, they were told. They retired early, so as to get an early start before the summer heat reached its full potential.

After a tingling shower the Loudons had breakfast at the same restaurant, ordering eggs, bacon, and hot cakes. The eggs were quite fresh, probably having come from a nearby hen house that very morning. Right--you don't get eggs that fresh in the big city.

After loading the car and gassing up, they were on their way again, making sure that they made the right turn to get onto 281 going north.

149

They saw a little bit of interesting country just north of St. Paul as they came to the North Loup river; but after that it was a long stretch of open country similar to what they had traversed the previous day. As before, they whiled away the time by singing and playing games.

After they had been on the road for about three hours the bus, that had been performing so satisfactorily, began to choke and sputter. The engine rapidly lost power, and finally the vehicle came to a stop as Janice pulled off onto the shoulder. Michael struggled on his crutches to the rear of the vehicle and lifted the engine cover, hoping to see something that would indicate what was wrong, and perhaps could be fixed on the spot. He knew almost nothing about Volkswagen engines, but poked around, perhaps to discover a loose wire or something else out of place. He found nothing of the sort. At his request Janice tried again to start the engine. There was a sputter or two, then nothing. What to do? There wasn't a building in sight--nothing but wide open country. There was not even an animal to be seen, to indicate the possible presence of humans in the vicinity. Even worse, at this moment there was no traffic on the highway. There was no air stirring, except for an occasional dust devil that scurried across a field and then dissipated in high weeds. The heat became quite intense and almost stifling. The Loudons sat in the shade of the bus, trying to decide what to do. Start walking? Forget it. Michael couldn't walk, and Janice couldn't go off alone. It might take hours even to find a farmhouse, with even then no guarantee of getting help.

Janice perceived a car in the distance, approaching at a high rate of speed. Michael struggled to his feet and tried to wave the car down, but it didn't even slow down. The driver, probably a tourist, evidently was taking no chances of a hold-up in this almost deserted countryside.

Another hot, steamy hour passed. Several cars passed, traveling at high rates of speed, and not stopping for a stranded vehicle. The Loudons were beginning to get worried. What if they were stranded here all night? They had no food or water, and there was no pond or stream in sight.

Finally they saw a vehicle of sorts, approaching at a slow speed, meaning that it was probably local. As it neared they could see that it was an old model T Ford truck, driven by an

150

elderly man dressed in faded blue bib overalls and wearing a shabby straw hat. In the back of the truck were two sheep, tethered to the side boards. As both Janice and Michael stood by the road and waved, the truck chugged slowly to a stop.

"You folks havin' some trouble?"

"Yes," Michael replied. "Our engine quit on us, and we haven't been able to find out what's wrong."

"Volkswagen bus, eh? Don't know much about them kind. Had a neighbor once as had one, havin' trouble with it all the time. Mind if I take a look?"

"By all means, please do!"

The old gentleman climbed out of his truck, went to the back of the bus where the engine was still uncovered, and stared at it momentarily.

"I ain't never seen one of these engines before. It ain't nothin' like a model T. Nossir, don't think I can help you much with this."

"Do you know where we might get some help?" Michael asked.

"Well, the nearest town is Bartlett, down thataway about ten miles."

"Yes," Janice said, "I think we came through there a while back. It was such a little town I scarcely even noticed."

"Tell you what I'll do," the old gentleman said, "I'm going that way, I know a feller there that's a pretty good mechanic, takes care of most folks around here--I'll tell him you're stranded out here, and likely as not he'll be out right shortly to see what's the matter. You folks don't mind waitin', shouldn't be too long."

"That will be fine," Michael replied. "We'll wait, and we thank you." The old fellow climbed into his truck and drove away.

There wasn't much the Loudons could do, except just sit and wait. They did not feel like playing games now. Ennui settled in as they began to feel, for the first time, that they might be starting to lose control. But discouraged? Not by a long shot. They knew that somehow they would manage to get out of this predicament. Well, if nothing else, a state patrol ought to be along sometime, and they always check stranded vehicles. Michael grasped Janice's hand, and they settled down to wait.

151

After about an hour they first heard, then saw, a beat-up old Chevy pickup rattling toward them from the direction of Bartlett. It came to a stop behind the bus, and the driver stepped out, a lanky fellow of perhaps thirty-five years, wearing greasy dungarees, cowboy boots, checkered shirt, and greasy baseball cap. His face was tanned and seamed from exposure to extremes of weather, and he looked as if he had missed shaving a couple of days. But the Loudons were glad to see him.

"Howdy, folks. My name is Zeke Flowers. Looks like you're the folks old Hank was telling me about. What happened here?"

"Well," Michael replied, "the bus was running just fine. We left Salina yesterday, stayed over night in St. Paul, and left there this morning. No problems, until we got to this point, when the engine started to sputter and choke, and then just quit. We've got plenty of gas. We tried to start it a couple of times, but no luck."

"Well, let me take a look." Zeke peered at the motor briefly, checked wires, belts, etc., then climbed into the vehicle and tried to start it. Nothing. He climbed out, took off his cap and wiped his forehead with his sleeve, and said,

"Well, folks, it don't take no genius to see what's wrong. You've got a busted fuel pump. There's no way it can be fixed, so I'll have to git you a new one, which might take some doin'. What I'll do, I'll tow your vehicle into Bartlett, where I have my shop. It'll likely take a day, maybe two, to round up a fuel pump. Ain't too many Volkswagens around, 'specially buses."

"What about overnight accommodations while we wait?" Michael inquired, thinking about the size of Bartlett and its isolation from larger communities.

"You'll be OK. We'll put you up with old lady Jones, she'll take mighty good care of you. Now, I'll just hook up to your bus and take her on in. You folks can ride in the pickup."

Zeke turned his truck around and backed up to the bus. He brought out a tow chain and hooked it onto the rear axle of the bus. That done, Michael climbed into the truck cab, then handed his crutches to Janice to throw in the back. Then she climbed in beside him. Zeke took the driver's seat and they were off.

It was only ten miles to Bartlett, but it seemed more like

twenty. The pace was necessarily slow, and it was quite hot in the truck cab, with heat from the motor added to the heat of the afternoon sun. The smell of grease and oil only made it worse. Finally they could see the water tower and grain elevator rising up out of the shimmering plains, and soon they were dismounting at the greasy shack that Zeke called his shop, amidst a half dozen old cars and trucks scattered around in various stages of repair and disrepair.

Michael got his crutches, and as he stood still to regain his balance he looked around at the town that apparently was to be their home for a while. Besides the water tower, and the grain elevator nestled up to a railroad track, there were several cheap frame houses, mostly one story, huddled together on the prairie. A few low buildings lining the highway told of past business activities, that now were mostly just memories.

"Now, folks," said Zeke, "here's how it adds up. I'll call up to O'Neill, which is about forty miles further up the line, and see if anybody up there has got a fuel pump that'll work on this type of Volkswagen. A guy might have to go clean to Omaha to find an original part for this, but I think maybe I can get a universal fuel pump at O'Neill. If they've got one, I'll run up there today and get it. If you'll just hang around for a few minutes, I'll put the call through right now. OK?"

The Loudons nodded their agreement. Zeke got on the phone, and soon they heard him saying such things as, "I need a fuel pump for a (designated) Volkswagen bus. Got one handy?" "Well, who do you think might have one?" "This is an emergency--I've got travelers here, they broke down about ten miles out, and are stranded. I'd like to get that part today if I can." "OK, I'll wait."

Then, to the Loudons, "This guy thinks he knows someone. who's got the part. He's gonna call me back right away."

After about ten minutes the phone jangled, and Zeke grabbed the receiver. "Yeah?" "That's great! Can I get it today?" "You're sure it will work on this model?" "Good! How much is it going to cost?" "Well, that's about standard, I guess. Thanks a bunch! I'll be there in about an hour. See ya!"

Hanging up, Zeke turned to the Loudons. "I guess you heard, this guy says he has located a univeral fuel pump that ought to work on your vehicle. It will cost you about fifty-two

153

dollars, he isn't sure of the exact price, plus labor to install it. I'll go up there now and get it. It will be late when I get back, so I can't install it 'til morning. I'll take you on over to Mrs. Jones's so you can get settled in, and I'll take off."

Mrs. Jones's house was close enough so they could walk, and Michael could manage on his crutches. The house was a square two-story, white frame building that had seen better days. Mrs. Jones met them at the door, and greeted the Loudons with a cheery, "Hello, welcome! I'm Adelaide. Come on in."

Mrs. Jones appeared to be maybe sixty-five or seventy, white haired, but still seemingly with abundant energy. One would think that she could handle herself adequately in almost any kind of situation, and be able to help others at the same time. "I'm the town hotel," she explained with a smile. "I'm glad to be able to help people."

Adelaide led the Loudons to a large, comfortably-furnished room on the second floor. "You can get whatever you need from your vehicle. The bathroom is two doors down on the left. You'll find towels, wash cloths, and soap. Supper will be served at 6:00 o'clock. Tonight we are having pork cutlets with applesauce, potatoes and gravy, and vegetables, and apple pie for dessert. If you have any special dietary requirements, let me know."

The Loudons thanked their hostess, and she left. Janice decided what they would need from the bus and left to retrieve it.

Michael noted that in spite of being on the second floor, the room was not hot. Evidently the entire house had been kept closed, with shades drawn, ever since the cool of the morning, to block out the heat of the day. Also, the house was probably well-built and better insulated than most in this part of the country.

After a cool bath in the large, old-fashioned bathroom, the Loudons dressed in fresh, clean clothing and descended at the appointed time for "supper." It was the kind of fresh, well-cooked country food of which they were beginning to be very fond. The atmosphere was pleasant as Mrs. Jones entertained them with amusing stories of her years in this house. The Loudons felt completely relaxed, and even began to feel that

154

having their bus break down right here may have been a blessing. In a way the event provided an initial introduction to the kind of life for which they seemed to be headed, a life on the vast prairie, amongst widely-separated small towns and genuine people.

After a good night's sleep, the Loudons had a tasty breakfast of pancakes, fresh eggs, and sausage, and lots of good, hot coffee. Now thoroughly rested and relaxed, they lounged in the cool living room, reading the Omaha newspaper and chatting occasionally with Adelaide Jones, who still had amusing anecdotes to relate.

After a while Michael hobbled over to Zeke's shop to see how things were going. Zeke smiled as Michael approached, and related that he had picked up the fuel pump last evening, and was now getting it installed. He figured they should be on their way before noon. He'd let them know as soon as it was finished.

Michael returned with the good news. Mrs. Jones said she would prepare a lunch for them to take along.

About an hour later Zeke came and announced that the bus was ready. The Loudons followed him back to the shop, where he started up the bus to demonstrate that it was working fine. Then he shut it off, climbed out, and went into the shop, where he did a bit of figuring. Finally he announced, "Well, folks, here's what she comes to--that's $49.50 for the pump, $20 for the trip, and $30 labor, comes to $99.50, and with tax, $104."

Michael was relieved, because he thought it could have been a lot worse. In fact the mechanic could easily have gouged them, since they knew nothing about this type of vehicle. Instead, it seemed to Michael that the fellow may have shorted himself on the time he spent. In that light, he paid the bill and added another twenty, which Zeke accepted with thanks.

Janice drove the bus over closer to the house and they loaded the small amount of stuff they had taken in the night before. Then, to the landlady, "How much do we owe you?"

Adelaide replied, a bit sheepishly, "I wish I could put you folks up for nothing, what with the trouble you had--I guess twenty dollars will do it. I hope that won't be too much."

"Adelaide, that's not enough!" Janice protested. "We had a

wonderful night's rest, and two nice meals plus a lunch--no way! Here's forty dollars. Take it!"

"Well, all right," replied Adelaide, blushing. "Thanks so much. I hope you folks have a good trip, and no more trouble. If you're ever by this way again, stop in and see me. I'd love to see you again!"

"We will," said Janice. "Thank you."

As they were on the highway once more Janice commented, "What a contrast with the city. I think we're getting a view of what people are probably like where we are going. People charging too little and bending over backwards to help, perhaps at their own expense, may take a little getting used to!"

"I agree," Michael replied, "but I don't think I'll mind getting used to that!"

The old bus continued to run just fine, although for a while the Loudons sort of held their breath hoping nothing else would go wrong. About noon they came to O'Neill, where Zeke had come to get the pump. It was a nice, medium-sized town. Since they had their lunch, and still plenty of gas, they breezed on through. Once well out of town, they stopped for lunch in a shady spot beside the road.

Underway again, in about an hour they came to the South Dakota border. They were now in sort of hilly country, and crossed the Missouri at Ft. Randall dam, Pickstown. Janice stopped and checked the map, to make sure they were staying on course. She noted that they were not far from Yankton, the town that Lawrence Welk came from early in his career; but it was not on their way.

Highway 281 jogged about ten miles to the east due to uneven terrain, but then pursued its usual straight course northward, clear to the North Dakota border. But they planned to cut west about mid state, South Dakota. Janice noted that she had misread the map earlier--281 would not take them into Huron.

She conferred with Michael, since it was late afternoon and the map did not show any good overnight stopping place in that vicinity other than Huron.

Michael commented, "I've heard about the Corn Palace in Mitchell. We might want to see that. How about stopping there? It's right on our way. And it's not very far, maybe thirty miles."

156

Janice agreed, so as they reached the city, situated right on I-90, a major east-west cross-country highway, they started looking for a motel. They found a nice one, with a pleasant restaurant nearby, and checked in.

The next morning after breakfast they toured the town. They found it to be larger than one might expect in such a sparsely populated state, but still of course a small town by most standards. And there was the Corn Palace, recognized as one of the wonders of the nation--a large building, completely covered on the outside by murals composed entirely of ears of corn and other corn parts, along with other grains of the region, boasting intricate designs depicting almost everything that characterized the state, such as Indians and their activities, farms, crops, cattle, industry, and famous scenic spots. The mosque-like turrets on top added a fascinating touch to the overall picture.

As the couple stared at the building Michael commented, "Imagine seeing something like this in this state. Quite a contrast to the thousands of acres of little more than farm land that we've been through lately."

Checking the map, the Loudons found that they were not far from where they planned to start looking for a landing spot. Leaving Mitchell they travelled the fifty-plus miles northward to where they could turn west on 14. Before long they observed that farm buildings were getting fewer and more widely separated, and flat fields were getting bigger and bigger. Towns were also getting smaller, and showing signs of economic decay. Wessington, Vayland, St. Lawrence. Miller, a little larger town; but beyond that, more wide-open spaces with few farm buildings in sight. Ree Heights, then Highmore. Here they began to see evidence of huge tracts of virgin prairie grass, suggesting the possible existence of cattle ranches. Along the way they did see herds of cattle. It wasn't exactly the old West, they decided, but close enough, maybe.

Highmore, a little larger town of perhaps a thousand population. They saw that the town boasted a nice-looking motel, so they decided that this would be a good place to light for a few days and get better acquainted with the country.

The motel did have a vacancy, and it suited them just fine, so they checked in and arranged to stay two or three days. They

157

were greeted by the lady who ran the motel, Judy Maseland, a plump woman of middle age, reddish-brown hair, and glasses, dressed casually in an attractive print dress. She was quite friendly.

"Where are you folks from?" she inquired, with a strong voice that suggested an outgoing personality. "We don't get too many travelers through here."

"We're from Oklahoma," Janice replied as Michael signed the register. As he finished Judy read the entry.

"Mr. and Mrs. Loudon," she said. "Are you--?"

"Yes, we are," replied Janice, smiling. "It seems our fame precedes us."

"Well, yes, we did hear it on the news. Folks around here are of the mind that you got a real raw deal. If you don't mind my asking, how have you been making out? We heard they, the government, I mean, took practically everything you owned and fixed it so you couldn't get a job--?"

"We thank you for your concern," said Janice sincerely. "We have had our problems, but have managed quite well. Folks up this way have been very nice to us, and we appreciate it. It is nice to know that not everyone thinks we are enemies of society."

"Well, you're among friends here. While you are here, if there is anything I can do to help, let me know. I mean that."

"Thank you very much," said Michael.

By this time Michael had recuperated to the point where he could walk a little without the crutches. He tried it gingerly at first, then since he did not experience too much pain, he tried a little more; but he decided not to rush it right now.

The couple spent the rest of the afternoon getting settled in and studying some local literature to get a feeling of what the country was like. They also went and had a brief talk with Judy, explaining briefly why they were there, and Judy suggested that they go talk to the lady who ran the restaurant, Alice Harkins, as she knew most of the ranchers thereabouts.

At the restaurant the Loudons spoke to Ms. Harkins, noting that Judy had sent them. Alice was a cheerful lady, blond, slender. She was busy, so suggested that they come in tomorrow morning about ten, as she expected a well-known rancher, Bill Halloway, to be there. The Loudons thanked her, then sat

158

down and ordered "supper," flank steak with mashed potatoes and gravy and corn on the cob (a nice treat), at a surprisingly low price.

It was a beautiful evening, warm, with smells of fragrant foliage filling the air. After dinner the couple decided to stroll through the town and get acquainted with it. There was the postoffice, the bank, a hardware store, grocery store, feed store, and other businesses established to serve the needs of farmers and ranchers. There were signs of changing times, but all in all the town appeared to have survived the economic blight that had affected so many of the smaller midwest towns. There was a nice school, even a public swimming pool: signs of community pride. Strolling back toward the motel, they noted the usual water tower and grain elevator by the railroad track, and a loading dock for unloading farm machinery and supplies from rail cars.

They liked the town. They liked the people of this midwest country. They were sure they would like the kind of life they were rapidly getting into. Thus they went to sleep that night with no doubts that they would be there tomorrow morning to meet the person who might be the key to their new life: rancher Bill Halloway.

CHAPTER NINE

There were moderate cooking facilities in the motel unit, so the Loudons fixed their own breakfast, supplemented by sweet rolls and coffee furnished by Judy. They busied themselves doing this and that until time to go to the restaurant to meet Bill Halloway.

When they arrived at the restaurant there were several people present, some of whom stared at them, evidently having been told who they were. Alice greeted them, and then led them to a table in the rear that was occupied by a tall, middle-aged man wearing a ten gallon hat, blue denims, western style shirt, a string tie, and cowboy boots. He was clean shaven. His black hair was moderately long, and well-trimmed. As the threesome approached he stood, holding out his hand, which Michael grasped.

"Hello. My name is Bill Halloway. You must be the Loudons."

"Yes, we are the Loudons," replied Michael. "I'm Michael, and this is my wife, Janice."

"Pleased to know you. Won't you have a seat?"

Once they were all seated, Halloway spoke, "I suppose Alice told you that I'm a rancher. She said you wanted to talk to me. What can I do for you?"

Janice remained quiet, letting Michael speak for them. Michael shifted in his chair as he tried to decide what to say. He finally chose these words:

"Mr. Halloway, you probably know by now what happened to us in Oklahoma. Maybe you know why, maybe not, but that doesn't matter. I'm a lawyer, former DA in Mallon County. Janice was a psychology professor at the college in Mallon City. She has her PhD in psychology. We have been black-balled in our professions, to what extent we don't know, except that we were denied employment in Salina, Kansas. We could look around, but after we got out of Mallon County and came north, we, well, we found we kind of liked being away from the hassle of the city and our professions. And then--we both found that deep down we had a yearning to get into ranching."

Halloway had been listening without expression, but now he spoke, "Well, folks, that is a most interesting story. So you

160

want to get into ranching. Just how? You want to buy a ranch, or what?"

"We don't know anything about ranching," Michael replied. "We want a chance to learn. How about letting us come to work for you, just for keep, until we get the hang of it. We don't have much money, but we have enough to last for quite a while if we don't have to spend it for food and lodging. And we will work, believe me, seven days a week if it comes to that. By the way, you didn't say what kind of ranching you do."

"I run about six hundred head of cattle over a spread of forty five hundred acres, most of it virgin prairie, grazing land. Not big by Texas standards, but big enough, because we've got more and better grass."

"That sounds like it's just what we want," said Michael. "So what do you think about our proposition? We work just for keep, until we learn the ropes. We learn fast, and it's what we want to do."

Halloway took off his big hat and ran his fingers through his thick hair. Soon he commented, "By jiminy, you folks top anything I've ever seen. A lawyer and a school marm on a big cattle ranch, probably never been on a horse in your lives. Oh boy!"

Putting the big hat back on, Halloway just sat and stared at the Loudons with an amused expression on his face, until the Loudons began to feel a bit uncomfortable.

Finally Halloway leaned back and shoved his hat toward the back of his head, and exclaimed, "By jolly, this takes the rag off the bush, for sure, but I think I'm goin' to give you folks a chance. How soon can you get away?"

The Loudons sat spellbound for a moment, then Michael sputtered, "Well, uh, yes, right away, I guess. Why not?"

"There is just one more thing," said Halloway, staring toward Michael's legs. "I saw when you came in you were sort of limping. Have you got a bum leg?"

"Oh, no," returned Michael quickly. "I had a bad sprain a while back, but it is just about healed. It should be 100% in a few days."

"OK, I'll take your word for it." Halloway then gave his full attention to Janice, asking, "How about you, Mrs. Loudon?

161

I haven't heard much from you--how do you feel about all this?"

Janice broke into a big smile and replied, "You needn't worry about me, Mr. Halloway. I agree with everything my husband told you. In fact I may be more excited than he is about getting into cattle ranching. I'm ready!"

"OK," said Halloway, standing to his full six foot plus, "go and get your belongings and meet me down in front of the bank. I'll be driving a red Ford pickup. Make sure you've got gas, because we've got about thirty miles to go, and no pumps in between." Halloway shook hands with both Michael and Janice, then added, "And please call me Bill!"

After likewise insisting on a first-name basis, the Loudons, now thoroughly excited, left to pack. On the way they thanked Alice, who was smiling broadly, very pleased with herself that she had a hand in helping this remarkable couple.

Back at the motel the Loudons told Judy the news, and expressed their regrets that they couldn't stay longer, as they had sort of promised. Judy was sorry she was going to lose them, because she felt privileged to have them there, but was very happy that they had gotten this break. Halloway? Yes, she knew of him, and had heard that he had an excellent reputation.

Michael did not try to pack the crutches. He found that he now could manage very well without them. He left them with Judy, to give to someone who might need them. The bicycle? Yes, be sure to take that. Everything else was quickly loaded into the bus. Check the fuel gauge. Might need some gas-- better fill up. Everything loaded, head for the gas station, fill up and get to the bank.

Halloway was surprised to see them so soon. "You folks sure move fast. All set now?"

"You bet!" exclaimed Michael. "We're ready!"

"Well, all right, let's get the show on the road. You just follow me."

Halloway took a main road out of town for about fifteen miles, then turned off on a gravelled road. After about ten minutes he turned again, this time onto a section-line road that was nothing but two tracks worn into the prairie soil. On the way the Loudons saw rolling country, many hay stacks, much grass land. They envisioned the huge herds of buffalo that must

162

have roamed here in earlier years, and pondered how millions of these huge beasts could have been slaughtered during the brief time that early white settlers shared the land with Indians. (In time they were encouraged by reports that extensive efforts were underway to restore some of the herds, and supposed that they might even see some of the shaggy beasts in this part of the country.)

Finally the road dipped down into a large lowland area, possibly the prairie equivalent of a valley. Ahead they could see a cluster of buildings which the Loudons supposed were Halloway's ranch buildings. Soon Halloway turned into a private road marked by a large overhead sign that read, "Lazy J Ranch--W. Halloway."

After about five hundred yards Halloway pulled up in front of the ranch house, a large one-story frame building with a wide porch across the front, protected by a railing composed of slender, peeled poles, with uprights of smaller limbs. About a hundred yards to the left was a large barn with hay loft above, evidently for sheltering horses. Beside the barn was a utility building that Loudon supposed was a combination blacksmith and machine shop. Near that building, and not far from the house, was a small frame building with windows that appeared to be a bunkhouse. To the right of the ranch house was an area of small to medium pens, separated from each other by high railings made of peeled poles. In one of the pens a few fine-looking horses stood idly near a fence, lazily switching their tails to thwart the ever-present flies. A bit farther away was a much larger fenced area, evidently a place to corral cattle ready for shipment. On one side of this area was a crude ramp, evidently used to load cattle onto trucks.

The open land surrounding the ranch buildings was dotted here and there with small groups of deciduous trees and patches of brush. High up on a neighboring hill they could see a herd of antelope, grazing on the native grass.

Beyond the barn were some huge stacks of baled hay, covered with tarps. (Halloway later explained that this was for winter feeding. Most cattle were sold off before winter, but they did keep a small herd for breeding purposes. At times they would also hold herds into the winter waiting for a better price. The winters were usually severe, but the cattle weathered

163

quite well as long as they had adequate food.)

Halloway dismounted from his truck, and the Loudons, taking the signal, dismounted as well.

"Well, folks, this is it. Not a big spread, but how do you like it?"

"I like it fine," said Michael. "It looks great."

"Me, too," said Janice. "It's beautiful!"

"OK, let's go on in the house and meet the cook, and get you settled in." Halloway led them across the porch and through the large, heavy door opening onto the large living area. The Loudons noted a huge stone fireplace, flanked by a large wooden table, and several large easy chairs, plus a huge sofa, all upholstered in leather. The walls were paneled in wood, and were adorned with Indian blankets and artifacts, plus a few stuffed heads of game animals. The floor, boasting heavy wooden planks, was richly decorated with a variety of sculptured rugs with colorful designs representing western scenes. Overhead were several massive beams supporting the high wooden ceiling. The room featured four large windows, flanking the entrance door and at either end of the living area.

Halloway stopped near the fireplace and pushed a signal button. Soon a small, heavy-set, homely woman, with short-cut, greying hair, appeared, dressed in print calico and a large denim apron.

"Folks, meet Betty, our able chief cook and bottle washer. Betty, meet Michael and Janice Loudon. They're going to be with us for quite a while."

Betty said nothing. Halloway smiled and explained, "Betty doesn't talk very much. But she's good. She takes care of this whole house, manages it like a hotel, very efficient. The Loudons will be here for dinner (lunch, to city folks), Betty. I know that's short notice, but it doesn't have to be fancy, and there's no big hurry."

Betty said "Yes, boss," and departed toward the kitchen.

"I don't think she's happy about seeing us here, especially on short notice," observed Janice.

"No, she doesn't mind that at all," said Halloway. "Just have a seat here and entertain yourselves, while I go out and check. A couple of riders should be coming in about now, for dinner."

164

Michael stood looking out a front window. He saw two young men riding in from the hills, walking their horses to avoid getting them too warm in the summer heat. They were clad in typical ranch garb, cowboy boots, slim-legged denims, wide leather belts with large, ornate buckles, farm shirts, and large, wide-brimmed hats. Their shirts were soaked with sweat. Approaching the waiting Halloway, the riders dismounted and the three engaged in conference, probably, Michael thought, about possible problems with the herd.

Halloway came to the house and invited the Loudons, "Come on out here and meet my riders."

Following Halloway's lead, Michael and Janice stepped outside and approached the young riders.

"Folks, meet Jesse and Hank, as good riders as you'll find anywhere. Fellows, meet Michael and Janice Loudon. They're going to be with us for quite a while, to learn all about cattle ranching."

The young men welcomed the Loudons with a smile and a handshake. "Happy to have you aboard," added Hank, who seemed to be a sort of leader (ranch foreman, they learned later.)

The cook announced that dinner was ready, so the two riders washed up in a basin set on a bench outside the room that passed for a cookhouse. They all seated themselves around a large oak table, on sturdy straight-backed rustic chairs. During the hearty meal the riders, with genuine curiosity, questioned the Loudons to learn more about where they came from, how much they knew about ranching, and did they plan to stay with it. The Loudons, in turn, wanted to learn more about the riders. Jesse Hawkins, born in a neighboring county raised on a small ranch, worked for Halloway about two years now. Hank Mac-Larty, a couple of years older than Jesse, been around these parts since he was a kid, worked for Halloway nigh onto four years, ever since the previous foreman went and joined the navy.

Dinner over, Hank and Jesse rested for a while in the bunkhouse, then rode off to work somewhere in the distance. Betty cleared the table and disappeared into the kitchen. Halloway showed the Loudons their quarters, a large bedroom boasting a queen-size bed with a huge, ornate canopy, probably

165

an antique, two swing rockers, two large dressers, a desk with drawers, and a large walk-in closet. The floor was carpeted with several individual pieces, each with colorful western designs. On the wood-paneled walls were two large pictures with mountain scenery, and several smaller pictures with ranch scenes.

"This has been our guest room," said Halloway. "But it's yours now. You can go ahead and bring in your stuff. I'm sure you'll have plenty of room for everything. So for now I'll leave you alone to get settled, and see you at supper." Halloway then left the house, and they didn't see him again that afternoon.

Michael and Janice both worked to bring in their "stuff," and get it stowed away.

They loved the room. Besides being very attractive and "homey," it was remarkably cool, indicating superb insulation. Michael observed that the walls were thick, made of heavy timbers. He wondered where all the timber came from--there were tons of it in the ranch buildings--and there was very little timber in the surrounding country (they later learned that most of it was brought in from the Black Hills by wagon, back in the days when the ranch buildings were built by Halloway's grandfather, circa 1900. Even most of the poles for fencing the corrals were brought in the same way, at the same time).

Once settled in, the Loudons walked around the premises to get better acquainted with the layout. In the bunkhouse they noted accommodations for several hands, although only two of them showed signs of occupation. Hung on the walls were saddles and other riding equipment, confirming the legend that ranch hands own their own saddles. Present also were lariats, two or three varieties.

In the barn there appeared to be accommodations for about twenty horses, each stall containing troughs and mangers for feeding both hay and grain. The harness room was well stocked with saddles and leather reins, as well as bridles, harnesses, and horse collars. Visible also were instruments for repairing and altering leather equipment. Behind the stalls, along the wall, were rows of manure forks and hay forks. The barn had the typical smell of animal sweat, manure, and hay.

The couple walked over to the corral where they had seen about a dozen idle horses. The animals had been moving about

166

aimlessly, but as the Loudons stood by the pole fence, two greys walked slowly over near them, close enough to touch. Janice reached through the fence and rubbed the nose of one of them, which tossed its head as though in appreciation. The other of the two greys moved closer to Michael and attempted to nuzzle him through the fence, perhaps checking to see if this visitor had any food. In a moment or two, having satisfied their curiosity, the two animals turned, kicked up their heels, and romped away. One of them made a feeble attempt to goad another horse into play, but soon settled into an idle, tail-switching stance.

Thus dismissed, Michael and Janice walked along a well-worn path out toward a shallow draw that could harbor something of interest. It was a beautiful day, not too hot, with no wind to stir up dust. In the draw was a small coppice of trees that offered some shade. Since nothing of special interest appeared, the couple decided to sit in the shade for a while. There were rocks aplenty, so each found one promising a degree of comfort and sat down.

After a moment of reflection, as he stared out over the rolling grass land, Michael took Janice's hand and said, "We had a dream, and now, by the grace of God, here we are, on the threshold of realizing that dream. I can hardly believe it--I keep thinking I'll wake up and find us back there somewhere, struggling to keep our heads above water."

"Me, too," offered Janice. "I can't believe that we are here, in ranch country. I am elated, but I still feel like something bad is going to happen and spoil the whole thing. I can hardly wait to get started with whatever we are going to do, to make it seem more real."

When the rocks they were sitting on started getting hard, the Loudons got up and started slowly back toward the ranch house. They spent the rest of the afternoon in the large living area, reading whatever they could find that would tell them more about the region they were in. There was much about the Missouri river, the state capital, Fort Pierre, and the Indians. They learned of several Indian reservations in this middle and western end of South Dakota--Standing Rock, Cheyenne, Pine Ridge, Rosebud, and not far away, Crow Creek and Lower Brule. They even found a Yankton Indian reservation down in

167

the southeast corner of the state. Close by they also noted some historic forts, Fort Kiowa (1822), Fort defiance (1842), and Fort Hale (1878). Michael commented, "What with all these Indian reservations and at least half a dozen forts within thirty or forty miles, we must be smack dab in the middle of one of the early territories with the heaviest Indian populations, which was probably also one of the most heavily contested areas between whites and Indians."

"Yes," added Janice, "and look at all these different tribes: I see references to Sioux, Mandans, Aricara, Kiowa, Cheyenne, Yanktonai, Oglala, Dakotas, and Crow. There's probably a lot more."

"I thought Oklahoma had about as much Indian history as anywhere, but there may be even more here," commented Michael. "Someone said the Custer massacre was in South Dakota--is that true?"

"I heard that, too, but not so. It says right here that it was in Montana."

"Well, I do see the famous Wounded Knee massacre site, down here in the southwest corner of this state."

"Another fascinating thing about South Dakota," said Janice, changing the subject, "is the Badlands. I've never seen them, but I'd like to. I'd like to see the Black Hills, too, and the world-famous Mt. Rushmore National Monument."

"The Black Hills has a lot of history connected with gold mining," added Michael. "The rush is long over, but I understand the Homestake Mine is still operating. It must be one of the biggest in the world. According to one figure, by mid-20th century it had produced more than $450,000,000 in gold."

"This really is a fascinating country," mused Janice. "When I think of the crowded, stodgy old northeastern states, compared to this wide open land, where you can see nature in its purest form, I wonder how those eastern people can stand it."

"But if they all moved out here, then this country would be just like the east--crowded and polluted," philosophized Michael.

"You're right! Let's not tell them!" agreed Janice, laughing.

Early evening. Halloway, Jesse, and Hank came riding in, dusty and tired. After they had cared for their horses, Halloway came on to the ranch house, while Jesse and Hank retired to the

168

bunkhouse to wash up and wait for the supper call. Halloway greeted the Loudons in passing, and after he had cleaned up a bit he came and sat down near them.

"Well, folks," Halloway began, "you haven't had much chance to size up the spread, but so far, what do you think?"

Michael and Janice stated emphatically that they loved it here, and could hardly wait to get started.

"Don't be in too big a rush," cautioned Halloway. "I don't think, from what I've seen, that you are properly equipped for ranch life. You need the right head cover to protect you from the weather, whether hot or cold. You need the right footwear. What the city slickers call cowboy boots were made that way for a purpose, to keep your feet happier in the stirrups. With ordinary work shoes, after a few days of riding your feet would be so sore you couldn't walk. I know those boots look awkward, but you'll find out, they work. And you'll need heavy-duty pants--forgive me, Janice but this goes for women too--else your clothes will be worn out before you can get back to town. And chaps--you haven't seen us wearing them yet, but you will--they are for riding through rough country where there's lots of brush. They protect your legs. You're probably saying that all this heavy duty clothing in summer can be hot as hades, and you're right, but you'll get used to it.

"Now, Janice, I've been talking like you are going to get out there and work like the boys. I figure if you want to learn ranching, that's how. Have I got it figured right?"

"That's exactly right," Janice assured him. "There may be some things I can't do, because I'm not strong enough, but I think I can handle most of it."

"Well, all right, here's what I suggest you do--both of you, drive into Pierre tomorrow morning. It's a little farther, but you find the best stores there. And take along a list of what you'll need. I'll help you with that. Get what you need for work. If you have enough money, it's a good idea also to get some dressy stuff, because you might be going to some of the doin's around here, like parties, dances, and box socials, and get in on the fun. In these get-togethers folks like to dress up a bit, makes them feel better. If you're a little squeezed on money, you can wait on the dressy stuff. There's plenty of time for that.

"Now, looking ahead, Janice, after you've learned the ins

169

and outs of ranching, you might like to take a whirl at the business end of ranch management, bookkeeping, budgeting, that sort of thing, 'cause some day you two might like to have a ranch of your own. But like I say, learn the ranching first, because then you'll know what goes on out there on the range."

They were interrupted by the call, "Supper's ready--come and git it!" So they proceeded to the cookhouse and seated themselves as before, the Loudons having learned, by one of the rare utterances from the cook, that in the cookhouse everybody always sits in the same place. They enjoyed a hot, well-cooked meal of mashed potatoes and gravy, corn, broccoli, T-bone steak, and apple pie, followed by hot coffee. When it was over, and they were back in the living area, Halloway asked the Loudons if they would care for a bit of after-supper sippin' brandy. The Loudons accepted with thanks. As they relaxed with a snifter of Napoleon, Michael mentioned something he had been wondering about.

"Bill, we were looking at the bunkhouse today, and I noticed there were bunks for several hands, but only two were occupied. I guess that was Jesse and Hank. I thought for a ranch this size you'd need several hands. How come just two?"

"Good point. What you hear about cattle ranching is how it used to be. In the old days the range was mostly wide open, and cattle could range for many miles. Herds were larger, because they lost a lot. Nowadays, around these parts at least, there's very little open range. It's all fenced. With the fences to contain the stock, you need fewer hands to keep track of them. And there are fewer losses. So about all the hands have to do, like during the summer, is take care of the little problems that crop up now and then. The cattle have plenty of grass, and we keep water tanks filled all the time with windmills on a device that when the water gets low, the mill goes to work. And we keep a good supply of salt out there, which the cattle have to have. During the busy times, like calving and shipping, we hire extra help."

"What about branding?" Michael asked.

"We don't brand in these parts any more, because the fences keep cattle from different outfits from mingling. Once in a while, like when there's a break in a fence, there can be some mingling, but then the different owners just divide up the mixed cattle, regardless of who they really belong to. It's a lot cheaper than branding. They do still brand in some open range areas out west."

"What about rustling?" Janice asked.

"There's some of that, but not like it used to be. And it's different. In the old days rustlers would drive stolen cattle away, but nowadays they mostly bring in portable butchering equipment, butcher the cattle on the spot, and truck away the meat. But there's a lot less of that now, because the state police and sheriff's departments, with better communication facilities and better transportation, have gotten pretty good at tracking down the thieves. We haven't had a loss from rustling here for about three years."

After listening to these dissertations, Michael commented, "Bill, you don't talk like most folks around here--you sound like an educated man. Am I wrong on that?"

Halloway smiled and replied, "Well, yes, thanks to my mother--my folks are both dead now, God bless them--I got a good education. Somehow or other she managed to put me through high school and college. So I ended up with a degree in business at South Dakota State at Brookings, with a minor in agriculture. I came back here to work on the ranch. My father died not long after, so I took over running it. Then about a year later my mother died of pneumonia."

"And you never married?" asked Janice.

"No, I never did," Halloway replied. "I did have a sweetheart once, but her family moved away, and she went with them. That shook me up so much I haven't tried it since."

"You must have loved her very much," commented Janice sympathetically.

"Yes, I did," agreed Halloway, appearing inclined to drop that subject. "Here, how about some more brandy?"

"No, thanks," said Michael, following a consenting nod from Janice. "We'll retire and let you get your sleep."

"It has been real nice talking to you," Janice said, as the couple got up to leave.

"Thank you," said Halloway. "I enjoyed it. We'll talk later."

The next morning when the Loudons arose and left their room they were greeted by the cook, who said their breakfast

171

was ready. Halloway and the two hands had long since gone.

After a hearty breakfast the couple followed Halloway's advice and drove to Pierre to shop for clothes. They found Pierre to be a big-little town, very interesting. They noted the bridge across the wide Missouri, and the domed capitol building. There was a moderate amount of traffic, and the town seemed to be a little bit sleepy on this hot summer day. Here the Loudons got their first view of local Indians, who would come in from nearby reservations to shop and to conduct official business with the state government. Although mostly clad in conventional white man's garb, many of the Indians still clung to some handmade garb with typical adornment of their tribes.

There were shops aplenty to meet the needs of ranchers. The Loudons wandered about, checking out the different stores before selecting one in which to do the bulk of their shopping. They noted a couple of stores that featured Indian crafts and artifacts, and browsed through them with much interest. Finally they selected a large store that seemed to offer the best selection of clothing and began to choose items from the list that Bill had provided. Hats: wide-brimmed, leather, moderate in style (several styles, they observed, were rather flamboyant, probably popular amongst the younger folk). Janice selected ladies' pants of heavy cloth, a mixture of cotton and polyester, one pair in light tan, another in powder blue. She found two blouses, again of a poly-cotton mixture, that seemed to promise durability, in tan and blue. Michael chose trousers of heavy blue denim with a small percentage of polyester, in the so-called boot cut style, i.e., with slim legs. Instead of the popular blue chambray shirts, he chose light-colored, light-weight polyester shirts with a typical western decorative pattern. Chaps? One pair of plain leather, passing up several styles decorated with fur, spangles, large brass buttons with leather strings attached, or what have you. Both of them avoided the dressy styles at this time, wishing to conserve their funds.

They tried on the clothes in the rooms provided. Getting the pants the right length was not difficult for either Janice or Michael, as both needed only standard sizes. Necessity for alterations would have meant another trip into town.

Then the boots. What a wide selection of styles for both

172

men and women, plain or fancy, of different kinds of leather in a wide range of prices. One pair in snakeskin was priced at twelve hundred dollars! All were expensive. The helpful clerk advised them to get a size larger than they customarily wore, to allow for heavy socks. Oh yes, need some socks. Okay, a pair of boots for each in the lower price ranges. Try them on. If they hurt, they're not right. "Good boots, properly fitted, do not have to be broken in," advised the clerk. Hmmm--the boots felt pretty good, not awkward, though that's how they look, with the high heel thrust forward.

The Loudons decided to wear one outfit each of their clothing purchases, plus their new hats and boots, to show them off to Bill when they got back.

"Do you get many 'tenderfoots' in here?" Michael asked the clerk with a smile.

The clerk smiled knowingly, "You bet we do. You'd be surprised. And we try to treat them right."

"You've been very helpful to us," said Janice. "We appreciate that."

They checked Bill's list to make sure they got everything. Bandannas? What for? Oh, yes, they were told: to protect your face and lungs from dust, mostly, but also to protect against driving rain, or whatever. Be out on the plains in heavy dust or inclement weather, you'll know what for. Bill's note: don't bother with outer wear, jackets and coats, or heavy underwear just yet. Gonna be hot for another six weeks yet, most likely.

Satisfied that they had gotten everything on Bill's list, the Loudons climbed into their Volkswagen bus and headed back to the ranch. The new clothing was hot, as Bill said it would be, but with the windows open and country air circulating freely through the bus, it wasn't too bad. They felt a little awkward wearing the big hats, but, they decided, they would get used to that too.

As they turned onto the gravel road they found themselves behind a truck traveling at a stiff pace and kicking up a lot of dust. Aha! The bandannas! Michael stopped the bus long enough for them to tie the brightly-colored, oversized handkerchiefs around their faces, over their noses; and then they knew for sure what for. Although the truck had gotten well ahead of

173

them, the heavy dust still hung in the hot air like a blanket.

As they turned into the ranch yard they saw Halloway working near the barn. As they came to a stop and climbed out, he came to greet them.

"Well," said Halloway as he looked the couple over, "you look pretty spiffy in your new duds. You did good. How do they feel?"

"Hot," said Michael.

Halloway laughed. "Right," he agreed, "but you'll get used to that. Come on in the house and we'll rustle up some cold drinks."

They moved on into the living area of the ranch house and settled into comfortable chairs.

"What'll you have--Coke, Pepsi, beer--you name it."

The Loudons both selected a cola.

"What did you think of our capital? " asked Halloway.

"It's a very interesting town," said Janice. "We saw a lot of Indians there, so they must come to Pierre rather often."

"Yes, I guess they do," replied Halloway.

"One thing I've been wondering about," said Michael. "In ranch country, you'd think you'd see some people wearing gun belts and pistols. But we haven't seen any. Apparently this country isn't nearly as wild as it used to be."

"Far from it," responded Halloway. "There's hardly any more violence around here than in most any other state. No need to carry guns any more."

"I notice that you and the boys carry rifles on your horses. What's that for?"

"Mostly for shooting predatory animals that prey on cattle. Believe it or not, we have seen cougars and wolves around here, and of course coyotes. They prey on the calves, or on cows weakened by illness. We don't have to use the rifles very often, but it's the sort of thing that when you do need it, there's no substitute for it. And of course there is the slim possibility that we might run onto some rustlers. We wouldn't want to shoot them, just scare them off. Some of them might get pretty bold if they knew we were out on the range unarmed."

Their drinks finished, Halloway returned to the barn. The Loudons put away the purchases that they were not wearing, then settled down in the living area to read until supper.

174

It wasn't long before Jesse and Hank came in from the range, tended to their horses, and cleaned up ready for supper. Soon the cook sounded her "Come and git it!" As they seated themselves at the supper table, Jesse and Hank playfully kidded Michael and Janice on their transformation from tenderfoot to cow hands, and expressed their mock concerns about losing their jobs to these newcomers. The Loudons fully enjoyed this lighthearted banter, and came back with their own repartee. The two riders then related some of their experiences on the range during the day, mostly the minor problems that crop up regularly in a large herd.

After supper Halloway again invited the Loudons to share the brandy. As they sipped he began to talk about the immediate future.

"First off, we'll have to pick out some horses for you. These will be your horses, and you'll learn how to care for them. They'll be easy ones at first, until you learn to ride. Then you'll get some younger, more spirited horses. As soon as that's done, the next step is to learn some of the work around the barn, cleaning it out, checking equipment, and so on. We'll get into the details later. Any questions at this point?"

"Well, yes, I do have one question," said Michael. "As we were on the way to Pierre and back we saw several ranchers driving around on their ranges with motor vehicles instead of riding horses. But you don't have any motor vehicles here except for your pickup. How come?"

"Good question," said Halloway. "Quite a few ranchers have gone to the mechanical stuff, but on this ranch the terrain is too rough, and motors would break down in nothing flat. And we're too far from town to get them repaired. I tried an all-terrain vehicle once, it lasted about a month. The same for most other ranch machinery that has come on the market recently. It breaks down, and it's too hard to get repairs. No, I'll stick with horses. Besides, they smell better."

"That suits me just fine!" responded Michael, laughing.

"Good!" said Halloway, as he rose from his chair. "Now, Mr. and Mrs. Michael Loudon, greenhorns, you'd better hit the hay, because tomorrow morning it's up bright and early. You're all set, so now, let's get to work!"

175

CHAPTER TEN

Mr. and Mrs. Michael Loudon went to work in earnest. They quickly learned to ride, and were soon assigned young and vigorous horses. They rode the range, learned how to herd cattle, and to move them from one grazing spot to another (to allow grass to recover, Halloway explained). They learned to detect signs of injury or disease that would require treatment, and to sort the individual animals out from the herd. They pitched hay (not as easy as one might think: there's a knack to it), shoveled manure, cleaned and oiled equipment, and curried horses.

Jesse and Hank, having been assured by Halloway that their jobs were not in jeopardy, assumed much of the burden of teaching the Loudons, who rode with them almost every day, to watch and absorb. They saw how the horses learn certain tasks and often perform them automatically as the occasion requires, with little or no prompting, often responding to such cues as knee pressure or even how the rider shifts his weight in the saddle. In short, in the rough and tumble of everyday life on the range, the horse and rider become a team, working together as would a team of skilled humans. And it became evident, first to Janice and then to Michael, that the horse really enjoys this interaction with the rider, and actually shows signs of chagrin or even disgust when the rider doesn't know what he is doing or can't make up his mind what he wants the horse to do.

Halloway stayed pretty much in the background, watching carefully the Loudons' progress, and allowing them to "learn the hard way," by making mistakes and profiting from them. It was soon apparent to him that he had two exceptional students, who were learning the ranching life at a surprisingly rapid pace.

As they progressed, the Loudons changed. They became lean and hard. They took on a tanned and weathered look, such that now nobody could identify them as tenderfeet. At first they suffered multiple aches and pains after riding the range all day, but after the first two or three weeks the muscles that had been complaining became inured to these new requirements.

Along with the physical changes came spiritual changes as well. Being so close to nature, and removed from the artificial constructions of man, they began to feel closer to God. Occasionally on a warm evening they would sit outside, in the near total darkness, and gaze up at the myriads of stars that graced the heavens, so bright that they seemed almost close enough to reach. At such times they pondered the depths of the universe, wondering if there was an end to it, and believing that in its vastness one could see the essence of God. As they studied the unsullied, wholly natural reaches about them, stretching seemingly to eternity in all directions, they thought, is not our nature, including ourselves, a part of the universe, and thus a part of God? They believed in God, but being seriously religious was not part of their family life as children, and it had never really come up as they became adults. Now, however, with their closeness to nature, they decided to start going to church.

Halloway had not been a church goer either, but as the Loudons expressed interest in attending, he decided to accompany them to a couple of meetings at least, to introduce them to some of their neighbors. The Loudons invited him to ride with them in the Volkswagen bus, which did seem to him to be preferable to his pickup truck for this occasion. In these and subsequent visits the Loudons did meet with a number of people residing in the region, some of whom had to drive as much as ten or twelve miles to get there.

They found all their neighbors to be very likeable people, who liked socializing. As a result they began to attend some of their social functions. Some of the families had homes large enough to accommodate sizeable groups (as many as fifty or sixty people, counting kids, might show up), while others had to wait until the hay was removed from their hay mows to host barn dances or other socials. In the summer evenings many socials were held outdoors, with mantle-type lanterns providing illumination. And there was always food. These ranch people were all hearty eaters, and welcomed any occasion to join with their neighbors in this activity.

Michael and Janice proposed to spend part of their remaining funds for dressy clothes for the social functions, but Bill gave them money, explaining, "You folks are learning so fast and getting so much work done, I'm going to have to start paying you. Here's five hundred dollars against future work--go on

177

and buy your fancy duds. We'll square up the bookkeeping later." So that they did, selecting garments similar in style to what most of their neighbors wore, distinctly western, attractive but not gaudy.

In their closeness to nature, Michael and Janice also felt closer to each other. Without their even noticing it particularly, their love deepened and became more structured. They felt no need to mention it. It was there, it was real, and that was sufficient. Somehow they knew it would be there as long as they lived, and would help them through whatever hardships might be their lot. They didn't even wonder about this remarkable experience. It seemed as natural as the world around them, and as enduring.

As the weeks went by and the Loudons became more and more proficient in all aspects of ranching, it seemed to Halloway that his students had completed their schooling, and now he had to think about the future. He had started to pay them, but was not in a position to offer them permanent employment. They could help out during the fall round-up, getting the cattle ready for shipment to market--but what then?

A possible answer soon came, with such superb timing that one might have thought it had been arranged by God, except that it was associated with tragedy. Halloway received word that his brother Gerald, who operated a cattle ranch in eastern Wyoming, died suddenly of a heart attack. Shortly thereafter there came a letter from the executor of the estate, asking what provisions should be made to transfer title to the ranch, as William Halloway was the sole heir. Urgency was advised, as the ranch was a large one and currently was being managed by the foreman, Jerry Alderman, who hadn't the administrative skills to keep the ranch out of financial trouble.

Halloway immediately talked to the Loudons. "Michael and Janice," he began, his voice expressing both hope and uncertainty, "I think I may have something for you--how would you like to have a ranch of your own?"

Michael spoke for the two of them. "What are you talking about? We have no money, and no property. How are we going to get a ranch of our own?"

"Would you take it if I showed you how?" asked Halloway, now, in fun, starting to bait them a little.

Both Michael and Janice began to suspect that Bill had something up his sleeve, but dared not hope that such a dream could become a reality for them.

Again Michael, after a questioning glance at Janice, spoke for the two of them. "Well, sure, we'd like to have a ranch of our own, but I don't see how--"

Deciding to get right to the point, Halloway told about his brother's sudden death and the urgency to get his Wyoming ranch title secured. He then asked, "Would you folks be interested in taking over the ranch?" He explained that the ranch was about the same size as this one, and was located in the eastern part of the state, not too far from the Black Hills of South Dakota.

"But," protested Michael, "We still have no money. What did you have in mind?"

"Okay, here's what I had in mind. If I couldn't sell the ranch right away, I'd have to go and manage it myself. And I'm not too keen on selling it to strangers, who too often misrepresent their means and end up in trouble, and then the property would come back on my shoulders. I know you folks, and know you can handle it, so I am willing to give you title to the ranch, with financial details to be worked out later. I'll even give you money for your expenses until you get settled in."

"We've never been in Wyoming," said Janice. "What's it like?"

"Wyoming is mostly mountains, the Bighorn Mountains in the middle, and the Rocky Mountains on the west and south. I think it is about the most beautiful and most interesting state of all. It has Yellowstone Park in the northwest corner, and lots of history. It has only about half the population of South Dakota, so you know what that means--not a lot of people to make trouble for you. And another thing, that ranch is open range, so that makes some difference in management problems, so I figure you ought to know that. But I still think you can handle it, if you're willing. How about it?"

As Michael and Janice listened they began to get excited, envisioning the realization of their dreams in such a beautiful and interesting state, even farther removed from the stress of city life than here at the Lazy J. But they were not given to hasty decisions of such magnitude.

179

"We'll have to talk this over," Michael replied. "We'll give you our answer tomorrow, if that's okay."

Halloway could tell by the looks on their faces what the answer would be, so he cheerfully granted them the chance to discuss it first.

The next morning the Loudons were working around the ranch yard, cleaning up and mending leather equipment. Halloway had gone out on the range with Jesse and Hank. About mid morning Michael noticed a plume of dust in the near distance, indicating an approaching vehicle. In all the time they had been on the Lazy J they had neither seen nor heard of any visitors, so this was an event of considerable interest. Janice joined Michael, as the two of them stood waiting for the visitor's arrival.

Shortly a large black sedan appeared and pulled to a stop near the waiting couple. The door opened and a man dressed in light summer clothing stepped out. The Loudons recognized him immediately.

"Dr. Folger!" screamed Janice as she ran and engaged the doctor in a vigorous embrace and kissed him on the cheek.

Dr. Folger reciprocated with a close hug, then turned to shake hands with the waiting and grinning Michael.

Janice was so excited she could hardly contain herself. "How nice to see you!" she squealed with delight.

"It is great to see you," agreed Michael, in somewhat more subdued fashion.

They invited their visitor into the ranch house and secured for him a cold drink as they seated themselves in the comfortable chairs.

"I had the devil's own time finding you," said Dr. Folger. "You sure covered your tracks well--or someone covered them for you. I had no idea where you had gone."

"How did you find us?" Janice wanted to know, still smiling broadly in her excitement.

"First I went to your landlord in Mallon City. All he had was the name and address of a motel in Salina. I went there, and they knew you all right, said you had rented a cheap motel in the same town, but it was shut down. The motel manager, I believe his name was Roger Harrison, said you had left town, probably heading for South Dakota to look for a ranch, but he

180

did not have your new address."

"I sent him our new address," protested Janice.

"I meant that he had a mailing address, but only a p.o. box in Highmore, South Dakota. Well, believe it or not, it took me almost two weeks to get that far. And then, at the Highmore p.o., all they knew was that a man named Halloway picked up his mail there. They didn't know where he lived. Some people around there knew the man, but didn't know where he lived, just that he was a rancher. I finally had to go to the hall of records to get his home location. But even then, they couldn't tell me how to get there; but they did pinpoint it on a map. When I started out in that direction I got lost, and it took me quite a while to finally get here. And until I saw you folks, I still wasn't sure I was in the right place."

"I'm glad you found us," said Michael. "We are real glad to see you. Now, let's have it--why did you come looking for us? Not more trouble, I hope."

"No, quite the opposite," replied Dr. Folger. "It's a long story, and I'll try to spare you the details as much as I can. You didn't know this, but I along with hundreds of other people across the country are volunteers in an organization called WOA, 'Watchdogs of America.' We have been personally selected by the president himself, after getting recommendations from well-known citizens of good repute. It is a secret organization, and the members are all sworn to secrecy. I am telling you only so you will understand, and I hope you will keep it secret.

"These members of WOA have but one chief function: to observe the behavior of government officials, watching for unethical or illegal actions or procedures, and to report such directly to the President.

"When you left, I knew you were in trouble, but I didn't think anything about it, because I knew you were expecting trouble, and were ready for it. So I wasn't worried about you. The newspapers didn't give a lot of detail, either, just that you had been ordered out of the county. Then I got a call from Madge Thomas--"

"She's a member of your organization?" asked Michael, incredulous.

"Yes, she's a member. Randy Cole kept her on as his sec-

181

retary after you left, because she knew far more about running the office than he did. Well, not long after your departure she happened to run across the agreement that you, Michael, had to sign to get out of jail, and she was flabbergasted. So she called and told me about it. I was flabbergasted, too. I had no idea they would pull a stunt like that. And taking away all your property and funds, including earned salary, that was the capper!

"So Madge and I got together, and decided this was one for the President. So I put through a call to the President, using the secret code that meant 'for the President, personal and urgent.' In the White House, staff are given firm instructions to give that code A-1 priority. When I told the President what it was about, without naming any names as yet, he asked me to come to Washington and meet with him personally, because this was a matter that could not be discussed over the telephone. So I did that, taking with me your signed agreement, and telling the President about the false charges against you.

"That was enough. The President immediately sent a special investigator down to Mallon County, with authority to see any and all pertinent documents and to interview, on demand, any person, any time."

"This is exciting!" exclaimed Janice, listening intently.

"Well, the investigator arrived within forty-eight hours, and went right to work. He talked with me first. He was a really nice guy, and not at all pushy or arrogant. After I told him what I knew, he went and talked to Randy, showing him your signed agreement, and demanded that he tell everything, and show evidence to support any charges against you. Randy tried to defend the charges, but when the investigator interviewed everyone Randy had named, it soon became clear that the whole thing was a cover-up.

"Well, Randy was arrested at once and charged with conspiracy to commit a felony. That leaves the DA slot open. Then the government got a grand jury indictment against Leonard Burnham and Franklin Dupree, of the Dept. of Vital Resources, and Clark Bennett, IRS. Charges are pending against local officials who were involved in the phony drug charges."

Michael and Janice stared open-mouthed upon hearing this report, first at each other, and then at Dr. Folger, their facial ex-

182

pressions revealing, at first doubt, and then delight--delight that the forces against injustice are there and working, even if one doesn't always see them.

After a sip of his cold drink Dr. Folger went on, "Word is that the parties named in the grand jury indictment are out of a job, and probably facing criminal charges.

"And now, Michael, you'll be glad to hear that Mallon County has agreed to reimburse you for salary withheld, to pay you substantial damages, and to give you your job back."

Dr. Folger now shifted his gaze and attention to Janice, with this report: "Janice, there's good news for you, too. The investigator talked to college officials, who revealed that they had been ordered by the Federal Government to fire you, or lose government support. They weren't sure who issued the order, but the investigator traced it to Burnham. Anyway, they agreed to give you your job back, with sincere apologies. I gather that they really felt embarrassed about what they did. They even agreed to pay part of the salary you missed."

Before the Loudons had a chance to reply, Dr. Folger drew an envelope from his pocket and held it up for them to see, saying, "Whatever your reply, I have been instructed to give you this." He pulled from the envelope a cashier's check, displaying it as he went on, "This is a check in the amount of eighty thousand dollars, drawn on the Mallon City bank, representing amounts deposited by the college and by Mallon County, as advance reimbursement for damages and lost salaries. A full accounting will be mailed to you later. The total authorized amount can be adjusted upward if you agree to come back and resume your jobs, but this check will be augmented anyway, regardless, as soon as they have the final figure. And by the way, the President asked me to extend to you both his sincere personal apology regarding the way you have been treated."

Dr. Folger handed the check to Michael, saying, "Michael, I'm sure it has occurred to you that you have grounds for a lawsuit against Mallon County and a chance to collect damages far beyond the amount of this check, perhaps up in the millions." As he spoke Dr. Folger watched Michael's expression closely.

Michael responded immediately, with obvious conviction, "No way. I know that has gotten to be pretty much a way of

183

life in this country, but I do not wish to be a party to it. I'm sure Janice feels the same way about it--." He glanced toward Janice, and received a nod of agreement.

"I was sure that's the way you'd look at it, and told the county officials so; so this check is not a sop, to get you to lay off. They honestly want to do what's right, I'm convinced of that."

"I'm sure you're right, " agreed Michael. "And by the way," he added, "just out of curiosity, did MAPS shut off any oil ship- ments, as Dupree said they would?"

Dr. Folger grinned and said, "Not a bit. When the Presi- dent got the news of what Burnham and his gang did, he got on the phone to Roshine and explained what had happened, so Roshine just switched his business to someone else. I don't know, he was probably using Burnham, because Burnham was so anxious to be a big wheel."

After the Loudons had gotten a chuckle out of the above story, Dr. Folger returned to the business at hand. "So, what do you say, about taking your jobs back?"

Michael looked at Janice questioningly, and Janice respon- ded with a slight but distinct nod, whereupon Michael turned his gaze back to Dr. Folger and said,

"I believe I speak for both myself and Janice when I say we are happier than we can possibly tell you that things have turned out this way. It supports our faith that people are basi- cally honest, and that it is a small minority that causes ninety percent of the trouble. On top of that, we can't begin to express our gratitude to you for what you have done. Of course we realize that you didn't do it just for us, you did it for all of the people, which is why you joined WOA in the first place; but you have our sincere thanks just the same."

Michael paused, looking down at the check, as he pon- dered how to phrase his next statement. Then, looking squarely at Dr. Folger, he said, "We are extremely grateful that we have been invited to resume our jobs in Mallon City, but we have already decided that if it came to that, we would decline. In a way, being booted out of Mallon County was a favor to us, in that it gave us a chance to think and search our feelings about what we really wanted to do. If we hadn't been forced out, we probably would have stayed in our respective ruts, and not

184

examined our true feelings about what we were doing and what we would rather do. As it was, we had the chance to see it all clearly, and we decided--or rather, we realized--that what we really wanted to do was to get into cattle ranching, closer to nature and far away from the stresses of our jobs. We have thoroughly enjoyed our life on this ranch. Now we have a chance to take over a ranch in Wyoming, and we are going to take it. Would you please extend our thanks and our regrets to the people back there?"

Dr. Folger was not surprised, but he felt that he still had something to say:

"I respect your decision, but it seems to me you folks have a lot to offer society, and society sorely needs people like you to lead the way and set an example for others. And you, Janice, particularly, you're one of the finest teachers in the country, certainly one of the brightest, and it seems to me that in teaching you have a special opportunity to shape minds along more constructive lines. And both of you have that rare quality, the determination to stand on principle, the things you believe are right."

This time Janice took the floor. "Yes, Dr. Folger, I believe that we have a lot to offer. The only thing is, I don't believe the world is ready to accept it. I could do wonders in my classes if given a chance, but I was never permitted to teach what I really wanted to. When I was fired, they told me it was because of some things I was teaching. I remember what Dr. James said at our final meeting: 'The Board of Regents told us that you have been teaching some things of which the college cannot approve--'." Janice related the specifics of the charges, then went on, "I know, they cooked up that charge, but the point is, they did consider it sufficient grounds for dismissal. If I had actually been teaching such things, and they found out about it, I would have been fired. And apparently the school was willing to go on record with that stand.

"I would be delighted to teach what I know could promote a more beneficial approach to the understanding and alleviation of human problems, but there are too many blocks in the way, blocks that have been deliberately set up and are currently being vigorously defended, apparently even by some universities. I believe that when people are ready to take a different

185

view about human behavior and problems, they won't need leaders to show them the way. Change will come when people are ready to change, and until then there is little that you or I can do about it.

"No, Dr. Folger, I am not abandoning the field. There are many others who can teach what I was teaching, and would welcome the chance to do so. Under the circumstances I much prefer to follow this new path that Michael and I have chosen."

"Well," said Dr. Folger, "I really can't fault you for leaving the fold. I could possibly have done something to change psychiatry if I had stayed with it, but like you, I didn't believe there was much I could do."

Dr. Folger put his empty glass aside and rose slowly, saying, "I'd best be on my way. I have quite a ways to go today, to make connections."

"Can you stay for lunch, or as they say here, dinner?" asked Michael.

"Thanks, but I really don't have much time. I really have enjoyed seeing you folks again, and I do wish you the best kind of success in your new venture. And one thing for sure, I'll never forget you!"

Janice and Michael saw the doctor to his car, again expressing their joy at seeing him again, and their gratitude for his efforts on their behalf. After the fervent goodbyes, they stood, arms about each other, and watched sadly as their very dear friend vanished from their sight, possibly forever.

With their arms still about each other, the couple trudged slowly back to the ranch house. They settled into the comfortable chairs to contemplate this sudden turn of events in their lives.

After a few moments of silence Michael stated thoughtfully, "This is something we can't possibly know, but with all these amazing coincidences paving our way into ranching, it wouldn't be too hard to convince some people that God had a hand in it, and is giving us His approval."

"Yes," Janice agreed, "it does sort of look like Divine intervention. Anyway, I hope that fortune will continue to smile on our venture. When you stop to think about it, even with our good fortune, what we are going into is pretty risky. We know very little about Bill's brother's ranch, what shape it's in, and all

186

that, and let's face it--we know very little about ranching. What is more, where we are going we won't have a good teacher like Bill. And," Janice added, looking impishly at Michael, "it isn't too late to back out!"

"No way!" exclaimed Michael with mock horror at the idea. "But seriously, I know it is a risk. We'll be starting out heavily in debt, and if something should happen to either of us, or for that matter, to Bill, we could end up in bankruptcy and lose everything we have. But," he recalled, "that's exactly where we were a few weeks ago, isn't it? So there!"

"I'm with you!" exclaimed Janice joyously, as the two of them jumped up and hugged each other. "Let's do it!"

"Wow," said Michael, "wait 'til we tell Bill. Won't he be surprised!"

It was a while before Halloway returned from the range, during which time the Loudons made their plans. It would be a couple of days before they could get away. They would probably have to get a new vehicle to replace the old Volkswagen bus, probably a pickup truck or van. They would have to find out who to see in Wyoming, to get settled in. They would definitely need someone to shepherd them through all the legalities involved in such a large and involved real estate transaction, an area in which they were both rather inexperienced. By the time Halloway got back, both of them were so excited they could hardly contain themselves.

As Halloway rode into the ranch compound he saw Michael and Janice standing waiting for him, arm in arm, grinning. He rode up to them, stopped, and stared at them, then said, "You two look like the cat that ate the canary. What have you been up to?"

"Have we got news for you!" exclaimed Janice.

"Well, wait until I put my horse away and you can tell me all about it."

When Halloway returned, the three of them entered the house together. After they were comfortably seated, Michael pulled out the check Folger had given them and held it for Halloway to see. "Look," he said, "eighty thousand dollars!"

Smiling uncertainly, Halloway inquired, "Great, but where in the devil did you get that?"

Between them, Michael and Janice told Halloway the story

187

of Dr. Folger's arrival and his news that they had been cleared back home. The eighty thousand dollars was for back pay and damages, and there would be more to come. It was not until after the main story had been told that they broke the news that they had been offered their jobs back. With this news Halloway's face fell, but Michael hastened to say, "But we turned them down. We told Dr. Folger that we had been offered a chance to buy a ranch in Wyoming, and--" Here Michael paused for dramatic effect, then burst out, "We decided to take it!"

At that they all jumped up and shook hands and hugged one another. Janice said excitedly, "We are so happy we can hardly believe it! First we are offered the chance of our dreams, and then someone comes along and gives us the money to at least make a down payment and get started. Bill, we love you!" she ended as she gave Halloway another big hug.

"Well, you know you didn't need this," reminded Halloway, pointing to the check, "but I know you're a lot happier having money of your own to start out with."

As they all sat down again, Halloway commented, "Well, now we can get busy with our planning. So, shall we get to it?"

With Loudons' happy agreement, they did indeed start planning and making appropriate arrangements. The Loudons did indeed trade the Volkswagen bus in on a new combination van and truck with money they borrowed from Bill, to avoid possible problems in getting that big a check cashed readily in a small community. As Bill got on the phone and made necessary legal arrangements and gave instructions to the executor, Janice and Michael got their belongings together and loaded the van.

Finally Halloway got off the phone and said to them, "Everything's all set over there. The papers are being drawn up, and when you get there you can drop into the executor's office in town (he supplied the name and address in writing) and sign them. A lawyer has been retained to check everything from the legal standpoint, so there shouldn't be any trouble there. To make you feel a little more like the ranch is really yours, I will accept a down payment of twenty thousand dollars. That should leave you with enough to get settled.

188

"I checked with the auditors, and they assured me that at the moment there is no sizeable encumbrance on the estate, just a few bills that can wait. Under the circumstances the creditors will be happy to give you time, because otherwise they might not get paid at all. No need to cash your check here, take it with you and deposit it there, then send me your check."

"Well," said Michael, "I guess we can get a good night's sleep and leave first thing in the morning."

"By the way," Halloway said, "I told the folks over there about you folks, who you are and what you are like, and they are all real happy about this arrangement. They are tickled pink to have people of your caliber taking over that ranch, because otherwise it could become a sizeable headache. So, believe me, you can be assured that you'll be amongst friends over there. You'll like them, too, because they are real fine people."

So the Loudons, excited though they were, did manage to get a good night's sleep, and were up at an early hour rarin' to go. After a hearty breakfast they said goodbye to Jesse, Hank, and Betty. Betty said nothing, but Jesse and Hank wished them all kinds of good fortune, and expressed their pleasure at working with them. The Loudons reciprocated with their own gratitude for the training they had received.

As the Loudons finished loading and were about ready to depart, Halloway added a final suggestion. "With an early start you'll have plenty of time to get there today, so take time to drive through the Badlands, and take the scenic route through the Black Hills. You won't regret it."

"We will," said Michael and Janice in chorus.

As they said their final goodbyes the two men shook hands warmly. There were tears in Janice's eyes as she gave Bill a final big hug and a kiss. "Bill," she said, "There's no way to thank you for all you've done for us. I know this isn't a final goodbye, because we will be seeing each other in the future, so let's just say, au revoir."

"That goes for me," agreed Bill, looking as though he might shed a tear as well.

Without further ado Michael and Janice climbed into their van and took off, watching Bill in the rear view mirrors as he stood waving to them until they were out of sight.

As Halloway had suggested, they drove through the famous

Badlands and marveled at the grandeur of the erosion-sculpted hills and monoliths, with their reddish color, set off here and there with patches of green grass. Then into Rapid City, and onto the highway that would take them through the most scenic part of the Black Hills. They saw wild turkeys, antelope, buffalo, and even some bears. They stared in awe at the huge, sculptured faces of four presidents in the Mount Rushmore National Monument. Otherwise they were struck by the rugged, often breathtaking, scenery of the mountains.

As they left the Black Hills they found themselves on a high plateau, featuring vast reaches of rolling hills covered with range grass and dotted here and there with patches of brush.

After about an hour of driving they turned off the main road, onto a graveled road. This they followed for several miles, now beginning to find low foothills with grassy valleys between. As they capped a high ridge that according to the map would be the last elevation before their destination, they spied, well below them, an immense valley, miles across and spreading to the right and left as far as the eye could see. Meandering through the middle of the valley was a small river, bordered by thick stands of small deciduous trees. The expanses of grass, brown from the summer sun, were punctuated here and there with large green fields, probably irrigated, around which stood huge stacks of baled hay. In the distance a few large herds of cattle were seen, grazing contentedly in the grassy reaches.

In the midst of this grand scene the Loudons could see, almost directly ahead of them, a cluster of ranch buildings which, according to the map, was to be their new home.

As they stared at this delightful setting, Michael and Janice dismounted from their vehicle and stood in awe, their arms about each other and their heads together, contemplating all that had brought them here, and their marvelous good fortune at being here. They had worn their "fancy duds" for this occasion, and now, as they viewed their future domain, Michael looked slim and handsome in his decorated western attire, and Janice, with wonderment in her face and eyes, was a vision in her ornamented high leather boots, draped tan western tulip-style skirt, adorned with silver conchs, ruffled sepia button-up blouse with long sleeves decorated with ruffles at the wrist, and her charming western-style, broad-brimmed hat, under which her long, curly, reddish-brown hair cascaded down almost to her shoulders. Tears welled slowly into her eyes as she and Michael embraced and engaged in a fervent kiss.

As they stood watching Michael mused, "My dearest, it appears that in the great courtroom of our world we have been tried by tribulation. Now the jury is in, and the verdict is, thank God, innocent--innocent by reason of sanity." Without a word they both bowed their heads in silent prayer of thanks for their blessing.

Then Mr. and Mrs. Michael Loudon, ranchers, mounted their van and began the final leg of their journey into their new life, one that was to be one of the most fascinating, and delightful, but in some ways the most troubling and exasperating, experiences they ever had. But that is another story.